"Don't move! You may have broken your neck."

Liz Matthews turned her head on a neck that was obviously still in working order, and looked at Mike Whitten. "I'm fine," she gasped. "Knocked my breath out." She put both hands on her diaphragm and pushed. "Better." She raised up on her elbows. "Nothing's broken."

Mike put one arm behind her waist and the other behind her knees and scooped her up. He began to walk as quickly as he could toward the stable.

"Hey!"

"Where are you hurt?" he asked, afraid for a moment he might have done her more harm than good.

"I'm not hurt, I'm mad as hell. I'm mad at the horse, mad at myself, and if you do not put me down this instant, I am going to be *really* mad at you."

"Fine." He dropped her legs. She limped toward the spot where the horse was standing. She obviously intended to get back in the saddle.

Mike watched her. She hurt considerably more than she was willing to let on. Maybe she'd cracked a rib. He ought to drag her to a doctor, just to be sure. She'd never go. Hard-headed, opinionated damned female. He caught his breath. *The kind of woman his daughter was growing up to be.*

Great, he thought, *now I've got two of them to worry about....*

Dear Reader,

Like many of you, I have experienced some of the struggles the hero and heroine of *If Wishes Were Horses* endure on their road to happiness.

Soon after my husband and I married, my teenage stepdaughter came to live with us. I was clueless. Even birth parents waffle between being too strict—our children's viewpoint—to not strict enough—our own gut feelings. While I knew that taking my own risks was scary, I found that letting this child I had grown to love risk heart or mind or body was downright terrifying. In the end I learned to close my eyes, cross my fingers, pray, and let her go for it. I didn't stop worrying. I just got better at concealing my fears.

I also firmly believe that riding horses can slide kids through adolescence with fewer problems. Without her horse, my daughter would probably have landed me in a straitjacket before she hit fifteen. Thanks to horses, I managed to cling to the sane side of loony until she was happily married.

Last, but definitely not least, I absolutely believe in lifelong love. It seems as though I've been married to the same man since before the American Revolution. But falling in love with a man who comes complete with children can be daunting, especially if we have absolutely no experience with kids. We have to handle special problems, and if lucky, we discover special rewards. I hope you'll agree that for Mike and Liz, love is worth the risk.

Carolyn McSparren

Books by Carolyn McSparren

HARLEQUIN SUPERROMANCE
725—THE ONLY CHILD

IF WISHES
WERE HORSES
Carolyn McSparren

Harlequin Books

TORONTO • NEW YORK • LONDON
AMSTERDAM • PARIS • SYDNEY • HAMBURG
STOCKHOLM • ATHENS • TOKYO • MILAN
MADRID • WARSAW • BUDAPEST • AUCKLAND

ISBN 0-373-70772-X

IF WISHES WERE HORSES

This edition published by arrangement with Harlequin Books S.A.

Printed in U.S.A.

For Ann Lee, who taught me to train horses and turned my daughter into a centaur, and for her daughter Liz, an extraordinary rider. For my own daughter Megan, and Karen, the stepdaughter I helped raise. For the people at St. Jude Children's Research Hospital, who fight death every day and seem to win more often than they lose, and finally, for my wonderful editor, who manages to stay cool even when I don't.

CHAPTER ONE

MIKE WHITTEN'S FIRST glimpse of the lush pastures and sprawling stable complex filled him with dread. He'd never been truly comfortable outside of cities, and even this close to town, these rolling pastures definitely qualified as country. He stifled an impulse to do a one-eighty and head his Volvo straight back to Memphis.

He'd never get away with it. Not with his eleven-year-old daughter Pat straining against her seat belt beside him. He couldn't remember ever seeing her so eager.

He stopped the car at the open front door of the stable, and Pat unfastened her seat belt and leaped out before he could turn off the ignition. She was in such a hurry she slipped on the gravel and nearly fell. Mike's heart lurched. He leaned across the seat as though he could reach her, steady her. "Hey, Pitti-Pat, watch it," he said.

This blasted place was already conspiring to damage his kid.

"Daddy," she said disdainfully. "I'm too old for pet names. I'm Pat, just Pat, remember? Now come *on!*"

He sighed, followed her and looked around this place where he did not want to be. The board fences were stained dark brown and were in good repair. The pastures had been mowed or perhaps eaten down by the horses, several of whom quietly chomped their way across the paddocks. The parking lot was edged with neatly trimmed shrubs, and beds of bright flowers—he had no idea what kind—surrounded the front door.

Something buzzed close to his ear. He slapped at it. A damned bumblebee! To his knowledge, Pat wasn't allergic to bees, but there was always a first time.

He called to his daughter, who scampered ahead of him into the shadowy recesses of the stable. He quickened his stride to catch up with her as she reached a broad transverse aisle.

Four dogs raced down the aisle toward them. An obese black Labrador retriever, a basset and a pair of small brown-and-white blurs that outran the others and launched themselves straight at Pat's face.

"Pat," he shouted, and moved forward to defend her.

"Aren't they adorable?" Pat cooed to the small dogs wriggling in her arms. "They're Jack Russell terriers. I've seen pictures of them in horse magazines."

They were licking Pat's face. Mike caught his breath at the thought of all those germs.

Meanwhile, the Labrador and the basset waddled over to Mike. He sidestepped them, his eyes still on his child. "Put them down, baby. They might bite."

"Oh, Daddy, get a grip," Pat said. The terriers stayed where they were.

Mike felt something soft brush against his ankle and looked down to see a fat black-and-white tabby doing figure eights around his legs. God, the place was a zoo. He thought he'd only have horses to contend with. The only animal he did not see was a human being.

He surveyed his surroundings once more, and was surprised at how clean the place seemed. The black-topped aisle was immaculate, and the barn smelled not of manure, as he'd expected, but of fresh hay. Despite that, he was sure the place was a disease factory. Pat's doctors said her immune system was normal, but could anybody's system stand the constant assault from the germs that likely populated the stables? He'd never even let her have a gerbil for fear of allergies.

The barn was built in a rough cross. They'd entered the short arm, and beyond was another set of open doors that he reckoned gave onto the riding arena he'd glimpsed from the road. Suddenly Pat crowed with delight and rushed past him with both terriers still hugged tight against her chest.

Outside in the arena, a woman in jeans, a T-shirt and some sort of tight brown leather leggings cantered into his field of vision on a horse big enough to pull a beer wagon. The pair sailed over a jump yanked off the Great Wall of China. Horse and rider landed with a thud and cantered off.

Mike closed his eyes. No way! He didn't want his precious, fragile child anywhere around this place. Every time he thought of Pitti-Pat on a horse all he could see was Rhett Butler cradling Bonnie Blue's broken body. Not his kid, by God!

He'd simply have to find a way to head her off, and that—as he knew from experience—was a hell of a lot harder than stopping a runaway train. How had he let her con him into this?

"Daddy! Aren't they wonderful?" Pat called from the fence. The rider and the horse cantered past to jump a tall stack of painted poles.

"May I help you?" a voice said at his shoulder. He turned to find a tall, slim woman with cropped dark hair that bore a single streak of silver along the right temple. She also wore jeans and a sleeveless T-shirt, and carried a pitchfork as though it were a rifle. She was in her mid-forties at least, but she had a beautiful smile and the taut body and unlined skin of a woman twenty years younger.

"I'm Michael Whitten," he said. "From Edenvale School. I have an appointment."

She set the pitchfork against the nearest wall, wiped her hands down the front of her jeans and extended her hand. "Oh, the chairman of the board of trustees. I'm so sorry. I should have realized who you were when I saw the blue suit and tie. But you're early."

Mike smiled grimly. He was always early for business meetings with possible adversaries. Threw them off balance, and sometimes he caught them in things they'd rather he had not seen. He said, "Sorry. Got away sooner than I thought I could. Didn't have time to change." He shook her hand. Her fingers felt callused. Her handshake was firm.

"I'm afraid you're bound to take home some dust on that suit," the woman said. "I'm Victoria Jamerson. I'm half owner and I manage this place. That's our trainer and co-owner, my niece Liz Matthews, out there working Trust Fund." She slipped past him and shouted to the woman on the horse, "Liz, Mr. Whitten's here."

"Bother," the rider said softly, but loud enough so that Mike heard her clearly.

She turned to stare at him from under a tight cap that might once have been black velvet, but had taken on a greenish cast. She brought the horse down to a walk and relaxed into the saddle. Mike could see the glint of sweat on the animal's flanks—hardly surprising on a July afternoon. The woman's blue T-shirt was soaked, as well, and her muscular arms glistened.

Mike caught himself staring at the curve of the shirt over her breasts and turned back to Victoria Jamerson. "And this is my daughter, Pat. Come here, Pitty—uh, Pat, and meet Mrs. Jamerson."

"In a minute, Daddy," Pat said, unable to tear her eyes off the horse and rider. She set down the terriers, climbed onto the bottom rail of the three-board fence and hung over the top.

"Bad case of equine adoration," Victoria Jamerson said easily. "There's something about horses that just seems to call out to little girls." She shrugged and smiled. "Happened to me, happened to Liz, and I already see the symptoms in your Pat. I'm afraid it's an incurable disease."

Mike felt his stomach roil. Mrs. Jamerson had no idea how her words affected him.

"I'm afraid you've only uncovered the tip of the iceberg," Mrs. Jamerson continued pleasantly. "Before you know it, you'll be the proud owner of a large pony. You'll spend your weekends cheering Pat in weather that you wouldn't put your dog out in. Comes with the territory."

At the words *proud owner* and *large pony,* Pat's head whipped around. Her eyes glowed with an inner fire that Mike had seen only when she was burning with fever—the day that he made her that fateful promise.

"My daddy's already promised to buy me a pony for my twelfth birthday," Pat said. "I'll be twelve in a month."

"Then we'd better get cracking," Mrs. Jamerson said and moved to lean beside Pat on the fence. "Large ponies that are suitable for beginning riders aren't very thick on the ground."

"We're getting ahead of ourselves," Mike said quickly. "Pat's never even been on a horse. She may hate it."

Both Pat and Mrs. Jamerson turned to stare at him with a "get-real" look that froze his heart.

In the center of the ring, the woman swung her long leg over the horse's back and dropped lightly to the ground. She patted the big horse's neck, slid the reins over his head and began to walk beside him toward them.

Mike saw the resemblance between the two women immediately. Both were tall, slim and had high cheekbones and broad foreheads that would probably keep them beautiful into their eighties. Mrs. Jamerson's eyes were gray, however, while Liz Matthews gazed at him from eyes the color of a jade Buddha.

Liz Matthews. Different last name. He knew Mrs. Jamerson was a widow. So Liz Matthews could be married. He checked the rider's left hand. No ring. Oddly, he felt pleased.

He liked the look of her, although she didn't seem overjoyed to see him. Probably didn't appreciate having her riding session interrupted. She walked with a long-legged, rangy stride emphasized by the tight dark leather encasing her legs. Her jeans sat low on her hips, but her T-shirt was wet enough to cling to her narrow waist and muscular rib cage. She reached up to pull her shabby riding hat off to reveal an unkempt mass of dark blond curls.

As she came closer, he saw that she was probably in her mid-thirties. There were tiny lines at the corners of her eyes, and a spray of freckles across a nose that had probably been broken at least once. Without that slightly crooked nose, Mike realized, she was simply a good-looking woman. With it, she was sexy as hell.

Since, as chairman of the board of trustees at Edenvale, he would make the recommendation either to employ her and her riding stable, or to look for someone else to start an after-school riding program at Edenvale, he'd expected her to welcome him effusively, maybe even do a little fawning. Apparently she didn't fawn.

She didn't offer to shake hands either, but walked straight into the stable, calling as she went, "Albert, can you cool down Trust Fund for me, please?"

"Uh-huh," came a bass voice from the shadowy reaches of the stable. A moment later a huge man opened one of the stall doors and ambled down to take the horse. "Hey, old fool," he said amiably, and walked the horse past them into the green area that surrounded the ring.

"Come on in the office where it's cool, Mr. Whitten," Mrs. Jamerson said as Liz came back to join them.

"Can I stay here, Daddy? Please, can I, please?" Pat whined.

"That's probably not a good idea, kiddo."

He caught a glimpse of Liz Matthews's raised eyebrows at Pat's tone.

"She'll be fine with Albert, Mr. Whitten," Liz said and turned to Pat. "Stay away from the stalls. Some of these guys kick and a couple of them will bite a plug out of you if you get too close."

"Sure," Pat said and skipped off after the big man and the horse.

Great, Mike thought. *One end kicks, the other bites.* "Pitti—uh, Pat, I'm sure this gentleman has work to do. He can't take the time to watch you. Better stay with me.''

Pat turned and glowered at him.

Albert had also turned, and gave him a broad grin that didn't quite hide the query in his eyes. "She'll be just fine, Mr. Whitten." He glanced down at the child. "Gonna put you to work, though, you stick with me. You can help me water the horses."

For the first time in her life, Pat seemed delighted by the word *work*. "I'll be just *fine*, Daddy." She shot him a look that dared him to stop her. Seeing Albert nod, he gave in and hoped he wouldn't regret his decision.

Somehow he'd find a way to keep Pat out of this summer riding camp, and before fall he'd make damned sure that he had enough ammunition to prove that Edenvale School did not need an after-school riding program.

If his Pitti-Pat wanted to learn to ride a horse, break bones, breathe dust, ingest dog and cat germs, chance disease and danger, she'd have to wait until she was grown and out of his control, and even then he'd go down fighting to keep her safe.

He'd come within a hairbreadth of losing Pat twice. The first time, being kept alive in an incubator, she'd managed to cling to life, but her mother, the only woman Mike had ever loved, had died bringing her into the world. That terrible loss had brought home to Mike, in a way that nothing else ever could, how fragile life was. One moment the child in his wife's womb was to be the crowning jewel in their charmed lives. The next he was alone and despairing, terrified of losing this tiny creature who was his only link to his wife.

The second time had come when he'd finally begun to relax a little, to think that he and Pat were safe.

Well, he'd finally learned. No way would he risk a third time. Not in his lifetime or hers. If she was angry with him, well, that came with parenting. He could face her anger; he couldn't face life without her.

He couldn't guard against every danger, but he tried to keep the risks to the minimum. If that meant going back on his promise to buy her a pony, he'd have to find a way to explain his reasoning to her. He'd only made that promise out of desperation when he'd seen her so small in that hospital bed, when he'd been afraid she'd never live to celebrate her twelfth birthday, let alone be able to ride a pony.

He'd do anything to keep her safe—even betray her trust in him, and that would be a very hard thing to do.

As he followed the two women toward the front of the stable, he felt a pang of nostalgia. He closed his eyes, inhaled deeply and remembered the two summers he'd spent at camp outside of Portland when he was younger than Pat.

He knew his parents simply wanted him out of the house, but still he treasured those memories—swimming in the lake, canoeing, campfires—a few months of paradise for a city boy whose every moment during the school year was carefully programmed to get him into the best schools, the best clubs, the most advantageous career when he grew up. Those two summers were the only time in his life he'd ever stepped off the fast track.

He wished with all his heart he dared allow Pat the same luxury, but her illness had left him more deeply scarred emotionally than it had her. To Pat, it was a horrible time, but it was over. Mike couldn't manage to get past his ever-present sense of impending doom.

Five minutes later Mrs. Jamerson, Liz Matthews and Mike settled in the air-conditioned clients' lounge with sodas at their elbows.

"Why should we pick your stable to run the after-school program at Edenvale?" Mike asked. He heard the edge in his voice and assumed the women would hear it too. Mike considered himself an equal-opportunity intimidator. Anything to get a better deal for Edenvale. Just doing his job.

Mrs. Jamerson glanced quickly at her niece. "Frankly, Mr. Whitten," she said, "there are bigger and fancier stables than ValleyCrest Farm in this area, but there's not a single one with a better atmosphere for the kids or a better trainer."

Mike turned to Liz. "What are your credentials?"

"Better than most," Liz said. "I have a B.A. in Equine Studies, and a British Horsemanship certificate. I grew up in pony club. I've been riding and training horses most of my life. I've ridden everything from short stirrup to grand prix, and I've started riders who've gone on to Indoors every year."

"What's all that mean to us common folk?" Mike said.

"It means I'm damned good."

"So if you're so good and so successful, why do you want to start this riding program with Edenvale?"

Mrs. Jamerson stepped in. "Good doesn't always equate with success, Mr. Whitten. Although Liz has done most of the training and all the riding for the last ten years, my husband, Frank, had the international rep-utation. While he was alive we always had a waiting list for lessons and stalls. Since he died, eighteen

months ago, some of our clients have moved to stables
with more famous trainers. We have to rebuild, recoup.
In the meantime, we need a steady cash flow. The riding program at Edenvale would give it to us.''

''And what do we get out of it?''

''We'll make your kids into horsemen—or should I
say horsepersons,'' Liz said. ''Not a bunch of snobs
who don't know anything about horses except which
end to get up on. And who never get any fun out of
the horses they ride.''

''Are you calling Edenvale's students snobs?''

''Not at all, but there are a great many kids who turn
into real brats when they start showing horses. We
won't let that happen.''

''How do you plan to prevent it?''

''Kids ought to have fun messing with their horses,''
Liz said, ''hanging out around the barn, learning to
clean tack and clean stalls, going on trail rides, just
becoming, oh, hell—horsemen. I've seen parents put
enormous pressure on kids to win—maybe live out the
fantasies they never achieved when they were young.
Riding is supposed to be fun. We try to keep it that
way.''

''On horses like that Trust Fund?'' Mike waved a
hand at the wall that separated them from the stalls.

Liz laughed. ''Of course not. He's a grand prix
jumper. He's a handful even for me.''

Her eyes crinkled, her mouth split into a broad grin,
the freckles on her crooked nose stood out and Mike's
blood pressure rose twenty degrees. He was stunned.
Women like this did not usually appeal to him. Even
dirty, there was something disturbingly sexy about this
one. Whoa. He'd have to watch himself. He didn't need
any further female complications in his life.

"We've got large ponies and small horses that have been teaching kids to ride for years."

"That you intend to sell the Edenvale children?" He knew he sounded truculent. He had to get control of himself and the situation quickly.

Mrs. Jamerson stepped in again. "Of course we'd love to sell every one of those children a horse or a pony to keep here in training—but we won't cheat anyone, and we're truly interested in bringing along the next generation of riders. Both Liz and I started in small riding programs at barns like this. Look where we wound up."

Hell of a selling point. Liz and Mrs. Jamerson were dirty and sweaty, fighting money troubles, and undoubtedly worked seven days a week. Just what every parent wanted for his child, a lifetime of drudgery in thrall to a bunch of animals who bit and kicked.

Then he looked into their eyes and saw a pair of supremely content human beings. He shot his starched cuffs and felt the constriction of his power tie. Maybe what he felt was envy.

"Do you give better care, better prices than the other stables?"

"The best care and competitive prices," Liz said. "Plus, we've got over a hundred acres here. Most training stables have a few paddocks and no place for the kids to trail ride."

Mike leaned forward and rested his forearms on his knees. "All right. As we discussed earlier, Edenvale is willing to give you a trial run. An eight-week camp for half a dozen or so kids from Edenvale—Monday through Friday, 9:00 a.m. until 3:00 p.m. They bring their own lunches. You provide drinks. Starting Monday week. I want a prospectus on my desk by Friday morning of this week detailing precisely what you plan to accomplish during that time.''

"That's crazy!" Liz yelped. "That's two days from now.''

"Come now, Miss Matthews, you keep saying you want to make horsepersons of these kids. You must have some idea of how to accomplish that.''

"How much?" Mrs. Jamerson asked softly.

Mike turned to her and smiled. He knew he looked like a crocodile that had just spotted a particularly succulent possum. He'd spent a great deal of time perfecting that smile. Let the negotiations begin.

The door to the lounge flew open. "Daddy, Daddy! I've found him! Come and see him. He's beautiful!'' Pat flew across the room, grabbed her father's arm and began to pull him to his feet. All four dogs tumbled into the room after her.

"Who's beautiful? What are we talking about here?" Mike asked.

"My pony! My very own pony! I've even got a name for him. Come and see him, Daddy. Right *now!*'' She flew out the door again.

Mike gaped after her.

"Terminal," Mrs. Jamerson said softly. "I did warn you." Smiling, she said, "We'll give you our price on Friday.''

Mike turned to Liz. "What pony?" He realized he'd been smartly outmaneuvered, but at the moment he was too worried about Pat's reaction to care.

"God only knows," Liz said. "Hadn't you better go see?''

CHAPTER TWO

"OH, DEAR," Mrs. Jamerson whispered.

"Uh-oh," Liz said. "She would pick that pony."

Mike glanced at the women and then at his daughter, who danced first on one foot then on the other in the stable aisle, pointing at one of the stalls halfway down.

"Come see, Daddy," Pat said. "Come see my very own pony."

Mike walked slowly to her, Liz and Jamerson following. In the stall stood a sleek gray pony. Even to Mike's untutored eye it was beautiful. Its coat glowed, its mane looked as though it had been beaten out of a single strip of silver.

"I'm going to name him Traveller, just like Robert E. Lee's horse, and he's meant for me. I know he is. I just know it."

"Not a good idea," Liz said quietly. "He's going to be a great pony eventually, but at the moment he's green as grass. Knows zilch."

Pat stopped dancing and her face took on that closed, mulish expression that Mike had learned to dread. In the hospital it meant that the doctors and nurses had a fight on their hands to get her to take her medication. He'd never blamed her. No kid likes throwing up a dozen times a day or going bald. There had been times when he'd chickened out, left the medical staff to handle her because he couldn't bear to watch her suffer another minute. They hadn't wanted him there most of the time anyway. Neither had Pat. Sometimes he thought she felt guilty about her illness, as though it were something she had inflicted upon him.

Her nausea passed, and her hair grew back, but unfortunately by that time she'd perfected her technique to get precisely what she wanted from him.

The look Pat gave to Liz Matthews would have curdled milk. "He is too my pony," Pat said. "I love him. We'll learn together." Then she took the next step in her prescribed ritual. Her eyes filled with tears, her lip began to quiver, her shoulders tightened. She grew visibly smaller right in front of Mike's eyes, as though she had taken one of Alice in Wonderland's shrinking potions. Mike closed his eyes and saw her on that bed again. He couldn't fight her and she knew it. "Daddy, you promised. If you love me, you'll buy him."

Liz snorted. Mike saw Pat glance at her coldly from beneath wet lashes.

"Listen, kiddo," Liz said matter-of-factly. "After he's had some training and you've learned to ride, maybe you'll be ready for a pony like this. But an inexperienced rider on an inexperienced horse is a recipe for disaster."

"No, it's not, it's not." Pat stamped her foot. "Daddy, buy him for me. Please," she wheedled. "If we give these people enough money they have to sell him to us."

Mike heard Liz Matthews's quick intake of breath at the same instant he felt all his plans to get Pat away from this place disintegrate under the force of her hazel eyes—her mother's hazel eyes—bright and earnest and intelligent and about as movable as Mount Kilimanjaro.

He actually looked forward to handling infuriated

business rivals. He knew half the investment community called him a ruthless bastard. So how come he couldn't handle one eleven-year-old girl?

"I think Traveller is a lovely name for him," Mrs. Jamerson said. "Much better than Iggy Pop, which is the name he has now." At the sound of his name, the pony raised his head and looked inquiringly at Mrs. Jamerson. She reached over and stroked his nose. "But you said your father promised you a pony for your twelfth birthday, and that's not for a while, right?"

Suspiciously, Pat nodded.

"So, there's plenty of time to find out whether you even like to ride, and meanwhile you can come over and pet him anytime you like. Who knows, you may fall madly in love with another pony."

"I won't."

"Possibly not. And he is a truly lovely pony. He's a registered Connemara—that's a rugged little breed from Ireland. You have good taste. Still, Liz is right. He doesn't know much about his job yet. So we'll take it slow and see what develops, all right?"

Pat took a deep breath, glanced from Mrs. Jamerson to Liz and back again. "Okay," she said, and Mike heard her whisper, "But he's mine."

Mike's relief that a full-blown tantrum had been avoided was tempered by the realization that now there was no way he could keep Pat out of the riding program. His only hope was that Liz and Mrs. Jamerson would be able to show Pat how little she knew. Surely she'd realize that she had a long way to go before buying even an experienced pony became an option. By then maybe she'd have discovered video games or tennis or shopping malls.

"Fine," Mike said, wanting to get Pat out of there

before this fragile truce disintegrated. He turned to Liz. "You'll have that complete syllabus to me by Friday morning? I want it on my desk early."

"We'll do our best," Mrs. Jamerson said when Liz didn't answer immediately.

Mike turned on his heel and walked back to his car. Pat followed silently. He knew damned well she'd start her campaign for that blasted pony the minute they were on their way. This was one time he'd have to put his foot down.

He felt an unreasoning resentment toward both Liz and Mrs. Jamerson. They were only trying to make a living, he knew, but they were complicating his life. Not their fault that they'd played into Pat's obsession or his worries as a parent. Still, he fervently wished they'd chosen some other day school to solicit for their stables.

As he drove away he watched Liz, standing beside one of the paddocks with all her weight on one hip. Damn! He certainly planned to come here for as many of Pat's lessons as he could. He'd arrange his schedule to get into the office late so that he could drive Pat every morning. That meant he'd be spending too much time hanging around Liz Matthews. Why couldn't she be as old and as wrinkled as her riding boot? And did her legs have to be that long? And that face. He tore his eyes away from his rearview mirror and concentrated on his driving.

He could find Liz Matthews sexier than Scheherezade for all the good it would do either of them. They were on completely different wavelengths. He glanced over at his daughter, who was completely preoccupied—no doubt planning her campaign for the gray pony.

At least Mrs. Jamerson seemed to understand children. He had a suspicion that Miss Matthews adhered to the drill-sergeant school of instruction. Pat didn't like to be corrected.

He smiled grimly. Liz might turn out to be the best ally he could have. A couple of days of her bullying in the July heat might well convince Pat to take up knitting.

"I'LL STARVE FIRST," Liz sputtered as she watched Mike and Pat drive away.

"The animals can't starve," her aunt said. "If a summer riding program for Edenvale is what it takes to pay the feed bill, we have to do it."

Liz threw up her hands. "That is a dreadful child, and her father isn't much better." She snorted. "He may be a big muckety-muck in business, but he's not doing that kid any favors by letting her get away with that kind of behavior in public."

"Well, we'd better keep her safe," Mrs. Jamerson said. "It's clear that Daddy will crucify anybody who hurts his little darling. We only carry half a million dollars in liability insurance."

"And you expect me to spend five mornings a week in ninety-five-degree heat with six or eight like her?" Liz said. "I cannot do it. I'll sell my body first."

Mrs. Jamerson looked her up and down. "It's a nice body, but it is thirty-seven years old and extremely dirty. I doubt anybody would pay five dollars for it."

"Oh, thank you so much for that vote of confidence."

"You could always marry a rich husband." She cocked her head in the direction of Mike's retreating Volvo.

"Pul-lease. I'll take the five dollars first," Liz said with a grin.

"That's your choice. But you'd better make believers out of Edenvale School and their little darlings, my dear niece, or we'll both be clerking at some discount mall before Christmas."

"If Trusty and I win the grand prix on Labor Day, we can add five thousand bucks prize money to the till. And maybe entice some of our old clients back. Besides, we haven't lost all our adult clients."

"Yet."

"Think positive. A couple of shows where Valley-Crest brings in championships and we'll be beating off new customers with a stick."

"We need a full barn and a full slate of lessons now, darling Liz. You've looked at the figures."

"I know, I know. But isn't there a better way than teaching half a dozen Pat Whittens to ride?"

"Come on, Liz, you're good with children."

Liz gaped at her. "What lifetime are we talking about here?"

"We could sell Mr. Whitten that gray pony for his Pat," Mrs. Jamerson said.

"No way! Edenvale has never been that sort of sleazy trader. We even kept Uncle Frank honest." She caught the look in her aunt's eyes. "I'm sorry, Aunt Vic. I know he was your husband, but he cut deals fine sometimes—or he would have if you and I hadn't been there to remind him where business stopped and horse-trading started."

Vic laughed. "He could have gotten away with a whole heap more, and the clients would still have loved him. I sometimes wonder how any of us put up with him when he was in one of his moods."

"He trained great horses and riders." Liz shook her head. "They adored him."

Vic sighed. "I wish I had Frank's charm. We could use a few hundred-thousand-dollar sales right about now."

"Charm? *Charm?* He made Marine boot camp look like a first-class cruise to the Bahamas."

"We won. We made money. We had a full barn. We had happy customers and top-notch horses. That's results."

"Results. Right." Liz turned away, her chest heaving. She'd finally learned to pity Uncle Frank about the time she turned twenty. Before that, he'd terrified her. He couldn't show affection, he couldn't praise the people he cared about, not even Vic. Certainly not his gawky niece.

Yet for all his grumpy bullying, Uncle Frank had taken her in after her mother's sudden fatal heart attack and her father's grief made living at home impossible for her. Frank had tried to love her, an eleven-year-old *de facto* orphan, in the only way he knew. He drove her to ride better, higher, stronger. And when she cried he seemed baffled. Memories of those sessions still made her hyperventilate. What would confrontation with Mike Whitten do to her breathing? She didn't doubt for a minute that he could bully with the best if he thought it would work for him.

The worst part was that despite his size and that lantern jaw, something about Whitten turned her on. He radiated confidence. He was in great shape. Probably played handball three times a week and had a personal trainer so he could impress the ladies on the tennis court at the racquet club. He wore no wedding

ring, and Angie Womack had told her there was no
Mrs. Whitten.

She wondered why such an obvious catch was running around without a wife in tow. Little Miss Pat
probably fed arsenic to possible queen consorts the
minute Daddy showed any interest in them. The girl
didn't seem eager to share.

The kid certainly had her father wrapped around her
little finger. Pat held the key to the Edenvale contract,
and if Vic said they had to get it to stay solvent, then
Liz would do everything in her power to make that
happen, even if she had to turn that kid into a centaur.

It wasn't that she didn't like kids. She rode against
kids every day in the hunter ring. But ValleyCrest had
always catered to adult riders.

As Uncle Frank's exercise girl from the time she was
old enough to sit a horse, Liz had been too busy after
school to make friends her own age. She'd moved into
the adult world when she was barely into her teens.
She'd had crushes on the few teenaged boys who rode,
but she'd been tall and so bony, and they'd always
gravitated towards the cute little debutantes.

So here she was at thirty-seven with nobody in her
life except her aunt and the animals, and that was the
way it was likely to remain. At least it was peaceful.
The dogs and cats never yelled at her.

She watched her aunt bending over the feed sacks,
Vic's youthful body lithe and strong. Liz often caught
the longing in her aunt's eyes when her niece swung
into the saddle. *Please God,* Liz prayed. *Let me never
lose my nerve the way she did, never cringe at the
thought of cantering down on a big fence.* She knew it
could happen to anyone, even someone as talented and
fearless as Aunt Vic had been.

Vic was a great manager, a great teacher, but Liz knew how deeply it must hurt never to sit in a saddle.

All those years that Uncle Frank had tried to bully and cajole her out of her fear, Vic never fought back. Liz finally told him if he said one more word on that subject, she'd leave. Since by that time Frank Jamerson weighed over three hundred pounds, and had no one but Liz to ride his horses, he'd tried hard to watch his mouth from that moment on.

He never knew that after their fight Liz had walked out of the room and thrown up. Only Aunt Vic and Albert knew that angry words wounded Liz much more deeply than broken bones and concussions.

Now Liz was faced with Mike Whitten and his whiny kid, and probably a bunch of other equally bratty kids with bullying mothers and fathers.

She walked up the front steps to her cottage, opened the door to the screen porch, made her way across into the cluttered living room and felt her sweat freeze in the air-conditioning as suddenly as though someone had thrown a bucket of ice water on her.

"What a jerk!" A raucous voice spoke from the shadowy corner.

"Am not." Liz said.

Jacko, her small gray parrot, hung upside down from the perch in his large wicker cage and regarded her over his shoulder with beady eyes.

"What a jerk?" he wheedled.

Liz laughed. "I wish you'd learn to say something else, anything else. How about 'I want my dinner.'" She reached for the parrot seed on the window ledge behind the African violets.

"What a jerk!" The parrot bounced up and down in ecstasy.

"Keep that up and I'll bake you into parrot potpie."

"What a jerk." The parrot sighed and stuck his beak into the seeds.

"You're probably right." Liz sank into the shabby sofa. It definitely needed new springs and new upholstery. She closed her eyes. Unbidden, Mike Whitten's face loomed up behind her eyelids. She blinked. "Oh, hell," she said. "That's just what I need." She pointed to the parrot. "And you, not one word. You got that?"

"What a jerk," the parrot replied. This time he sounded as though he meant it.

CHAPTER THREE

THE VAN FROM Edenvale School arrived fifteen minutes late on a cloudless Monday morning. By nine-fifteen the temperature already hovered around eighty-five, but a steady breeze kept the humidity down.

Liz had been up doing her chores since six. When she heard the van, she turned off the water hose and set it down, walked to the front door of the stable and watched as three girls and two boys tumbled out of the van.

No Pat Whitten. Liz gave a sigh that was half relief, half disappointment. She wouldn't be burdened with the kid, but she also wouldn't see Mike Whitten. Why on earth she should want to was beyond her. The man was one step short of an ogre. That little Friday trip to his office to present him the syllabus for the camp had more than proved that.

After making such a big deal about the blasted syllabus, Whitten kept them waiting fifteen minutes, then barely glanced at the sheaf of papers Vic handed him. He hadn't been rude exactly. Just cool. No, dammit. Downright cold. She'd been certain he'd turn them down.

But he hadn't. He'd called late Friday afternoon to accept their terms without a quibble. Vic had set down the phone carefully, then turned a relieved face to Liz. "At least we can pay the feed bill," she said.

"Yeah, but can we stand what we have to do to get the money?" Liz answered.

Today would definitely answer that question. Liz lounged against the open door to the stable. The kids formed a ragged line in front of her and eyed her warily. Only then did she introduce herself.

A moment later Aunt Vic and Albert came out of the stable. Liz introduced them to the children and made her first stab at learning the campers' names.

They stared at Albert's bulk with awe. The broad grin on his dark face made him look like a ravening wolf. Liz knew he was the gentlest, kindest man alive, but he'd try not to let the kids see that. Not right off, at any rate. He always said he liked to get the good out of folks while they were still scared of him. Unfortunately for Albert, most people caught on very quickly that he was about as scary as an oversize stuffed bear.

"Okay, let's get started," Liz said. "Lunch boxes in the fridge. I'll show you around and give you the ground rules first. Then we can start to sort out who gets which horse."

As she turned away, Mike Whitten's Volvo pulled into the driveway. *Oh, damn and blast*, Liz thought. *That's all I need.*

Pat opened the car door and stepped out. The other kids wore ratty jeans and T-shirts. She wore new jodhpurs and shiny brown paddock boots. She carried an equally new black velvet hard hat under her arm.

Two steps from the car Pat clearly realized what the other kids had on, and stopped dead. Liz felt sorry for her. She remembered how important it had been at that age not to be different, not to stand out from her peers.

One of the boys snickered. Pat kept her eyes straight front, but her face flamed.

"Morning, Pat," Liz said casually. "You're late."

Mike Whitten climbed out of the car and answered for his daughter. "I had to take a transatlantic call." No apology, merely a statement of priorities.

"It might be easier for Pat to be on time if she rode in the van with the others," Liz said, trying to keep the edge out of her voice.

"Unnecessary," he snapped. "In future we won't be late."

"Whatever. Come on, kiddo, join the group. We're about to take the nickel tour." She turned to the rest of the group. "Are you with me?"

"When do we get to ride?" the same boy who had snickered at Pat asked. He was a compact towhead who looked younger than the girls.

"You start out on the lunge line."

"What's that?" a redheaded girl asked.

"That's when somebody holds one end of a long rope in the middle of a circle and the horse goes around the outside of the circle attached to the other end of the rope with you on top of it," a cheerful brunette girl answered. "On top of the horse, that is, not the rope." She giggled.

"That's right, uh...?"

"Janey." The girl smiled smugly. "I know how to ride already. I have a pony at my gram's in Missouri."

"Fine. Then you can go first and show the others how it's done."

"Oh, no," Janey groaned. "Not first."

"First. Okay. Aunt Vic will show you around."

"What do we call her?" Janey asked. "We can't call her Aunt Vic."

"Why not?" Vic said. "Everybody else does. You'll get used to it." As she started in the door, she turned to Pat, opened her arm in a gesture of inclusion and smiled at her, "Well, come on, child. Don't just stand there."

Pat took a deep breath and followed, keeping a good five feet between her and the rest of the group. She didn't even glance at Mike.

Mike's eyes followed her.

"I'm sure you have things to do, Mr. Whitten," Liz said. No way did she want him hanging around.

"I'll stay through her riding lesson," Mike replied.

"That's not necessary."

The eyes he turned toward her were icy. "Yes, it is."

Liz took a deep breath, but it didn't do an ounce of good. This man hit every hot button she owned. "Mr. Whitten," she said, trying to keep her voice level, "Edenvale signed a contract with ValleyCrest. We'll fulfill our part, but we can't do it with you or anybody else breathing down our necks. For heaven's sake, do you plan to go to college with her?"

"She won't fall off college and break her neck."

"She won't fall off horses either if she's listening to me and not watching you. There's really no nice way to put this, Mr. Whitten. You can go alone or take your daughter with you, but you absolutely cannot lurk."

"Pat is my child, not yours. And my responsibility."

"Fine. Then take her home with you." Liz turned to walk into the barn.

He followed, caught her arm and spun her to face

him. "Listen, there are special circumstances. Pat's not like the other kids."

"In what way?"

He took a deep breath. "I can't explain, but she isn't."

"Fragile bones? Fragile psyche?"

"She's been ill. She's fine now, but I...oh, hell."

"Tell me. If there's anything I should know..."

"I've said too much already. I promised her I wouldn't tell you or anyone else."

"The kids don't know?"

Mike shook his head. "Not even her teachers at school know."

"What can't she do? Surely you can see I have to know her limitations."

"The doctors say she's perfectly well, completely healthy, but I'm her father. I worry."

Liz looked into those cold eyes. Didn't seem so cold when he spoke about his child. "She doesn't have the stamina to keep up with the other children? Is that it?"

He snorted. "At the moment she has enough stamina to run me ragged. That could change if she got sick. This is not exactly a sterile environment." He waved a hand at a pair of cats snoozing in a patch of sunlight.

"The rest of the world isn't sterile either," she said. "Mr. Whitten, I have several clients who are asthmatics and one who is actually allergic to horses. With medication they manage fine. Is Pat on medication?"

"No. Listen, I shouldn't have opened my mouth. If Pat finds out I've talked to you she'll kill me. Think of me as being here to worry about her so that you won't have to."

"What a truly comforting thought."

Mike's heavy jaw tightened. Those eyes of his had gone glacial again.

Liz continued before she lost her nerve. "I have to establish my authority with these kids if I'm going to get anywhere with them. That goes for Pat as well. Oh, hell, let the child have some space, why don't you? You saw how the other kids treat her. Is that what you want for her? Total isolation?"

"Of course not."

"Then please go to work, Mr. Whitten. And try not to worry. You can pick her up this afternoon." He made a sound deep in his throat that sounded to Liz like a pit bull about to attack, then seemed to think better of it.

He turned on his heel. "Her nanny, Mrs. Hannaford, will pick her up. She'll have identification with her."

"Oh, really."

"Surely you wouldn't release a child to a stranger?"

"No, no, of course not. But the other kids ride in the van."

He said over his shoulder, "My child will not ride in the van. She will be picked up." He got into his car and slammed the door so hard that Liz jumped. He dug a six-foot gash in the gravel as he peeled out.

Liz's heart was pounding. She could almost feel the acid attacking her stomach lining. She'd won this round, but she suspected the man didn't retreat often. Liz took a deep breath and went back into the barn. She looked down and saw that she was running her fingers over her arm where Whitten had held her. He hadn't grabbed her hard, but she still felt his fingers on her skin. He had strong hands. She grinned. No doubt they were a hell of a lot softer than hers and a darned sight better manicured.

THE MORNING WAS BUSY, but by ten the campers knew what was expected of them, what they could and could not do. They'd made a passable job of grooming and tacking up one of the beginner horses and the old campaigner pony. Vic and Liz were now ready to take the kids—two at a time—to either end of the arena to lunge.

"Just thirty minutes each?" The towheaded boy, whose name was Josh, sounded disgusted.

"Trust me," Liz answered. "Thirty minutes on a lunge your first morning is plenty. Once everybody has had a turn, we'll have lunch, rest in the cool for a while, and then if you've got the energy and there's time, we'll do the lunge-line routine for another thirty minutes. Depending on how well you do, we can assign your horses tomorrow."

"I'm ready now!"

Liz shook her head. She looked up and caught Albert's eye. He nodded. If young Josh wanted to keep busy, Albert would make certain he went home with his tail dragging.

Eddy, the other boy, was an entirely different matter. He was tall for his age and shy. Liz suspected he'd be a timorous rider who'd need a gentle hand and some extra nurturing. She fitted all the kids except Pat with hard hats owned by the barn. Pat had her shiny new one. It stood out like a sore thumb among the ratty hats parceled out to the campers.

Despite her objections, Janey was first in the saddle. Liz showed the kids the basics—then she smashed a broad-brimmed straw hat onto her mop of hair, picked up the lunge line and walked Janey and the pony to the ring with the other kids trailing.

Liz noticed that Pat dragged along sulkily. She had

her father's jaw, if not his eyes. Hers were hazel and were emphasized by her short, straight brown hair.

This was a different kid from the one who had bounded onto the arena fence the day Mike came out to see the place. Liz understood that the other children had elected her group freak. Having been the freak in her own sixth-grade class, Liz felt for Pat.

Liz had managed to break out of the mold. Pat could, too. She simply needed to make a couple of friends. But unless Pat stopped acting like Mrs. Astor's Plush Goat, that would not happen.

Liz concentrated on Janey and the pony. Wishbone was a real packer who could teach kids in his sleep. She could tell immediately that Janey had done more than gallop bareback around her grandmother's pasture. She'd had lessons from a good teacher. Liz was so impressed she clicked off the lunge line and let Janey trot and canter on her own.

Liz had a sudden idea. Janey would be perfect for the gray pony, Iggy Pop. He'd be a challenge for her, and she'd be good for him. Liz had not planned to use him for the campers, but having somebody like Janey work him would teach them both. Liz glanced at Vic, caught her eye, mouthed "Iggy" and received a nod of agreement.

Liz motioned to Pat.

"I want to go last," the girl said.

"My stable, my choice," Liz told her. "Come on, Wishbone is all warmed up for you."

"I want Traveller."

"No way. Come on. I'll give you a leg up."

"Fraidy-cat," the girl with the red hair, whose name was Kimberly, whispered to Pat's back as she passed.

Liz saw Pat stiffen, but the girl said nothing. Liz decided to speak to Kimberly later.

Pat reached the pony, who turned his head to stare at her with chocolate eyes. She stepped back.

Kimberly was right, Pat really is afraid, Liz thought. *I was sure she'd be raring to go.*

Liz held Pat's stirrup. After two tries Pat got close enough to the pony to actually put her foot into the stirrup. As her bottom hit the saddle, Wishbone snorted. Pat froze. "What's the matter with him?"

"He's lazy. He's just realized he's going to have to work some more for his supper."

"He'll be mad."

"Wishbone? He doesn't know what mad is."

"I don't want him. I want Traveller."

"You're not ready for Trav…Iggy. Start with the basics. Ready?" Wishbone walked to the end of the line and began to circle Liz at a walk. Liz watched Pat with narrowed eyes. She could see Pat's chest heaving. The girl held tight to the front of the saddle. Her lower lip trembled.

Suddenly she hauled back on the reins so hard that Wishbone nearly sat down on his tail. "Stop! No. My daddy says I get to ride whoever I want to ride."

"If your daddy said that, which I doubt, he was wrong."

Pat turned a furious face to Liz. Now she looked like her father, except her eyes smoldered while his froze. "I want my very own pony. You're not the boss of me." Without waiting she threw her leg over the saddle, dropped to the ground and ran as hard as she could straight into the stable.

"Told you she was scared," Kimberly said smugly,

moving forward to take Pat's place. She looked over her shoulder, "Scaredy-cat, stuck-up scaredy-cat!"

"Cut that out," Liz snapped. She glanced over at Vic, who stood frozen in the center of her circle with a horrified expression on her face. "Oh, da...drat!" Liz said. "Albert?"

"Uh-huh."

"Where'd she go?"

"She's in the barn. I'll keep an eye on her."

"Thanks, Albert." Liz turned back to Kimberly. "Okay, your turn. And remember that anybody who is not scared at some time on a horse is just plain dumb. Got that?"

Chastened, Kim climbed aboard.

The rest of the morning went smoothly but with no sign of Pat. When they came into the barn for lunch, Liz raised her eyebrows at Albert. He jerked a thumb overhead. The hayloft. Oh, great. Momma Kat had a fresh litter up there, and if Pat tried to bother the kittens, Momma Kat would rip her to shreds.

"I'll do lunch," Vic whispered. "Go."

Silently Liz climbed the hayloft ladder. Bales of hay were stacked like stairsteps across the big platform. The ceiling fan kept the shadowy air circulating.

Liz waited for her eyes to adjust as she searched for Pat. At first she saw nothing except hay, then movement at the far back caught her eye.

"Lunchtime," Liz said matter-of-factly.

"Don't want any lunch."

"You brought it, you eat it."

"Not with them."

Liz walked toward her and was vastly surprised to find Momma Kat curled against Pat's thigh and all five kittens asleep in her lap. Pat's dusty face was streaked with sweat and tears. "Quite a coup," Liz said, pointing to the kittens. "Momma Kat avoids people when she's got kittens."

"They're beautiful," Pat said, stroking a small gray kitten who was busily stropping its needle-sharp claws on Pat's fine new jodhpurs.

"You can have one when they're old enough, if your daddy says its okay."

"He won't let me. He won't even let me have goldfish. They carry germs."

"So do you."

"Tell him that, why don't you?"

"I did already." Liz sat on the bale nearest to Pat but on her level.

"You're kidding! What did he say?"

"Never mind. Tell me what happened out there this morning?"

Pat turned away. "I want to ride Traveller and not that stupid pony you put me on."

"That wasn't it. You froze."

"Liar."

"I know what I saw. Incidentally, don't ever call me a liar again. It's rude, untrue, and I don't like it."

"Who cares what you like? My daddy says—"

"We're not talking about your daddy, we're talking about you." Liz realized her tone was harsher than she'd planned. And Vic said she had such a great way with kids.

Abruptly, Pat dumped the kittens, who protested loud enough to wake Momma Kat, and stood up.

So did Liz. "We don't run from things in this barn, especially the things that frighten us and embarrass the hell out of us."

"You can't make me."

"Sure I can, but I shouldn't have to."

Pat sank onto the floor, put her head down and began to sob.

Whitten would have this kid home and that contract nullified before dark at the rate she was going. She reached out and touched Pat's shoulder as though it were a hot stove.

Pat flinched. "All right, I'm scared, I admit it. Now are you satisfied? You can just throw me out right now and I'll never come back, never get to ride, never get my pony, never..." The sobs turned to wails.

Liz was stunned. She sat down. "Come here, Pat," she said and opened her arms. Pat sniffled and knee-walked over to her. "Lesson number one. Everybody gets scared."

"I'm scared all the time."

"Trust me, you do not give that impression."

"I know!" Pat wailed. "My daddy thinks I'm tough, but I'm so scared something will happen to me and then he'll just die and it'll be my fault."

Mike Whitten, I will have your hide!

"Bull. Nothing's going to happen to you, and if it does, it won't be your fault, and your daddy looks like a pretty tough character to me."

"He's not, he's not. You don't know what he's been through."

"Then tell me."

"No!" Pat cried.

Liz opened her mouth, then remembered she wasn't supposed to know anything about Pat's illness. "Okay. Forget your daddy for the moment." She gestured toward the floor and the office below. "Did you know Aunt Vic was an Olympic rider?"

Pat sniffled, suddenly interested. "Really?"

"Yep."

"Oh, wow."

"Great teacher, great barn manager, best friend I have in the world."

"Uh-huh." Pat regarded her suspiciously.

"She hasn't put her foot in a stirrup for twenty years."

"Why not?"

"She was warming up her jumper at Madison Square Gardens, and some fool crashed into her."

Pat's eyes widened.

"Broke her collarbone, her pelvis and one leg. Nearly killed her."

"And she got scared?"

"The other rider was one hundred percent responsible for the crash, but that didn't help Vic. The horses came out without a scratch. She was hurt, but at least she lived."

"He died?"

"Broke his neck." Liz realized suddenly this might not be the absolutely perfect story to tell a kid who was terrified of walking around in a circle on a quiet pony at the end of a lunge line.

But Pat seemed absorbed. Liz plunged ahead. "Vic couldn't ride for nearly eight months. The first time she tried to get back onto a horse, she completely freaked. Everybody knows about it, and they don't laugh at her. She works around horses, lunges, feeds, does everything else, but she can't get up and ride. You can."

"But..."

"Make you a deal. Call your nanny and tell her to pick you up at four o'clock this afternoon instead of three—make up some excuse. Not unusual to run late the first day. After the other kids are gone, you and I will work through your fear."

"On Traveller?"

"Absolutely not. No temper tantrums, and you do what I tell you when I tell you or the deal's off. Take it or leave it."

"But..."

"My way or the highway."

Pat stared at her for a long moment, then she nodded. "Okay."

"Good, now get your tail downstairs and eat lunch. I'm starved."

"Nunh-uh, not with them."

"Fine. Deal's off." Liz walked to the hayloft ladder.

"They'll laugh at me."

"Big deal. Give you a tip. However big a to-do they make over this morning, you make a bigger one. If they accuse you of being scared, tell them you were positively petrified. If they laugh, laugh louder. Confuse the hell out of them."

"I don't know."

"Try it. It may work, and if it doesn't, you're no worse off than you are now. And call your nanny from the office after lunch."

Albert stood at the foot of the ladder with the cordless phone. "It's Whitten."

"Drat." Liz took the phone and adjusted her voice. "Yes, Mr. Whitten, what can I do for you?"

"How did Pat's lesson go?"

Pat stepped off the last rung in time to hear Liz say her father's name. She made a face.

"Beautifully. She did fine. Got the makings of a good rider." Liz grinned at Pat, who bugged out her eyes and pointed at her chest with an exaggerated "me?" sign.

"Excellent. I've decided to pick her up myself."

"Damn." Liz whispered. "That's fine, Mr. Whitten, but we're running a little late today—first day and all, shakedown. Could you come about four…"

Pat was shaking her head and holding up five fingers.

"Uh, better make that five. Give everyone a chance to cool down."

Pat nodded and grinned.

Liz heard Mike's heavy sigh. "Yes, all right. Five. On the dot. Put Pat on the line."

Pat pantomimed "no." Liz raised her eyebrows. "Of course, but please be quick. We have a schedule to meet. You're cutting into her rest period." *That ought to get him.*

Pat put both hands around her throat as though she were strangling herself and stuck out her tongue at the phone. Liz snickered and handed it to her anyway.

"Hey, Daddy. Yes, I did great." She listened and looked up at Liz in panic. "No, you can't see me ride today. Uh…the horses get fed at four-thirty."

Liz put thumb and forefinger together in a circle in the "that's perfect" sign.

Pat nodded and grinned. "Tomorrow?" She made a face. Liz shook her head violently.

"No, Daddy, That's too soon. I want to be able to show off what I know. Give me time to learn something, okay?" Pat listened for another moment, said goodbye and handed the phone back to Liz. "He wants to speak to you again."

"Miss Matthews, I apologize for my rude behavior this morning," Whitten said. He didn't sound one bit apologetic. Maybe he expected Liz to apologize in turn.

"Think nothing of it. Goodbye." Liz clicked the phone off and met Pat's high five in midair. "Go get your lunch. And laugh like he...heck."

The moment Pat's back was turned, Liz stuck out her tongue at the phone and handed it back to Albert.

"What you up to?" he asked.

"I have no idea what you're talking about."

"Doesn't do to get between a daddy and his little girl. He finds out, he's gonna whip your tail."

"Him and what army?"

As she turned away she realized that Albert, as always, was right. She not only had to keep Whitten from finding out about her private session with Pat, she had to keep the other kids from finding out as well. And Pat Whitten did not seem like the most reliable ally. How did she get herself into these things?

As she turned the corner and saw Pat sitting on the sofa between Janey and Kimberly and laughing like a demented hyena, she grinned. *Because she reminds me of me.*

CHAPTER FOUR

THE VAN PICKED UP the campers at three that afternoon. At three-twenty Pat mounted Wishbone while Liz held his bridle. At three-thirty Pat allowed herself to be played out on the lunge line.

At a quarter to four Pat decided she could walk around all by herself—no lunge line.

At ten minutes to four Liz sat down on a jump in the center of the ring while Pat walked around the perimeter all by herself. By four-fifteen she decided she was ready to trot. Pat didn't bother communicating this to Liz. She simply kicked Wishbone hard in his sides. Surprised, he woke up, grunted and obligingly trotted forward.

Pat dropped the reins, dug both hands into the pony's mane and yelped. Liz ran to her and grabbed Wishbone after five strides.

"Our deal is that you do what I tell you, young lady, and not what you think you'd like to try," Liz said.

Pat threw her leg over the pony's side. "I want to get down now."

"No way. Quit now and you'll never get back on."

"But my daddy says..."

"Your daddy is not here. Get down now and don't bother to come back tomorrow."

Pat sniffled, picked up her reins and walked forward.

She gulped when Liz let go and stepped away, but she stuck it out for another five minutes.

"Okay. Now you can dismount. It's hot and the pony's tired." Liz instructed Pat in the proper way to dismount—a way that did not involve throwing the reins up in the air and yelling like a coyote. "Walk him in and give him a bath. Albert will show you how."

Pat took the pony's reins and began to move toward the stable door.

"Oh, and Pat?"

Pat looked over her shoulder.

"You did good."

"I did, didn't I?" Pat's face glowed.

As Liz walked into the stable behind Pat she heard the telephone ring and raced to pick it up. "Valley-Crest," she breathed.

"Hey, Liz," a familiar female voice said, "This is Angie." She sounded subdued. "Are you still speaking to me?"

"You mean, since you left ValleyCrest and went over to the competition? I guess so. What's up?"

Silence, then a deep breath. "I need a favor. A really big favor. This afternoon."

Liz waited.

"I don't know whether anybody told you, but I decided to breed my mare Boop."

"I heard."

"Thing is, she's due to foal any minute now and I have absolutely got to go to Europe for a few days on business. I'm leaving tomorrow."

"Uh-huh."

"I'm terrified she'll foal while I'm gone. Kevin refuses to be responsible. Says he delivers human babies, not horse babies.''

"So, doesn't Mark have a stall available?"

Another deep breath. "I don't trust him to handle the birth, either." Angie went on in a rush. "He's never foaled a mare in his life, and he couldn't be less interested. He's furious that I even bred her."

"So he won't take her?"

"Oh, he'll take her, all right, but I have no intention of leaving her with him unless I can't con you." The voice became a wheedle. "Please, Liz, please. I know I was a total monster to abandon you and Vic the way I did for Mark's barn. I've learned my lesson."

Liz felt a wave of elation. Angie Womack was an excellent rider who kept two very expensive hunters on board and training year round. Her OB-Gyn husband provided her with unlimited funds. If she came back to ValleyCrest, others might follow. The Womacks were good people. Besides, no way could Liz let that mare foal under Mark Hardwick's tender mercies. "Sure," Liz said. "Bring her on. I'll have a double stall waiting for her."

"Oh, thank you thank you thank you!" Angie said.

Liz smiled and went to tell Vic and Albert that they were back in the baby business.

Angie's big two-horse trailer pulled into the yard ten minutes later and Angie jumped out. She wore baggy jeans and an Olympic T-shirt with the sleeves ripped out. Her hair was almost as short as Albert's and nearly as curly. She was burned brown by the summer sun, and she was grinning from ear to ear. She ran to Liz and Vic and hugged them both. "Yell at me, I deserve it."

"Let's get that mare bedded down first," Vic said

and smiled at Angie. "Then we'll yell at you. You did bring the foal predictor kit? I'm not sitting up with this lady every night until you get back."

"I've got it in the car." She smiled over Liz's shoulder at Pat, who stood in the doorway. "Hey. I'm Angie."

Pat nodded, obviously fascinated.

Two minutes later a broad chestnut mare backed out of the trailer.

"Wow!" Pat said and ran to pet the mare.

"Be careful, she's pretty grumpy. She wants that baby out of there," Angie said as she led the mare into the barn with complete familiarity. Vic winked at Liz.

"Can I help?" Pat asked as she trailed along. "Daddy won't be here for another thirty minutes—if he's on time. Half the time he's not."

"Come on," Angie said amiably.

"You do that, kiddo," Liz said. "I've got to get on Trust Fund before feeding time."

She was still riding when Mike Whitten arrived and found Pat sitting on a tack trunk helping Albert wash down stirrup leathers.

"You're too early," Pat wailed.

Mike checked his watch. "Actually, I'm five minutes late. Are you supposed to be that dirty?"

"Oh, Daddy. I've been riding and grooming, and come see the mare who's about to have a baby." She pulled her father down the aisle. Outside in the arena he glimpsed Liz cantering by on that same big horse.

"Daddy, I've got to finish helping Albert," Pat said. "You go on outside and wait for me."

"Pat..."

"Daddy! It's my first day!"

He gave in, but instead of going to his car he walked out to stand beside the arena and watch Liz.

She hadn't even acknowledged Mike's presence, not that he expected her to. She turned the horse down the center toward a pair of big jumps. Mike felt his heart in his mouth. Trust Fund sailed over the first and cantered down to the second.

The horse stopped dead one stride from the fence and dropped both his head and his shoulder. Mike didn't expect that. Apparently neither did Liz. She did a somersault in midair and came down on the far side of the jump flat on her back with a whump that raised a cloud of dust. She didn't move.

Mike vaulted the fence, raced to where she lay and knelt in the dirt beside her. The horse shied away.

Liz was on her back, her eyes open and staring, her mouth wide. She didn't seem to be breathing. As his knees hit the dirt she sucked in a huge breath that sounded like a death rattle.

"Don't move," Mike snapped. "You may have broken your neck."

Liz turned her head on a neck that was obviously still in working order. "I'm fine," she gasped. "Knocked my breath out." She put both hands against her diaphragm and pushed. "Better." She raised onto her elbows. "Nothing broken."

Mike put one arm behind her waist and the other behind her knees and scooped her up. She was no lightweight, but at that point he figured he had enough adrenaline pumping to move Brooklyn Bridge. He began to walk as quickly as he could toward the stable.

"Hey!"

"Where are you hurt?" he asked, afraid for a moment he might have done her more harm than good.

"I'm not hurt, I'm mad as hell. I'm mad at Trusty, mad at myself, and if you do not put me down his instant I am going to be really mad at *you*."

"Fine." He dropped her legs.

The instant she touched down she wrapped her arms around his neck and clung to him. "Oh, heck. Just let me stand here a minute until I get my breath back."

Mike suspected that small request cost her dearly.

It cost him as well. She stood in the circle of his arm, her breast and hip against his side, her breath against his cheek. He closed his eyes and relished the feel of warm woman against him. Too long since he'd felt it.

After a moment she let go of his neck, but he kept his arm around her waist in case she should feel rocky again. And because he liked having her in his arms.

She disengaged herself carefully and took a couple of steps toward the horse, who stood at the far side of the ring eyeing her sheepishly. "Trusty, you old fool, come here."

The horse meandered over. Mike caught his reins.

"Thanks," Liz said. "Give me a leg up."

"You're not getting back up there!"

"Of course I am." She sounded surprised. "If I let him get away with that nonsense, he'll do it again."

"You need to be checked over by a doctor before you ride again."

"The hell I do. Now, are you going to give me a leg up or what?"

She bent her knee. Mike tossed her into the saddle so hard that she nearly tumbled over the other side.

"Wow!" she said. "You try tossing Pat that hard and she'll come down in the back pasture." She moved away and said over her shoulder, "Better get out of the way while Trusty and I have our little prayer meeting.'' She trotted off.

He watched her bottom rise and sink in the saddle and discovered he was having visions that he should not have about his child's riding teacher. He dusted himself off and walked to the edge of the arena. This time he used the gate. He turned to see Liz heading for that pair of huge fences again. He crossed his fingers and held his breath.

Trusty sailed over both jumps perfectly. Liz pulled him down to a walk immediately and came over toward Mike. "That's enough. What you saw earlier, Mr. Whitten, was an example of 'quitting dirty.'''

Mike opened the gate.

"Most of the time horses telegraph that they don't intend to jump. Trusty occasionally stops with his toenails in the fence. This is the first time he's gotten me off, but I've held on to his ears a couple of times.'' She grinned and patted the big horse's neck. "Quitting dirty is a very bad habit.'' She smacked Trusty lightly on his thick neck. "Remember that.''

Albert came out of the barn and stood with his hands on his hips. "What's the matter with you?'' he asked. "You look like you've rolled in the dirt.''

"I did.''

Albert took the reins and glanced at Mike. "So does he. And he's not dressed for it.''

Liz swung off and leaned against Trusty's shoulder for a moment.

"You okay?'' Albert asked.

"My bruises are having bruises as we speak, but yeah, I'm fine. Just rang my chimes a little bit.''

Albert shook his head and led the horse off. Liz put

both hands in the small of her back and stretched, then took two steps toward the stable.

"Ow!" she yelped, and grabbed the back of her left thigh. "Ow, ow, ow, *ow!*"

Mike reached for her. She snaked her arm back around his neck and held on.

"Charley horse." Liz grimaced in pain. "Ow, ow, ow," she repeated.

She hobbled to the mounting block with Mike's help. Pity she had to be in pain before she'd let him near her.

Mike lowered her so that she sat on the block, and he knelt in front of her. "Stretch your heel down."

"No way!"

He grabbed the heel of her boot and pulled down hard. She yelped again, but she kept it down when he took his hands away. He reached around her thigh and began to knead. He could feel the knotted muscle. After a moment it began to loosen. He heard her sigh.

He, on the other hand, felt other portions of his body tighten and hoped nobody would notice. He was entirely too susceptible to this woman. His attraction to her had been powerful and immediate. That had only happened to him once before—the first time he laid eyes on Sandi. Sandi, at least, had liked him—loved him, in fact. Liz Matthews made no bones about her dislike.

"You're good at this," Liz said and leaned back with a sigh.

"Tennis and handball are notorious for tying up your muscles. You either learn to unkink them fast or walk with a cane."

"Thanks," she said. "I'm sorry I snarled at you. I

hate having anybody see me fall. Makes me feel like a fool.''

"No problem.''

She began to giggle. ''You're as dirty as I am.''

He shrugged and stood in front of her. ''Dry cleaners clean.''

"Yeah.'' She pulled herself up. At that moment, Pat came around the corner followed by Vic and Angie. "You fall?'' Vic asked with studied casualness.

"Trusty quit dirty on me. I'm okay.'' She cocked her thumb at Pat. ''I think your daddy's ready to go. And Pat, better wear jeans tomorrow.'' She limped toward the lounge.

Mike watched her. She hurt considerably more than she was willing to let on. Maybe she'd cracked a rib. He ought to drag her to a doctor just to be sure. She'd never go. Hardheaded, opinionated damned female. He caught his breath. Great, he thought, now I've got two of them to worry about. *Where in hell had that thought come from.*

"WHO WAS THAT masked man?'' Angie asked as she flopped down in one of the shabby leather club chairs in the clients' lounge. The sound of Mike's Volvo on the gravel driveway was just fading.

Liz lay stretched on the equally shabby leather couch.

Angie continued, ''There's something really— *grrrr*—sexy about him.''

"I hadn't noticed,'' Liz lied. ''You're a married woman. You shouldn't be growling at other men.''

"Shoot, I growl at everybody.''

"Unfortunately, so does he.'' Liz sat up slowly. She was really beginning to stiffen up. ''He's Mike Whitten, the chairman of the board of trustees at Edenvale School. The guy we have to convince to give us their after-school riding program this fall.''

"*That's* Mike Whitten?" Angie began to laugh. "God help you. Kevin knows him from the racquet club. Says he's rumored to drink a quart of antifreeze every morning just to keep his blood circulating."

"I can believe it." Liz began to knead her shoulders. "He's Mr. Iceberg to everyone except that kid of his."

"Well, I think he's gorgeous in a craggy sort of way. Anyway, enough about the intimidating Mr. Whitten. Am I back in your good graces?"

"Partially."

Vic came in, dug a diet soda out of the refrigerator and took the club chair across from Angie. She looked her niece over carefully. "You really okay?"

"Sure. And feeling foolish."

Angie sighed, leaned forward and dropped her brown hands between her knees. "Liz isn't the only one feeling foolish."

"Why did you leave us?" Vic asked.

Angie hunched her shoulders and took a deep breath. "After Frank died, I stopped winning. I knew it wasn't your fault, but I thought if I went over to Mark I could start winning again. And I did, too, for a little while."

"What went wrong?"

"God, everything. He started badgering me to sell both my horses and let him find me some better ones—meaning more expensive. He was furious when I refused, and even more furious when I decided to breed Boop against his wishes."

"Why did you?" Liz asked.

Angie blushed. "It's being around Kevin and all those babies. I wanted a baby—*something* to love, even

if it was a foal. And I'll move Charlie here too if
you've got room for another jumper.''

"Absolutely," Vic said.

"Okay," Angie said. "I'll leave you a letter of au-
thorization to pick up Charlie tomorrow and bring him
here.''

"And the problem of not winning that Mark was
supposed to solve for you...?''

Angie shrugged. "I can't ride Boop until her baby
is six months old and weaned. Then it'll take another
three months to get her in condition to jump again. That
puts us into next spring, so I won't be riding any hunters unless I can pick up a few rides for some of your
clients, or maybe even for Liz, if she's got too many
horses to ride.''

"We'll be glad to have you," Vic said.

"So you don't care about winning any longer?" Liz
asked. "Don't believe that for a second.''

Angie sat up straight and held her hands out. "Hey,
you two are far and away the best trainers I know. I
intend to win with *you*. ValleyCrest is developing clout
again with the pair of you. The people that matter are
noticing you.'' She raised her eyebrows. "You're even
starting to scare a few people like Mark. Goody,
goody.''

LATER, after Liz and Vic shared a salad and a chicken
sandwich, Liz bedded all her animals for the night, including Jacko the parrot, and climbed into her old
clawfooted tub to soak her bruises in a herbal bath. As
she sank into the blissfully hot water, she wondered
what Mike Whitten was having for dinner with his
Pitti-Pat. Healthy junk. She smiled. He had no idea she
and Pat were conspiring against him.

She felt a tingle in the pit of her stomach as she remembered the feel of his muscular arm around her, his long fingers on her thigh. Much to her disgust she agreed with Angie. He did exude a kind of wild sexiness.

Liz hadn't been interested in any man in a very long time. Not only were the pickings slim, but she told herself she didn't have time for another relationship that would wind up going nowhere. Men did not like to share her attention with the horses. They resented the fact that the horses came first. Always had, always would. And so would the dogs, the cats and the parrots. Animals didn't break your heart. Men invariably did.

But maybe it wouldn't be so bad to feel Mike's arm around her again. Would it be worth falling off a very tall horse to get him to touch her?

"Nah," she said aloud and closed her eyes. "Although I could always fall off a shorter horse."

CHAPTER FIVE

DURING DINNER, Pat gave Mike a replay of every moment of her first day at camp.

Mike thought she seemed happier than he had ever seen her. Her face was flushed...

He reached across the table and laid the back of his hand against her forehead.

"Oh, Daddy," Pat snapped. "I don't have any fever."

"You've got a lot of color in your cheeks."

"The sun does that." Pat snorted. "Get a grip. I feel great!" She told him for the third time how she'd trotted that pony all by herself. A couple of times she nearly slipped and told him the truth—about how she stayed behind so that Liz could help her work through her fear. She managed to catch herself in time.

She was used to giving her father a heavily edited version of her activities. She knew he'd have a cat fit if he ever caught on to some of the things she did when he wasn't around, and Mrs. H. had promised not to snitch on her. It wasn't lying exactly. She didn't want Mike to worry—well, not any more than he did, at any rate.

Maybe when he saw how much fun she was having he'd loosen up a little. She checked to see how he was taking all this. He had a goofy grin on his face. She got up to kiss his cheek.

And she kept up the chatter. Mike found he was listening with a tinge of jealousy. Pat was the only person left in his life who loved him. God knew he loved her. And now she seemed to be developing a crush on Liz Matthews. All his colleagues had warned him that sooner or later Pat would grow up and begin to move away from him.

Strange. He'd never rebelled against his parents. He'd felt no more for them than they had for him. They saw him as a certificate of deposit—tend it properly and the dividends would be worth the expense.

Well, he'd paid off handsomely by presenting them with a large trust fund that would make their years of retirement from the faculty at Berkeley more than comfortable. And then he'd walked out of their lives.

That was almost twenty years ago. He doubted they noticed that he no longer called or came to see them. His father would still be writing stuffy papers about the state of the economy for academic journals, and his mother would be so engrossed in her mathematical formulae that she'd forget dinner.

When they'd sent him to prep school at age twelve, he'd never had a moment's homesickness. Probably because he'd never felt at home with them. Even as a small boy, he'd often wondered whether he should introduce himself to his parents at breakfast. They never seemed to know quite who he was or what he was doing in their cloistered lives.

Wiping her hands on a linen towel, Mrs. Hannaford came in from the kitchen. "Enough. Time for bed, young lady."

"No. It's too early." Pat's statement was flat. "Did I tell you…"

"Tomorrow comes early."

"I'm too keyed up to sleep. I'll just lie there and toss and turn until daylight."

"So look at the ceiling and think about tomorrow," Mike said. "Mrs. H. is right. Take your bath and go to bed. Now."

"Daddy, I've had one bath this evening. I do not intend to take another, thank you very much."

"Point taken. So brush your teeth and things."

Pat stalked off toward her bedroom with her head high. She could usually get around her father except when it came to her health. Bedtimes were not negotiable. At the door she paused and turned to say dramatically, "I can hardly wait to get to college and away from here. I plan to drink, smoke pot and date the entire football team."

"You do and I'll lock you up in a dungeon until you're ninety," Mike answered.

"I'm already locked in a dungeon." She slammed the door behind her.

"Just like you." Mrs. Hannaford's voice was gruff with affection.

"I drink very little, I don't smoke pot or anything else, and I have never ever dated anybody's football team."

"You might consider dating the girls' volleyball team."

Mike laughed. "They're about six years older than Pat. Besides, at my age all that sex would kill me."

Mrs. Hannaford gave him a cool appraisal. "I doubt that. You going out tonight?"

"No, I'm going to bed. Rachelle is at some real-estate dinner thing."

"Oh, really."

At the housekeeper's tone, Mike raised his head

from the back of his chair. "I don't know why you dislike Rachelle. She's beautiful, has a great career of her own so she's not after me for my money—her alimony has left her a wealthy woman—and she and Pat are even civil to each other most of the time. In one year Pat will be thirteen. She needs a mother to—oh, teach her how to shave her legs."

"I have already taught her that."

"You have?" Surprised, Mike pulled himself out of the chair and walked over to Mrs. Hannaford.

"Mrs. Hannaford, I don't know what we'd do without you. Promise me that even if I do marry again, you'll always be with us."

She turned away and casually flicked her linen towel at an imaginary dust mote on the polished glass dining-room table. "A new wife will want to do things her way."

"Not negotiable. You're family."

"And who says I'd want to stay under those circumstances? I could always get another job." She began to polish harder, making tight little whorls on the glass.

Mike felt a jolt. Melba Hannaford had only been with them for a little over two years, but from the beginning he'd never thought of her as an employee. She'd seen too much of their lives, been too much a part of the bad times. He cleared his throat and moved to the window. His hands worked at his sides. When he spoke, his voice sounded colder than it had before. "No doubt you could. You are extremely competent."

"That nonsense won't work with me," she said. "I know you too well. But sooner or later Pat is not going to need either of us, you know."

"That won't happen for years." He felt much more relief than he would admit. "And I don't plan to marry anyone until I am absolutely positive that it will be the right thing for all of us."

"I would never presume to tell you who to marry," she said. "But you should not remain celibate for the rest of your life."

"Who says I'm celibate? And how would you know?" He smiled as he turned and saw the color rise in her cheeks.

"I did not say chaste, Mr. Whitten. Look up celibate in the dictionary. It merely means unmarried, whatever you young people think. All I'm saying is that once Pat goes off to college and starts making a life for herself, you are going to find yourself very much alone."

He walked over to the cabinet in the corner and pulled a bottle of light beer out of the small refrigerator. He leaned against the closed door, popped the top and took a deep swig. "The wrong woman would be a hell of a lot worse for Pat than celibacy."

"So find the right one. For both of you." Mrs. Hannaford sat on the black leather chair and propped her feet in their shining white tennis shoes on the glass-topped coffee table. "Oh, that feels good."

Mike sat across from her and propped his Top-Siders on the other side. "You don't think Rachelle is the right one?"

"You're the one who's got to live with her if you marry her."

"True enough." He took another long swig of his beer, then dropped his head back and closed his eyes. Pat's exuberance wore him out.

"Hmmph." Mrs. Hannaford pulled herself to her feet and stalked off to the kitchen.

"One more thing," Mrs. Hannaford spoke from the

kitchen doorway. "What on earth did you do to that blue suit you were wearing?"

Mike laughed. "You do not want to know."

"Indeed." Mrs. Hannaford slammed the door behind her.

All his women seemed to be slamming doors on him tonight.

Mike was alone with his thoughts. He tried to conjure up Rachelle's elegant face. Instead, he found himself staring at a vision of Liz Matthews, dirty face, freckles, wild hair and all. He blinked and sat up.

She was the last woman in the world for him. She was so different from Sandi. He turned so that he could see the vibrant portrait above the fireplace. The woman whose eyes met his was darkly sleek, almost fiercely beautiful. Even in a big blow on Puget Sound in their sailboat, she'd always managed to stay neat. Until that final afternoon. He sighed and closed his eyes against that terrible image.

Every woman he'd ever dated since Sandi's death had possessed that same elegance.

So why should Liz Matthews with her crooked nose and her grubby jeans attract him? She was so damned sure of herself, so career oriented. She crashed into his life like a freight train.

He set the empty beer bottle down on the coffee table as the realization hit him. Damn. All those qualities were exactly like Sandi. She'd spend all weekend designing one of her fancy Puget Sound houses and forget to eat or sleep. She dragged him to art galleries and theater and ballet and the opera—and taught him to love all of it. She'd exploded his miserable life like a rotten melon.

Four years out of Yale he'd been bored with making

money, fed up with the ruthless negotiation and cliff-hanger days when ten minutes might make the difference between a million lost and a million won. He'd needed something—or someone—new in his life.

He remembered the night he first saw her. He'd been alone, as usual, propping up the wall of the office reception room while a cocktail party raged around him, waiting until he could go home without seeming too rude.

She wore a loose red silk dress and the highest heels he'd ever seen outside of a topless bar. She stood out like a peony among all those navy and gray suits. Her long black hair was pulled back tight in a heavy bun on the back of her head. She caught him gaping at her, worked her way through the crowd until she was close enough to lay her hand on his arm. She said, "Do you believe in love at first sight?"

He stammered, "I do now."

He took her to bed two hours later, and six weeks later they were married. She was two years older than he, but that made no difference. They had six years of happiness. He bought her a forty-six-foot sailing sloop. Her career as an architect took off. He regained his pleasure in the money game. They seemed to live in a golden glow where everything they attempted turned out perfectly.

It had ended in four hours on a rainy Friday afternoon. She'd gone into premature labor, had an emergency C-section and burst a blood vessel in her brain that killed her twenty minutes later and left him with a two-pound baby daughter that he never intended to see.

He'd felt only rage. Rage at himself for giving in to her and getting her pregnant, rage at the child who had killed her, at Sandi for leaving him with this tiny little thing on his hands, at the doctors, the hospital, heaven itself.

He sailed their sloop out into the Sound so that he could open the sea cocks, sink the boat and join his wife.

He'd never doubted that it was Sandi who stopped him as he reached for the first plug. He turned the boat around, sailed back to the dock and drove at once to the hospital. He stood outside the neonatal intensive care unit looking at his blue-black stick figure of a daughter as she fought for her life. She was the ugliest small animal he'd ever seen.

As he stood staring in at his child, Sandi gave him her final gift. She filled his heart with love for this child for whom she had died. He sat down with his back against the wall and howled so loudly that two interns tried to sedate him.

He'd had his one great love. He couldn't expect another. In the years since, he'd only sought to find a friend, a colleague, an ally to share his life and help raise Pat. Most marriages had considerably less going for them than friendship and collaboration.

Liz Matthews wasn't his ally or colleague, and she didn't act as though she'd ever consider him a friend. Yet she stirred his blood. He felt a tremor of disloyalty to Sandi, then he seemed to hear Sandi's laughter. She never let him get away with nonsense like that.

Suddenly he had to get out of the apartment, drive somewhere, anywhere. He told Mrs. Hannaford he'd be back in an hour or so and escaped from the apartment as though he were being chased by the devil himself.

"TRAVELLER'S MY PONY," Pat screamed and started up the ladder to the hayloft.

"Get down from there," Liz said. "I don't feel up to climbing today."

"I won't."

Liz sighed and began to follow, groaning at every step.

Halfway up the ladder, Pat stopped and glared over her shoulder at Liz. "You really hurt?"

"I am stiff and sore, thank you."

Pat said nothing for a moment, then she started down. "Get out of the way."

Liz stepped off the ladder and stood waiting in the aisle with her hands on her hips. "Come into the lounge so we can discuss this properly."

Pat slouched ahead of her, dropped onto the leather couch, crossed her arms over her chest and pouted.

"Did we or did we not have an agreement about tantrums?"

"You gave that stuck-up Janey my Traveller. How could you?" Pat wailed.

Liz blew out her breath and sank gingerly into one of the chairs. "Janey is an experienced rider. I'm too big to work Iggy, and Vic doesn't ride. Every step Janey takes on that pony teaches him."

"But I want to ride him now."

"Forget it."

Pat set her jaw and glowered. Liz did not react.

After a moment Pat sighed and said, "Okay. But only if I can stay late for an extra lesson every day this week."

"God, you drive a hard bargain. Anything for a peaceful life." Liz pulled herself to her feet. "So go get Wishbone tacked up and get yourself into that arena.'' She walked out.

Pat uttered a deeply put-upon sigh and heaved herself off the sofa just as Vic stuck her head in the door.

"You're in my class today,'' Vic said. "I warn you, I don't put up with bad manners. One fit and you're out.''

"Everybody's always trying to throw me out.''

"No, we're trying to keep you in. You just make it darned difficult for us.'' She put her arm across Pat's shoulders. "Listen, you've got the makings of a good rider.''

Pat shook off the arm. "How come you don't ride? You're scared, right?''

Vic caught her breath. "Boy, you go for the jugular, don't you? Okay,'' Vic continued. "I used to think I stopped riding because I was scared for myself. That's not it. I'm terrified that somebody else will do something stupid and will get hurt because I'm not good enough to get out of the way. I can't take that chance again.''

"That's silly.''

"You asked. I told you. Now get Wishbone ready. We're ten minutes late.''

PAT'S LESSON WENT smoothly enough. She did everything Vic asked of her including trying to post at the trot. Toward the end she seemed to click into the rhythm. She *did* have the makings of a rider.

Janey, meanwhile, handled Traveller beautifully. At the rate she was taking him, he'd be jumping small fences in a week.

At four o'clock Liz found herself hanging around inside the barn waiting for Mike Whitten to pick up

Pat. When the silver Volvo pulled into the parking lot ten minutes later she felt her heart lurch. It sank as a plump lady climbed out of the driver's side.

"Hey, I'm Melba Hannaford come for Pat." She presented a note from Mike.

"Oh? Where's Mr. Whitten?"

"Had to go out of town for a couple of days."

Pat saw Mrs. Hannaford, and after a moment's hesitation, took her on the same tour of the barn she'd dragged her father on.

She wasn't so lucky at dragging out her visit, however. "No. I've got to stop by the store and get dinner in the oven," Mrs. Hannaford said. "You'll be back tomorrow."

Pat stormed off to the car, climbed in and slammed the door. Through the windshield, Liz, Vic and Mrs. Hannaford could see her staring bullets at them.

"I hope he'll be back in time for the barbecue and sleepover Friday night," Vic said.

"Sleepover?"

"The parents are all coming for dinner, then the kids will stay over in sleeping bags on the lounge floor."

"Oh, dear, I don't think Mr. Whitten would allow that. Pat has never slept over at anybody's house."

"Time she started, then," Vic said.

Mrs. Hannaford smiled. "You're right. I'll talk to him. Oh, can he bring a date?"

"Sure," Liz said. Her voice sounded like a croak. "Now, I've got to go work out my jumper before my next lesson shows up. Nice to have met you."

Of course Mike Whitten would bring a date. He must have dozens of women—beautiful, fashionable, *clean* women. Why did it bother her so badly? She turned to find Vic at her elbow and asked, "What's this about a barbecue? We can't afford it."

"We can't afford not to. Albert and I have everything arranged."

"I should have guessed."

"This is a family barn, Liz. Time we started treating it that way again. Show Whitten what a marvelous atmosphere it is for kids."

"He'll never let her eat barbecue in the open. He probably prefers pheasant under glass—suitably disinfected, of course." Liz stomped off with Trusty's halter in her hand.

Vic raised her eyebrows at Albert, who was straightening the wash rack and surreptitiously watching Liz. He nodded and grinned. "Uh-huh. Thought so."

CHAPTER SIX

FRIDAY THE CAMPERS brought sleeping bags and paraphernalia for the sleepover. All except Pat. Mrs. Hannaford explained to Vic. "Mr. Whitten gets in from San Francisco at noon. I've talked to him on the telephone about the sleepover and the party, but he hasn't made his decision yet." She patted Vic's arm. "I think I can persuade him to let Pat stay. I'm off to buy Pat a new sleeping bag. He can bring it with him tonight."

Because all the kids were staying late, there was no extra lesson for Pat in the afternoon. She really didn't need one. She had worked hard all week, and was progressing as well as everyone else.

Much to Liz's amazement, Pat and Janey were becoming a team. They giggled together, ate together, played with the kittens together. Pat had become accustomed to Wishbone, but Liz caught her looking at Traveller wistfully, particularly now that Janey had progressed to trotting the pony over poles on the ground and cantering low jumps.

Liz knew Pat was still scared, although she hid it well. She did fine at the trot, but so far she'd categorically refused to try to push Wishbone into a canter. Each day she told Liz she'd try, and each day she reneged.

Now the barn was spiffed up, the horses were groomed and fed, the barbecued ribs and shoulders were turning over a slow hickory fire in the parking lot, the tables and chairs were set out and ready.

Parents and clients began to arrive at six, and within minutes, pandemonium reigned as proud youngsters introduced their parents to the horses.

Liz, who usually loved parties and liked meeting new people, found herself strangely absentminded. Mike Whitten was late. She was curious about his date. Probably some long-stemmed beauty with painted toenails and expensively streaked hair.

At seven the silver Volvo pulled into the parking lot. Liz held her breath. Mike climbed out and walked around to open the passenger-side door. Liz blinked. He was wearing tight black jeans, a black linen shirt open at the neck and polished loafers without socks. He really did have a great body. She gulped, saw the woman emerging from the car and began to laugh.

Melba Hannaford climbed out and pulled a new sleeping bag and duffel from the back seat. She loaded Mike down with his daughter's gear, turned, saw Liz, smiled and waved. Mike saw her at the same moment. He frowned.

"This is against my better judgment," he said without preamble.

"Good grief, why?" Liz asked.

"Pat sleeps in filtered ionized air. She's not used to sleeping on the floor surrounded by dust and pets."

"Maybe it's time she started." Liz took the duffel off Mike's arm. "Come on, Melba, meet the crowd." She led them into the party.

Mike hated parties. He was lousy at making small talk with strangers. He glowered. That generally kept people at a distance.

Not tonight. A tall, graying man with a cherubic face

and pink cheeks strode up to him with hand out-stretched. "Hey, Mike. You may not remember me. I'm Kevin Womack. Your locker is two down from me at the club."

Womack clapped a hand on Mike's shoulder and began to introduce him around. Everyone was speaking at once and seemed to be having a great time. Mike searched the crowd for Pat, who had vanished.

"She's in the hayloft with Janey," Vic said from behind his left shoulder. Mike began to make his way through the crowd. He wanted to see his daughter.

As he turned the corner, he heard one Edenvale fa-ther say to a rotund, middle-aged man, "That's Mi-chael Whitten. Increased the endowment three hundred percent. I'm glad he's on our side. I hear he's a bad enemy." Mike smiled grimly. At least his reputation was intact.

"Pat?" he called up to the hayloft. He was answered by a pair of squeals. A moment later two heads, Pat's and a dark girl's, appeared over the edge of the hayloft.

"Did you bring my stuff?" Pat asked.

"Are you sure you want to stay?"

"Daddy! Of course I'm staying. This is my friend Janey."

Janey's head bobbed.

"Yes. We brought your stuff," Mike answered.

"Great. Come see the kittens. Liz says I can have one when they get older." The two heads disappeared.

Oh Liz does, does she?

He began to climb the ladder to the hayloft, saw that there was no guardrail in front of the platform and re-alized that the drop to the asphalt aisle was a good twelve feet. Pat could easily fall off the thing and break her neck. Didn't these women have a bit of sense? He made a note to speak to Mrs. Jamerson about installing a rail immediately, even if he had to pay for it.

"Come down from there," he told Pat. "And be careful."

"Sure." The two heads reappeared. "It's nearly time to eat."

He waited on the ladder to catch the girls if they should fall. They didn't.

Suddenly music filled the stable. Golden oldies. Big-band sound. The girls listened a moment, then made gagging sounds.

"Eeuw, as if!" Janey squealed. Pat squealed backup, and the two ran back to the party. Mike suddenly felt very, very old.

Liz slipped out from under an adjacent stall door and brushed her hands together. "You do this stuff?" she asked.

"What?" Mike looked at her questioningly. She was wearing fresh jeans and a silk shirt that flowed over her breasts like thick cream. She'd pulled her wild hair back with a barrette or a bow or something. She even had on lipstick.

"Can you dance?" Liz asked.

"I had to learn in prep school."

"Show me." She held out her arms to him.

"I'm rusty."

"So am I."

He slipped his hand around her waist and heard the slight catch in her breathing. He wondered if she regretted asking him to dance—to touch her. He resisted the desire to slide his hand lower.

He began to move slowly to the music. Her curves meshed perfectly with his. Too perfectly. She followed his lead as though she could read his mind.

It was probably just as well she couldn't. He felt like a teenage boy who couldn't control his hormones. Did she realize how aroused he'd become in just these few seconds? He should back off, put some distance between them, but he didn't. He held her close and wished that he could slide his palm beneath the thin silk of her shirt to run his fingers up her spine, wanted her to shiver with awareness of him. Only fair considering how aware he was of her.

Her slim fingers curled through his, and he ran his thumb gently over the throbbing pulse in her wrist. She jumped, but after a moment she relaxed and laid her cheek against his shoulder.

He only had to turn his head to drink in the scent of her hair. Moonlight and meadows. He closed his eyes and brushed his lips against her ear.

Her muscles stiffened, and he pressed his palm against her back, closed his fingers around her right hand. He couldn't let her go. Not yet.

He knew they'd stopped dancing. Now they swayed to some inner rhythm older than music.

She looked up at him. Her eyes were wide and wary, but her lips were parted, full, inviting.

He bent his head.

His lips touched hers—barely a kiss, but even that small touch ignited his senses.

She sighed and leaned into him.

In that instant he knew he wanted much, much more.

Somebody shouted, "Hey, everybody, samba!"

She broke away. "This is out of my league," she said shakily.

They weren't talking about the samba. "I'll teach you."

She shook her head and wrapped her arms across her body. "Not tonight."

He held her with his eyes.

"You dance well," he said.

"No, I don't. I never learned to…dance. I'm clumsy and awkward and I don't know the steps."

"Let me teach you."

"Maybe. Someday." She bolted like a skittish mare.

He took a moment to get his breathing—and his body—back in control.

"Someday," he whispered. "Someday soon."

TEN MINUTES LATER, Mike found Melba Hannaford serving barbecue as though she were a member of the family. At her shoulder stood a tall man with a deeply lined face and a fringe of gray hair around his balding head.

"Oh, Mr. Whitten," Melba said. "I'd like you to meet Walter Simpson. He brought young Eddy to the party. He's Eddy's great-uncle. Walter and I have run into one another a few times when he's come to pick up Eddy."

Mike extended his hand. "Nice to meet you, Mr. Whitten." Simpson smiled at him. "You're a lucky man to have Melba here to look after you."

Mike stared at Melba. The woman was actually blushing. "Uh, yes," he said, and moved away quickly. He glanced back to see Simpson looking down at Melba with a tender grin on his face.

Mike thought back to his conversation with Melba. Was Walter Simpson the reason she was so eager for Mike to remarry? Did she want to know he and Pat would be okay if she left them?

"I do believe we've got a budding romance," Angie whispered. Mike glared at her.

"Uh-oh," she said. "You look like Juliet's daddy facing a gang of teenage Capulets. Or was it Montagues? I forget which was which."

"Mrs. Hannaford is my employee. Her welfare concerns me."

Angie grabbed his arm, turned him around and led him off down the barn hall. "Don't glare. Walter's a very nice guy. I've talked to him some. Retired, decent income, widower. He's not some gigolo out to take advantage of her."

Mike stiffened. "That's hardly my concern. Or yours."

"Lighten up. Come look at Miss Fat Boots. This is Boop, my mare. She's the size of a tank. Due to foal any minute."

Even Mike, who knew nothing about pregnancy in horses, was impressed. The mare was vast.

"She's feeling really hateful," Angie said. "She tried to kick my head off this afternoon when Pat and I were walking her."

Mike caught his breath. "She tried to kick Pat?"

"No, silly. Me. Pat was well out of the way. Keeping us company. That child sucks up every bit of information she can get about horses. She's turning into a regular horseman—horseperson. Whatever." She turned him around again. "Come on. It's feeding time for us human animals, and I intend to slurp up as much of that barbecue as I can stuff in my face."

Angie walked ahead of him, leaving him to contemplate Pat as a horseperson. Fooling around with other people's ill-tempered horses. His heart sank. There didn't seem to be a thing he could do about it.

He ate almost nothing, though people kept pressing food on him, clapping him on the shoulder, inviting him to join them. He found his usual position at such functions. He propped one foot against the wall at the edge of the crowd.

And watched Liz. He followed her progress throughout the evening. Several times she glanced his way and smiled tentatively. He avoided smiling back.

As soon as people began to clear the plates, he went in search of Melba, and found her dancing cheek to cheek—actually cheek to chest—with Walter Simpson. He tapped Simpson on the shoulder.

"Cutting in?" Simpson said, smiling, and offered Melba's hand to Mike.

"Not precisely. Mrs. Hannaford, I have some work to do at the office."

He saw her face fall and felt guilty. "Uh, do you think...?" He looked at Simpson.

"I'd be overjoyed to take the little lady home," Simpson said, still holding her hand. "She is a truly fine dancer. And I do love to dance."

"Mr. Whitten, if you don't need me...?" Melba said anxiously.

"No, that will be fine. Pat's staying here. Please have a good time."

"Oh, I will. I am." She smiled up at Simpson.

Mike nodded and turned away just as the music changed into a fast forties jitterbug and Kevin Womack pulled Liz onto the dance floor.

Mike didn't want to watch, but he couldn't take his eyes off her. She was actually laughing out loud. She was also glowing. Damn! That Womack was married to Angie, but that meant little to some men. He spotted Angie, standing at the side of the group clapping and egging her husband on. She didn't seem in the least concerned, so why should Mike feel this incredible stab of jealousy? It was just a dance. Liz was three feet away from Womack, not close against his body as she'd been against Mike's earlier. The memory gave him a jolt. He'd danced with a million women. Why should this one be memorable? And why on earth had he kissed her? He turned the corner and went into the lounge so that he couldn't see them any longer. He needed to get away before he did something truly stupid.

He double-checked all Pat's things to be certain she had everything she needed. He found her, Janey and the two boys from the camp sitting cross-legged on the grass under the trees by the front paddock. They were laughing.

"Pat," he called. "I'm going home. Call me the minute you get up tomorrow, please."

She barely turned her head. "Sure."

He hesitated. "You have everything you need?"

"Uh-huh." She and Janey began to giggle. The boys eyed him warily.

God! Surely it was too soon for boys!

THE LIGHT ON HIS answering machine was blinking when he got home. He clicked it and heard Rachelle's southern drawl. "Michael, dahlin', you must be off gallivantin' again. Do call me when you get home." A soft chuckle. "I don't care how late."

The clock read barely ten-thirty. He could call. She'd join him at the club for a drink. If he asked, she'd come flying over to his apartment. So far he had resisted getting himself too deeply involved with her, but tonight he was tempted. Why not? Everybody else seemed to have someone.

He shook his head. Not Liz. She seemed to be as alone as he was. Oh, she was surrounded by people, but there didn't seem to be anyone special in her life. Any special *man*, he meant.

He decided not to call Rachelle. He wasn't being fair to her. He wasn't in love with her. He should probably allow their relationship, if that's what it was, simply to peter out.

He dropped into his leather chair.

He'd long since decided he no longer had the capacity for love, but if a woman like Liz Matthews could stir his blood so thoroughly, then he still must have the capacity for passion.

He went to the window of the penthouse and stared out at the lights of the city beneath him, then let his eyes wander farther, past the dwindling lights of suburbia to the tiny pinpoints of light where city met county along the horizon. In that direction lay Valley-Crest, Pat and Liz. He wished he had a crystal ball so that he could watch what was happening at the sleep-over. Watch over Pat. And Liz.

He might as well admit it. For the first time since Sandi died he deeply desired another woman. The wrong woman. What the hell was he going to do about it?

"THE BEST PARTY EVER," Vic said as she and Albert folded the last tablecloth.

"It was all right." Liz said and covered the dregs of the coleslaw.

"Come on, Liz, you know everybody had a ball."

"Not Mr. Bigshot Whitten. He snuck off the minute my back was turned."

"He doesn't do parties," Albert said. "Shy, most likely."

"Shy? Come on, Albert. Your judgment is usually infallible, but Mike Whitten shy?"

"I said it. I mean it. Man's shy. Get the feelin' he hasn't been around real people much. Just people he does business with. Bet the man hasn't got a friend to his name."

"Poor man," Vic said and looked at Liz. "Maybe we can fix that."

"Oh, and how do you plan to do it? Intimate dinner parties with a few select billionaires?"

"Man needs a good woman," Albert pronounced. "Not natural for a man to live alone like that."

"He apparently prefers it that way."

"Not anymore." Albert walked out the front door, whistling a low-down blues tune.

CHAPTER SEVEN

WITH THE BIG, nationally rated Labor Day horse show on the horizon, the ValleyCrest adult riders wanted more and more lessons. The campers arrived every day like clockwork, expecting to be taught as well. Finally, the horses that were at ValleyCrest to be trained had to be ridden daily so that they would be in perfect shape for the show.

The long days in the heat were beginning to take their toll on horses and people alike. Liz and Vic both dropped five pounds. Even Albert looked slimmer.

Pat took her extra lesson each afternoon for the two weeks following the party. Mrs. Hannaford chauffeured the girl to and from the stable. She mentioned that Mr. Whitten was in Singapore and Korea, on business. He couldn't say when he'd be home. Meanwhile Pat was paying for her extra lesson by working with Albert each day. She followed him around like a shadow. Albert snapped and snarled at her the way he did at everyone, but Liz could see that he was fond of the child. She obviously adored him.

All in all, the camp was a huge success.

Good thing, since everything else seemed to be crumbling.

The stable could ill afford the five-hundred-dollar fee to enter Liz and Trust Fund in the Labor Day grand prix jumping class. During a ten-minute break between the campers leaving and Pat tacking up Wishbone, Vic, Liz and Albert sat around Vic's rolltop desk and pondered the figures.

"All the campers plan to ride in the show," Vic said. "That means they'll be paying ValleyCrest extra fees while they're on the showgrounds."

"But then the camp ends, the kids all go back to school, and unless Edenvale signs the contract for the after-school riding program, that's the end of that particular revenue stream," Liz said with a sigh.

"Whitten will sign," Albert said and dug into the pocket of his oversize jeans for a plastic bag full of salted pecans.

"If the man ever gets home long enough," Liz snapped.

Vic and Albert glanced at one another.

"We've still got our adult clients," Vic continued. "If everyone does well in the horse show, we'll come out on the winning side and maybe make a few people sit up and take notice of us again." Vic leaned back. "Especially when you and Trusty win the grand prix."

"*If* we win." Liz dropped her head into her hands. Her hair felt grimy between her fingers. Her skin felt dry and dirty. She probably looked like a boot. No wonder the closest thing she had to a male companion was a smart-ass parrot.

"Think positive. Even if you come in third or fourth you'll still make more than the entry fee."

"And if we crash and burn?"

Vic's eyes narrowed. "What's with you? I've never known you to doubt yourself like this."

"Oh, shoot, call it PMS." Liz knew it was a good deal more than hormones—well, not that particular combination of hormones at any rate.

The telephone rang and Vic went to answer it. Albert pulled himself out of the captain's chair and headed for the door. Liz sighed and waited for Vic to finish her conversation.

"The feed man is getting a little snarky about his bill," Vic said as she hung up the phone. "Not to mention that all the horses need their fall shots, and their feet trimmed and their shoes reset before the show." She leaned back and closed her eyes.

"We've got to buy a trailerload of hay to set us up for winter," Liz said. "If we wait much longer we'll have to pay premium prices." She slid lower in the chair. The green canvas across the back of it was frayed along one edge. Liz shifted and heard a tiny tearing sound. "One of these days this chair is going to rip and dump me on my bottom."

"Better you than a customer," Vic said with a sigh. "Unfortunately, redoing the furnishings is way down on the list of priorities. The horses are our main concern."

"I realize the animals come first, Vic, but it would be nice if you and Albert and I could keep eating too. We need to sell a couple of horses."

Vic took a deep breath. "Uh, that's something I need to talk to you about."

Liz sat up. "Oh, God, what now?"

Vic took a deep breath, avoided Liz's eyes, picked up a pencil and began to work it over and under her fingers like an expert cardsharp. "Mrs. Morehouse called me this morning. They're thinking about buying Traveller for Janey."

Suddenly Liz couldn't breathe. "Oh, damn."

"You said yourself Traveller and Janey fit well together. They're willing to pay the Jessups their asking price and keep him stabled here on training board. It's one less horse we've got on consignment, and the hefty commission plus the back stall rental and training board will increase our bank balance substantially.''

Liz dropped her head in her hands. She felt tears fill her eyes. After a moment, she raised her face. "What on earth am I going to do about Pat Whitten?"

"What choice do we have? We need the commission from the sale. There's always another pony, maybe even a gray one. Whitten can afford to buy a real packer, a Class A pony for Pat that will win everything in sight.''

"It's not the same thing."

"Pat's never even been on Traveller."

"I know, but she grooms him every afternoon, she lunges him for me, she brings him carrots and apples and...oh, hell, if she loses him to Janey it will break her heart!''

"She'll get over it. I told Janey's parents I'd discuss the situation with you.''

The door opened. "Hey, Liz, Wishbone's all ready," Pat said.

Liz swallowed and wiped her eyes on the tail of her T-shirt.

"You okay?" Pat asked.

"It's just the dust. Come on, let's get to it."

Before she followed Pat to the ring, Liz whispered a few words to Albert. He raised his eyebrows at her, then nodded.

Liz's stomach was churning. Pat was riding darned well, but she was terrified of moving to the next level. She had no idea what was at stake. And it was all Liz's fault.

Maybe there was a way out. If Pat passed the test.

Unfortunately, she wouldn't even realize that there *was* a test. "Today you canter. You promised me yesterday you would."

Pat was silent.

"Remember?"

"Yeah, okay. I promise."

Twenty minutes later Liz said, "Okay. Canter. You know the signals. Use them."

"I don't want to." Pat answered. "Maybe tomorrow."

Test failed, horse lost, dream destroyed. Damn! How dare this kid get between her and the proper business decision? Liz walked toward the gate without a backward glance.

"Hey, I've still got ten minutes," Pat said.

"Lesson's over. You broke your promise." She kept walking.

"Wait!" Pat said and trotted the horse in her direction. "I'll do it tomorrow. I'm not ready."

"You're more than ready. Bring Wishbone in."

"You can't make me!"

Liz hadn't heard that tone for a while. She kept walking.

"Come back here! I want my lesson."

Liz reached the arena gate.

"I hate you!" Pat screamed.

Liz headed for the barn.

"Please." Pat sobbed. "Please come back."

Liz stopped and turned toward her. Pat's tears cut muddy swaths down her dusty cheeks. Liz felt like a monster, but she couldn't see any other choice. "Then canter that horse."

"I'll fall off."

"You won't."

"He'll run away."

"Wishbone? Not likely. Pat, you are ready. You have been ready for a while. You're a good rider. Do you trust me?"

Silence. Then a reluctant nod.

"Try him at a trot, then push him into the canter. Now."

Pat's chest heaved. After a moment she clicked at Wishbone, turned him to the rail and trotted away.

A moment later Liz watched her back stiffen. She set Wishbone up and clucked. Instantly he broke into a slow, rolling canter hardly faster than his trot. As Pat came around the end of the ring so that she and Wishbone faced Liz, Liz saw not fear but wonder on her face. Liz let them make another complete circuit, then held up a hand in time for Pat to stop beside her.

"I did it! I did it!" Pat leaned down and wrapped her arms around Wishbone's neck. "It's not hard. It's fun."

"So try it again."

"Hey, yeah."

Ten minutes later they walked Wishbone into the barn. Albert stood grinning beside the wash rack. All tacked up, Traveller stood on the wash rack.

Pat was so excited she didn't even see Traveller at first. Vic stood at the door of the office watching them with troubled eyes.

"Mrs. Hannaford won't be here for another twenty minutes," Liz said. "How tired are you?"

"I feel great!" Pat crowed.

"Then we're going to try an experiment. Give Wishbone to Albert."

Pat looked at Liz, then her eyes widened as she realized that Traveller wore both saddle and bridle.

"You get up on him and you walk—only walk—until you are both relaxed. You got that?"

Pat nodded.

Albert handed Traveller's reins to the little girl. Liz couldn't breathe, and she wasn't certain anyone else in the stable was breathing either. She checked the stirrup length, then gave Pat a leg up. Traveller snorted and danced sideways. Pat froze momentarily, then picked up her reins with an air of grim determination and walked the pony into the arena.

Liz glanced at the side of the ring. Vic and Albert stood side by side. Albert had his big arm draped across Vic's shoulders. Vic was crying. Liz thought Albert's eyes looked a bit more luminous than usual as well.

"Reverse and walk." Liz began to snap out commands.

Nobody paid attention to the time until Mrs. Hannaford ambled out of the dim recesses of the stable to stand beside Vic and Albert. "My, I've never seen her ride before. Doesn't she look pretty?"

"Uh, I just needed her to do a little extra work on this pony for me," Liz said. "Pat, walk him out. Melba is here."

"Do I have to? Can't I canter him too?"

"Not today."

Pat patted Traveller's neck. The pony wickered softly. "See," Pat whispered. "I told you you were my pony."

Liz nearly broke down completely.

After she walked Traveller cool and handed him to Albert, Pat seemed subdued but elated.

"Your daddy's home," Mrs. Hannaford said as she and Pat walked toward the Volvo.

Liz's heart turned over.

"Great! Now I want him to watch me ride. Now I'm ready." Pat jumped into the front seat.

As they drove away, Vic and Albert leaned against the wall watching Liz. "So?" Vic said.

"Okay, the way I see it is this. Thanks to Janey's work on him, Pat really can ride Traveller if she listens to me and only rides him under supervision. You agree?"

"Dicey, but yes."

"Pat adores that pony. I think he even likes her. Janey's just another rider to him and he's only another mount to her. She needs a Class A horse that's going to win for her. She's already good enough to ride Small Junior horses instead of Pony classes. I'm going to talk to the Morehouses and tell them that."

"Where you gonna find a horse like that this late in the season those folks can afford?" Albert asked.

"It just so happens I know one," Liz said.

Vic raised her eyes and her hands.

"No, listen, Vic. Christine Vickery leaves for college orientation in two weeks. She told me at the last show that she wants to lease Candy Bar for the next year."

"You think the Morehouses would go for a lease?"

"If they don't, they're crazy."

"We don't get a commission on leases," Vic said.

"I know, I know."

"I understand how you feel, but we need that money."

"Don't mention any of this to the Morehouses until I talk to Christine. After that I'm going to call Mike Whitten and ask him to buy Traveller for Pat's birthday."

Liz tried four times to call Mike Whitten that night. Each time, she broke the connection before she dialed the last digit. Finally, at ten o'clock she completed the call. When Mrs. Hannaford answered, Liz asked whether it was too late to speak to Mr. Whitten. A moment later he was on the line.

Liz took a deep breath. "Mr. Whitten, I need to see you."

Dead silence. He cleared his throat. "First of all, isn't it about time we started calling one another by our first names? Mine is Mike."

"Uh—Mike."

"Is it about Pat? Has something happened?"

"Yes, it's about Pat, and yes, something's happened, and no, it is not something bad. It's very good."

"Really."

"I'm not sure I can explain over the phone. Could I come to your office tomorrow afternoon?"

"I'll drive Pat tomorrow morning. We can talk then."

"No!" Liz closed her eyes a moment. "I don't want her to know I'm talking to you."

"What's she done?" Mike snapped. "Or should I ask, what have *you* done to *her?*"

Liz's stomach churned. She was six inches from slamming the phone down when she stopped, took another deep breath and squared her shoulders. This was for Pat. "Will you see me or not?"

"Of course. I'm going to have a long day, but I assume we both have to eat sometime. How about dinner tomorrow evening? I'll pick you up about eight, if that's not too late."

Oh, good grief. "Someplace informal?"

"Anywhere you like."

When Liz put down the phone she realized she was shaking. Dinner with Mike Whitten. Spending an hour or more face-to-face with him.

While she tried to convince him to buy a pony that less than a month earlier she'd told him would be a disaster for his child. What fun.

CHAPTER EIGHT

WHEN MIKE RANG her doorbell the following evening, Liz jumped and looked down at herself with trepidation. Her best black designer jeans, red silk shirt, earrings, even real shoes. True, the shoes had flat heels, but at least they weren't paddock boots. The best she could do. She pulled a brush through her hair one last time.

On impulse she picked up the bottle of Mandarin perfume that Vic had given her for Christmas. She sprayed her wrists and the base of her throat. The doorbell rang again.

"Just a sec," she called as she ran to answer it.

Mike stood on the doorstep in a duplicate of the outfit he'd worn to the party—black from head to toe. Maybe it was the only outfit he possessed that didn't come with a vest. Or maybe he liked looking like a gunfighter. Add a black Stetson and he'd be perfect for Black Bart in the old-time Saturday serials.

"Hi," she said breathlessly. "Just let me grab my purse."

He followed her inside.

"What a jerk."

Mike's head whipped around. A small parrot inside a large, ornate Victorian birdcage hung sideways from the chain of his perch and regarded Mike with disdain. "What a jerk," it told him solemnly.

A parrot. The things carried psittacosis. At least Pat wasn't likely to come in contact with it. She stayed at the stable. Or Mike assumed she did. He realized that he'd been out of town so much lately that she could have been spending half the day up here without his hearing about it.

"Okay," Liz said, appearing a moment later.

Walking across her screened-in front porch was like plunging through the Amazon rain forest. Ferns, potted palms, rubber plants, hanging baskets full of blooming somethings-or-other. Mold spores. Wet dirt.

"If you don't mind, I have to stop by the barn for one second. Boop's close to foaling." She didn't wait for him to open the car door for her.

"We have time. Our reservation isn't for thirty minutes." Down the hill he pulled into the parking lot and Liz bounced out. He followed more slowly, his hands in his pockets. Her perfume lingered in his nostrils like the scent of the South Pacific flowers he remembered from his years crewing on sailboats.

She'd obviously made an effort for him. He felt flattered until he remembered that Pat was the reason for this meeting. And Liz probably planned to use the opportunity to sweet-talk him into the fall contract with Edenvale. He should be so lucky she had dressed up to entice him. Nice thought. Fat chance.

They'd be together for a couple of hours at least. Whatever her ulterior motive for the evening, it gave him a chance to get to know her better, to see whether that tingle of unbridled lust he felt whenever she came within range held up. He still wasn't certain what to do if it did.

"Hi, Mike," Vic said from the door to the mare's stall. Then, "Probably not tonight," she said in answer to Liz's unspoken question. "Possibly tomorrow or the next day. There's a cold front moving through in the morning."

The mare was immense. She munched on her hay and seemed completely relaxed. "What's the weather got to do with it?" Mike asked.

"Mares invariably wait for the worst storms of the century. Tornadoes and earthquakes will do very nicely, thank you. If there is also a full moon, chances are that baby's coming."

"And tonight," Mike added, "the moon is full."

"But no storms predicted before morning. You two go on," Vic continued. "I'll call Angie and tell her she might want to stay close to a phone tomorrow. At least she made it home from Europe in time for the blessed event." She leaned over and kissed Liz's cheek, took a deep whiff and raised her eyebrows.

Liz blushed and turned away.

"Have a good time," Vic called after them.

THE RESTAURANT WASN'T overly fancy, but it was above Liz's price range. As they waited for their spinach salads to arrive, Mike put his elbows on the table and said, "Why did you need to see me so urgently?"

"Can we talk after dinner?"

"I'd prefer to know now," he said. "Are you having difficulties with Pat?"

That familiar burning sensation right below Liz's heart kicked in. "Why would you assume that?"

"I realize that to some people she can seem difficult, demanding."

Boy, is that an understatement.

"She comes by it naturally," he told her.

Churn, churn.

"It's in her gene pool. My side of the family," he said, and smiled.

Liz had never seen him smile before. Really smile. She'd seen that crocodile grin of his on a couple of occasions and didn't ever want to see it again. But this smile softened the planes of his face. He looked almost warm. She couldn't say one good thing about the man, and yet, along with a churning sensation in her stomach was another much more dangerous reaction lower down. He excited her.

Why not? Crazy horses and rank stallions excited her, too. Didn't mean they wouldn't stomp her, given the opportunity.

Liz took a deep breath. "I think you should buy Traveller for Pat's birthday."

"I beg your pardon?"

She plunged ahead. "She's come a long way fast and so has the pony."

"Pat's never been on his back."

"Yes she has," Liz said and saw Mike's eyes ice over as quickly as a blacktop road in a sleet storm. How much should she tell him? She decided to get it all out—most of it anyway. She prayed he wouldn't fire her. If he did, she'd have to sic Vic on him in hopes that her aunt's diplomacy could smooth things over. "Pat was so terrified that first day of camp, she bailed out on me and hid in the hayloft."

"You said she did fine."

"I lied."

"Really."

"You've got her so scared, she was paralyzed."

"Me?"

"Yes, you." Liz felt her anger begin to rise. Oh, boy, this was really not how she'd planned to handle the evening. "She was so afraid that you'd go to pieces if anything happened to her, she wouldn't take even the smallest risk."

"I sincerely hope not," he said coldly.

"Well, she's over it now," Liz said with satisfaction. "Today she rode Traveller all day in class while Janey took over one of the more advanced horses."

"You put my child on that crazy pony?"

"She adores him, and he seems to like her. He certainly performs beautifully for her. Most of the time. Yes, he's still green, and yes, she needs constant supervision and training when she's on him, and yes, she still needs to learn on Wishbone, but the thing is..." Liz took a gulp of her wine and nearly choked. "If you don't buy her that pony, and I mean now, I'm afraid Janey Morehouse's folks are going to snatch him right from under your nose."

He stared at her silently. "I see."

"You do? Thank God."

"I run into this tactic every day, Miss Matthews. 'We already have two other tentative offers for this plant, Mr. Whitten. If you don't snap it up right this minute you'll lose it.'" He threw his napkin down beside his plate. "I had expected better of you."

Liz gaped at him. "You *are* a jerk!" she said. "Listen to me. I am not bidding up the price of that pony. I could have sold him to the Morehouses this morning for the total asking price and made a hell of a commission, which, frankly, we need desperately. I've been on the telephone all morning trying to tie down another horse for Janey that she'll be happy with just so your darling daughter, who you keep swearing means a great deal to you, will not lose the pony she wants more than life itself. How dare you?"

"More than life itself." He seemed to be speaking to himself.

Liz longed to get up and storm out, but she was twenty-five miles from home and had only ten dollars in her purse. If she called Vic she'd have to wait around in the parking lot. She took deep breaths and tried to steady herself.

He still excited her, damn him. He had already stomped her, and here she was standing up and begging for more hoofprints on her behind. "Listen, you," she began, but he interrupted her.

"I'm sorry," he whispered. "Most horse traders have a reputation for making a fast buck any way they can."

"Horse traders *all* have reputations. I have one too, as an honest person. Check around, Mr. Whitten. I don't make bad deals for my clients."

"Can Pat ride him safely?"

"If she pays attention and does what I tell her, and if she signs a contract not to ride him alone or try anything without supervision. No horse is a hundred percent safe, Mr....Mike. Not even Wishbone."

He thought that over, and after a moment, he picked up his napkin and dropped it back into his lap. His next words were, "How will the Morehouses react if I buy Traveller out from under them? Janey has become Pat's friend. I don't want to see her suffer, either."

Liz sat back and let all the wind out of her lungs. He actually gave a damn about somebody other than his own kid. Miraculous! There might be hope for him yet. "I don't plan to let Janey suffer," Liz answered. "I've already found her a horse that's much better suited to her needs right now. It's a lease, so it's also less money. His owner brought him over this afternoon and Janey tried him out. She's crazy about him.''

"How much does the pony cost?''

"Only seventy-five hundred. By the time Pat is ready to move up to a horse, he should be worth much more. Think of him as a good investment as well as the pony Pat truly wants.''

"Seventy-five hundred dollars is not exactly chump change. And I've seen your stable fees. This is a not a cheap sport.''

"No, but it's a darned low profit margin for us. ValleyCrest operates on a very tight budget and with the bare minimum staff. Pat's been helping out every afternoon after her private lesson...'' Her voice trailed off. She could have kicked herself. Any hope that Mike wouldn't pick up on her words faded the moment she saw his eyes widen.

"Private lesson?''

She hit her thigh with her fist. "Bother. I promised Pat I wouldn't say anything, and now I've opened my big mouth. It's no big deal. She's been staying late every afternoon and working with me one-on-one.''

"Since when?''

Liz made circles on the linen cloth with her fork.

"I didn't hear you,'' Mike said.

"The first day,'' Liz whispered. She raised her head and glared. "Well, she needed them, dammit.'' Churn. Churn.

"How is she paying you?''

"I told you, she's helping Albert. And she really is a great deal of help.''

"Hardly sufficient compensation.''

"That's our business. I'm satisfied, and she's happy.''

"I won't have Pat taking advantage of you. Send me a bill. I'll write you a check."

"The hell you will," Liz said, and this time she did stand up. "This is between Pat and ValleyCrest Farm."

"Sit down, please, Liz," Mike said softly and reached a hand across the table.

Liz sat. She had precious little choice. A cab ride would cost more than twenty dollars.

"What's our next step?" Mike asked. His hand still lay on the table.

"How do you mean?" She glanced from his hand to his eyes and wondered for a moment whether he was still talking about the pony. She swallowed. She was being silly. No way was he coming on to her. Unfortunately.

"Pat's birthday is exactly five days from today. I don't want her to know I'm even considering buying that pony for her. So what needs to happen next?"

The waiter set plates in front of them.

Although she was ravenous, Liz didn't glance at hers. She felt the rising tide of excitement she always felt when she was about to buy the perfect horse for a client. She tried to sound very businesslike. "I call our veterinarian or you can choose one you know. He vets the pony to be certain he's sound, x-rays to be sure the horse's knees are closed, and at five they should be. Traveller already has an official card from the American Horse Shows Association that proves he is a bona fide large pony and not a horse, and eligible for pony classes. We'll have to do some paperwork to change his name, but we can do that anytime. Then you hand me a cashier's check, we sign a contract for training board with the barn, you and Vic sit down and order tack and grooming supplies and a tack trunk and…"

"Whoa! It would seem that buying the damned pony is the easy part."

"Right. Although Pat can use the barn's tack if she needs to."

"No, I can afford whatever she needs. Can we get everything together before her birthday?"

"Pay for overnight delivery and you can."

Mike picked up his fork. "Call your vet first thing in the morning. If the pony checks out, you have a deal. I pray it doesn't come back to haunt me." He dug into his salmon. The subject was closed, the deal concluded. Just like that.

Liz couldn't think of a single thing to say. Apparently Mike couldn't, either. They ate in silence, barely even glancing at one another. What did they have in common except Pat? Liz wondered. She couldn't talk international finance and Mike wasn't interested in horses. He apparently considered this a business dinner. Period.

Mike raised his glass of Chablis to her. "To a successful negotiation."

Liz raised hers. Great. Just what a woman wants to hear. She took a very large gulp. Normally she didn't drink, but she needed something to help her through the evening.

Eventually Mike looked up from the remains of his salmon and asked, "How did you get involved with horses anyway?"

Liz smiled. "What's a nice girl like you doing in a business like this?"

He smiled back. Not the crocodile smile, either, but a really human smile that actually touched his eyes.

Liz felt her heart buck and spoke quickly to cover her confusion. "Actually, it would be weird if I'd managed to avoid them. I spent summers with Aunt Vic and Uncle Frank from the time I was about, oh, four or five. I guess my mother must have been experiencing some of the heart problems that eventually killed her and needed a vacation from me, but at the time I thought I was escaping straight to paradise. I was Albert's shadow, just like Pat. Even Uncle Frank's tough teaching couldn't take the bloom off. After my mother died when I was about Pat's age, Uncle Frank and Aunt Vic took me in permanently." She had no intention of regaling Mike with tales of her father's alcoholic depression after her mother's death, his swift remarriage and the miserable year she spent bidding for his attention by getting into as much mischief as she could.

"Your father gave you up?" Mike sounded incredulous. "I could never give up a child."

"In this case it was best for everybody. Daddy had...problems. I wasn't an easy kid to get along with. Vic rescued us all. It was a good fit from the start." She finished her wine and held out her glass for a refill. Mike complied, then glanced at his own half-full glass. Liz set down her glass without tasting her wine. She loathed drunks—drunken women especially. As unaccustomed to alcohol as she was, she might qualify very quickly. Instead she buttered a roll and nibbled on it. "Nobody should ever call my Aunt Vic a coward."

"Why would anybody say that?" Mike asked in surprise.

"After she quit riding, Uncle Frank used to call her a coward every time he got angry at her. She was an easy target because she never fought back. Secretly I think she agreed with him. Uncle Frank eventually put on so much weight that there was no way he could ride a horse. We tried to slim him down, but nothing worked. Angie thinks he kept all those layers between him and his feelings. He didn't want to see Vic's pain. Mine, neither, for that matter. Congestive heart failure killed him.'' She reached for her glass, then thought better of it. ''And his death may well mean the end of ValleyCrest too, if Vic and I aren't careful and lucky.''

For a moment Mike considered offering to help them out financially. He was even more surprised to realize that he hadn't been thinking of a loan, but a gift. Why should he even contemplate such a foolish thing? Completely unbusinesslike. No return on investment. Besides, that pair of hardheaded women would never agree.

Then he realized he might not be so crazy after all. Pat needed ValleyCrest. She was growing in ways he'd only begun to discover, and if he wasn't exactly pleased with all the changes, he had to admit she seemed happier than she had in years.

He could never offer either of those women money openly. He'd have to find some way to prop them up without their catching on. He didn't want Liz to go under. Liz? Not Vic and Liz?

Pat might need ValleyCrest, but he was beginning to think he needed Liz. Definitely *not* a good fit, but there didn't seem to be much he could do about it.

''Anyway, I've been with the horse business ever since. Don't know anything else, don't want to do anything else.''

''Very narrow.''

''Yes, but so time-consuming that there's not much energy left over for the ballet and opera.''

''That's what I said once upon a time. Someone proved me wrong.''

After Mike paid the check they walked out to find

that the cold front had already invaded. The pear trees that edged the parking lot bent almost double under the force of the wind. Liz's hair whipped across her face. She spat it out. "Moon's gone," she said. "Temperature's dropped." She wrapped her arms across her body. This time she let Mike open the car door for her.

"You're cold," he said when he got in. "Would you like to go somewhere for an after-dinner drink? Or cappuccino to warm you up? We could go to the club. Celebrate my buying that blasted pony."

He sounded almost eager, as though he really wanted her company. Liz glanced at the wind-whipped trees and shuddered. It was going to be a bad night. "Thanks, but I'd better get home in case Vic needs me."

The Volvo was a big sedan, but nowhere near as wide as Liz's huge truck with its double set of tires. There was no avoiding a sense of Mike's presence. Some men wore too much nasty sweet aftershave and cologne, but Mike smelled clean and slightly lemony. She felt her toes curl. She needed to get out of this car quick before she said or did something she'd regret.

A bolt of lightning streaked sideways across the sky in front of them. A moment later thunder rattled. Liz yipped and gripped the armrest.

Mike glanced over at her. Even in the dim light he probably saw she was shaking.

She caught his glance and tried to laugh. "Sorry. I hate storms." She spoke through clenched teeth. "I hate riding horses in the rain and I'm terrified of lightning." She closed her eyes and was immediately transported to that awful afternoon when she'd cradled her mother's dying body on the sidewalk and screamed at the storm that drenched them both.

From that time on, one lightning bolt, one raindrop, and her father opened the vodka. He never forgave his wife for dying on him so young and leaving him with a nine-year-old daughter. He took out his feelings of abandonment and betrayal on Liz. He never hit her, but he treated her as though she alone were responsible for her mother's death. No matter where she hid, his cold rage followed her, his words drummed into her ears no matter how she covered them. In a way, she would have preferred a physical beating. He always apologized afterward and swore he'd never drink again, but he always did. In her mind the fury of the storm was forever linked to those anguished moments when she felt her father hated her.

"I didn't think you were afraid of anything."

"Little you know." Another bolt crashed beside them and Liz jumped. "Oh, damn!"

"Relax. It's miles away."

"You say." She clutched her arms across her chest and tried to make herself very small.

"Do the horses get upset by storms?"

"Not when they're safe in their stalls. Blast, here comes the rain."

Mike slowed. The first gust of rain drove across the windshield at right angles.

"This is the kind of storm that knocks down trees," Liz said. She tried to sound rational. A man like Mike would undoubtedly laugh—or worse, sneer—at her fears.

"I drive this car because it's the safest on the road. And I am an excellent driver. I won't let us get hit by a tree. Promise."

Liz turned to him and for a moment relaxed her grip on the armrest. He hadn't sneered. He'd made a simple statement of his expertise as though reassuring her was the most natural thing in the world. As though her terror were normal. He couldn't control lightning. He couldn't keep trees from falling onto their car, but still she felt safe with him.

If she were home, she'd pull a pillow over her head and drag all the dogs into bed with her. If she were riding a horse on course, she'd try to concentrate on keeping the horse from falling in the muck and killing them both before she could get out of the ring to find shelter. Either way, enduring storms was grim. But having Mike beside her seemed to make things easier.

Mike was concentrating on his driving, so she concentrated on him to keep her panic at bay. He had a good—if somewhat battered—face. In profile she could tell that his nose was even more crooked than hers. He wasn't classically handsome, but he looked strong and appealing and extremely male. His big hands turned the steering wheel casually, despite the weather.

Watching a sexy man drive a car always gave her a rush. With Mike it threatened to escalate from rush to major desire. She told herself to get a grip. She wondered if she was imagining the escalation of tension in the car. Or was something going on between them that had nothing to do with buying a pony for Pat?

He carefully avoided a fallen branch on the road and turned into the ValleyCrest driveway.

"See, I promised I'd get you home safely." He drove past the barn and pulled up in front of her house.

She felt a stinging regret that the trip was over, storm or no. She wished she'd taken him up on that offer of cappuccino. Anything to keep the evening going a little longer.

The next bolt of lightning gave her an excuse to keep

him around. The rain seemed to fall in a sheet as solid
and impenetrable as rock. "You can't drive home in
this," she said. "Come in until the worst is over. I can
actually make coffee if I read the directions real carefully. Not cappuccino, but hey, you can't have everything."

He hesitated, then said, "Thanks. I'll even help you
read."

Before she could respond, he jumped out of the car
and ran around to open her door.

"You're getting drenched," she said as she exited
the Volvo.

"I'll dry."

They ran toward the house. Just as they reached the
bottom step a clap of thunder shook the whole house,
and a moment later tremendous lightning bolts lit the
sky for miles. Liz yelped and crossed her hands over
her head.

Mike put his arms around her waist and half carried
her up the stairs to the shelter of the porch. She turned
and buried her face against his shoulder.

GREAT, he thought. The rain had soaked their clothes,
their shoes, dripped into their ears and onto her eyelashes. He knew because he lifted her chin so that he
could see her in the shadows thrown by the dim porch
light. He should never have accepted that offer of coffee. If he didn't get back in his car and drive away this
minute, he was going to do something that would get
his face slapped.

She was only offering to give him shelter because
of her own fear of the storm. Earlier, she couldn't get
away fast enough, even though he'd have offered her
champagne to keep her with him a little longer.

They were both breathing as though they'd run a marathon. She was plain scared. He was scared too, but not of the thunderstorm. Scared he was about to make a mistake. Scared he'd misread the signals. But he had to take a chance.

He bent his head to kiss her eyelids and tasted the rain on his lips. She didn't resist, so he moved to her mouth. Just a little comfort and reassurance, that's all.

The hell it was. The moment he tasted her lips he felt as though he'd been kicked in the head by one of those blasted horses. The instant her lips opened, her arms encircled his waist, and he knew he hadn't been wrong. He deepened the kiss and felt her respond, felt her wet body melt against him. Felt passions ignite that he thought had abandoned him forever. He wanted her.

He wanted to possess her completely. Nothing less than total war and total surrender. His tongue probed her lips, and she opened to him, met him, painted his mouth with fire.

It was as though he were being lowered into a vat of burning oil, but all he felt was the heat without the pain.

Her hands caressed the back of his head, moved down his back to stroke the muscles beside his spine.

He longed to strip her and lay her down and take her right then and there while the lightning struck at them and the thunder rolled like artillery in the background.

She broke the kiss. She gasped up at him. Her eyes shone in the dim glow. She looked as confused as he felt. "I didn't...I mean..."

He shut her up in midsentence. She didn't seem to mind. She moved her hips against him as his hand slid down to caress her breast. He could feel her nipple erect under the wet silk and the thin bra. She moaned and dug her fingernails into his back through his wet linen shirt.

At that moment he knew he could do anything. He could carry her to her bed, strip them both of their soaking clothes and make love to her until they both screamed.

He reached down to scoop her up in his arms, and was hit full in the face by a pair of headlights. A horn blared. He froze.

Liz jumped away from him. Mike turned away. It was obvious he was aroused. So was Liz, but the condition of her nipples might be put down to chill and damp. Only one thing could cause his condition.

"I'm so sorry," Vic called as she opened the door of the pickup truck. "I mean, I apologize—it never occurred to me. I saw the headlights coming in and I couldn't get you on the phone and, oh, hell, Liz, the mare's about to foal and I need you."

Not now! Mike's mind screamed. Not the damned mare now.

"I'll be right there."

"Put on some dry clothes first," Mike said. He didn't want her catching pneumonia.

"There are some cotton jumpsuits in the barn." She stammered, "I'll—I'll ride down with Vic. Thank you for...oh, hell." She started for the truck.

He caught her arm. "I'll follow you. You may need my hands."

She raised her eyebrows.

"To help with the mare."

"Oh. Of course."

Mike slid his wet rear end onto the leather upholstery of his car without a thought for the mildew. Of course

Liz had to go if the mare needed her. But horses had babies all by themselves all over the globe. Couldn't this one have waited at least a couple of hours before she went into labor? He was being unreasonable and didn't give a damn. The mood was broken.

But at least he knew now that she was as hungry for him as he was for her. Okay, so maybe not *that* much, but he obviously didn't repel her. They could never hope to have any sort of lasting relationship. But, God, how he wanted her! And he hadn't truly hungered for a woman in years.

Another night they'd finish what they started.

CHAPTER NINE

IN THE MOMENTS it took car and truck to drive from Liz's house to the barn, the storm charged to the east and left only an occasional grumble and spark to mark its passing. The puddles on the gravel looked as large as lakes. Gouts of water ran off the eaves and pelted the flower beds, but the rain had slowed to a drizzle. In the west the clouds were already breaking up.

The temperature had dropped twenty degrees. Mike's shirt was nearly dry, although his jeans still felt clammy. He hadn't worked in damp clothes since he gave up sailing, but the familiar sensation didn't bother him much. Liz, however, would undoubtedly be chilled in that silk shirt. "Go put on some dry clothes," he commanded.

"In a minute."

Dusk-to-dawn halogen floodlights illuminated the mist from each corner of the barn's roof and from over the front door. Inside, however, the stable was shadowy, except for a dark red light above the mare's stall. The horses slept leaning against the walls of their stalls or stretched flat out and snoring.

A yellow tabby materialized from the darkness to weave around Liz's ankles. She stooped to pet him. Purring, he trailed them down the aisle.

"Why the red light?" Mike whispered.

"Bright light upsets her," Liz answered. "Besides, that's a heat lamp for the foal."

Not all the horses slept. Those on either side of the mare and across the aisle from her were pacing their stalls, occasionally stamping or snorting nervously.

"I've already scrubbed her and put a clean bandage on her tail," Vic told Liz in a normal voice, then turned to Mike. "Boop's ten and this is her first baby. No idea whether she'll be a good mother. We may have a problem getting her to let the baby nurse. Poor old girl, she knows something's wrong, but she has no idea what."

To Mike, the mare looked pretty ticked off. She had paced a big circle into the thick wood shavings that bedded her stall, and from time to time she'd stop and kick at her stomach. Her shoulders were damp with sweat, and milk dripped from her udder. At least Mike supposed it was called an udder—not as big as a cow's, but bigger than it had been the last time he'd seen her.

He found himself getting interested and at the same time flashing back to the only other birth he'd been a part of. He clenched his fists. It was only a horse, dammit. Yeah, but it was still a miracle. A dangerous one.

Vic and Liz seemed completely at ease. He was the one with sweaty palms.

"Could be a minute or an hour," Liz said. "You don't have to stay, Mike. We should be fine." She sat on a hay bale against the far wall.

Sounded like a dismissal.

"But if you'd like to stay," Vic said, "we may need the extra help, and if you've never seen a mare foal, it's pretty exciting."

"How long does it take?"

"Once the process starts—" Vic snapped her fingers "—about that long. Unless there's trouble."

"And if there is?"

"We fix it quickly or we lose them both," Vic said flatly.

Mike nearly bolted.

LIZ COULD CHEERFULLY have throttled her aunt. Vic had seen Mike's kiss and Liz's reaction. Liz had refused to open her mouth on the ride to the barn, and now Vic was getting back at her by practically hogtying the man to get him to stay. And those remarks about birth? Vic knew Pat's mother had died when she was born. Even a mare in foal was bound to dredge up terrible memories for Mike. Liz glared at her aunt. Vic smiled in dewy innocence.

"Vic, would you mind helping me find the iodine?" Liz asked through clenched teeth. Once she got her aunt into the office she'd give her Hail Columbia and tell her to knock off the matchmaking. It was embarrassing as hell to Liz and, kiss or no, she suspected Mike would resent it.

"Right here, dear." Vic held up the bottle. "I do believe I have absolutely everything we're going to need. There's no time to call Angie. She couldn't get here anyway. We'll call her if and when that baby gets here."

She was actually simpering! Liz tried to think of something suitably cutting to reply, but before she could open her mouth, Mike, who had been leaning over the stall, turned to them.

"Does that mean anything?"

A sound like Niagara Falls came from the stall.

"Water's broken. Here we go!" Vic said, and opened the door of the stall.

Liz jumped up and joined her. She said over her shoulder, "Stay out here."

MIKE STAYED. He'd never felt more out of his element. He worried about dirt and germs for Pat's sake, not his own. He'd both seen and experienced his share of bloody injuries in school and on the sailing vessels he'd hired onto. He'd even sutured a nasty shoulder wound one of his shipmates had ripped on a burred halyard.

But this was different. This was some atavistic female rite that he could never be a part of. Besides, he had no experience of animals, large or small, and certainly not pregnant ones.

The two women closed the stall door behind them as the mare began to sink onto her belly. The moment she was down, a translucent white sac began to protrude from under her tail. Vic held the mare's halter, while Liz squatted beside the mare's rump and watched.

"What we got?" Vic asked.

"One front foot. Here comes a nose! Oh, hell! Get her up! Quick! The other foot's caught somewhere."

Vic began to pull on the mare's halter. She grunted and refused to budge.

"Mike, help," Vic said. "We've got to get this mare onto her feet right now!"

Liz heaved up on the mare's tail and dug her toe hard into the mare's fat rump while Mike went to Vic and took the other side of the halter.

Talk about deadweight. The mare stretched her neck and grunted at him, but stayed on her belly.

"Get up, you idiot horse," Liz screamed. "Get on your damn feet right now!"

They'd never have strength enough to haul her up

the way they were going about it. Mike ducked under the mare's neck, leaned his shoulder into her chest and shoved her back onto her rump. Something had to give. She grunted and pulled her front legs around until she sat on her haunches like a big donkey. A big *mad* donkey.

"Watch her. She's scrambling," Vic shouted.

Mike felt an excruciating pain on his instep and yanked his foot out from under the mare's hoof before she put all her weight on it. Should be an interesting bruise. And a limp to go with it.

The mare lunged to her feet.

"Thanks, Mike. I can keep her up," Vic said. "Go help Liz."

Liz was trying to shove the white sac back into the mare. Through the translucent membrane, Mike could see the foal's liquid brown eyes. They blinked once as the whole mass slid slowly back inside the horse. Liz stuck her arm all the way to the shoulder in behind it. "No time to put on a glove."

"What the hell are you doing?" Mike asked, stupefied.

"Damn! I can feel that foot. It's caught behind the pelvic bone, but it's not turned backward. I think I can pop it loose."

Mike realized she'd never had time to change clothes. She stood armpit deep in the rear end of a horse, wearing a wet silk shirt that would never be the same. "Anything I can do?" Mike asked.

"Yeah. Pray she doesn't have a contraction while I'm in here or she'll break my arm in half a dozen places."

Instinctively he reached out to pull her away. "I'll do it. Tell me what to do."

"No time! Let go of me!" She shouldered him away. "All right. Gotcha!"

Mike heard a tiny pop.

Liz pulled out her arm, and before the mare could begin to lie down the sac reappeared. It slid quickly toward the ground. Now both front feet preceded the nose.

"Grab it!" Liz shouted.

Mike grabbed and realized he was holding on to an incredibly slippery bag that held a wriggling animal weighing several hundred pounds. Liz pressed against his back, slid her arms through his and around the foal's belly. Under ordinary circumstances he'd have enjoyed the feel of her, but at the moment he had to concentrate on holding this greased package. Together they slid the baby to the ground, and Liz began to rip open the sac. For an instant the foal's great brown eyes seemed only mildly interested, then he caught on and began to thrash free.

The umbilical cord broke and a stream of warm blood drenched the sleeve of Mike's shirt. He barely noticed.

He glanced at the mare. Those big hind hooves were directly in line with Liz's skull. Would the mare kick out at this strange being that had caused her so much pain? "Watch yourself," he told her. At that moment the foal caught him across the left kneecap with both front hooves. They were small, but they cut like steel.

"*Careful*," Liz said.

"Now you tell me," Mike gasped through the pain. He propped his back against the side of the stall.

"You okay?" Vic asked.

"Fine," he said through gritted teeth. "Are we having fun yet?"

At that moment the mare swung around to get a good look at the thing on the ground. The foal froze, its eyes wide with apprehension. The mare snorted and drew back. Then slowly, she stretched forward, bent her big head over his, bumped him gently with her muzzle, placed a single hoof delicately against his rib cage and called to him softly. He raised his nose to sniff his mother's face and nickered.

"Oh, yeah," Liz said in a gentle tone he'd never heard her use. "We're having fun."

In the glow of the red lamp he saw tears streaming down her face. Vic was crying too. He felt some moisture in his own eyes and told himself it was just the pain in his knee.

Liz was spattered with blood from the tip of her nose to her ankles, her clothes were ruined and her hair looked as though she'd been hit by one of those lightning bolts. She was so beautiful he felt that if he looked at her for long she'd strike him blind. "Yeah," he whispered. "I guess we are."

LIZ HAD TO GIVE Mike credit. He'd managed to get that mare up, then he'd hung in there, blood and all.

And he was still sticking around. Maybe he thought there'd be a repeat of that kiss after all this was over. Wrong.

Kiss, hell! A damned incendiary device with a short fuse.

Every time she thought of the way she'd wound up in Mike's arms, Liz felt her face flame. He must think she had rounder heels than a kid's punching clown. One shove and over she tipped. If Vic hadn't shown up when she did and hit them with her handy-dandy headlights, Liz might well have spent the remainder of the night staring up at Mike from a distinctly supine position.

And faced his daughter in the morning knowing that she'd allowed herself to be seduced by the man with antifreeze in his veins.

The thought of making love with Mike Whitten turned her insides to melted butter. Not a good thing. Had to be the storm. She'd felt vulnerable, he'd acted protective. Voila! Instant passion.

He was no kid, no casual horse-show acquaintance to flirt with. He was used to getting what he wanted—on his terms. Tonight he'd selected her for dessert and she'd come damned close to going along with him. Simple lust, that's all it was. She was out of his league and he was definitely out of hers.

She had never met a man who curled her toes just by driving through a storm. She didn't even like to remember what that kiss did. Toes were the least of it. The last time she saw stars she'd had a concussion.

The foal tried to stand on her big toe. "Ow!" she yelped, and snatched her foot out of harm's way. "That's what I get for not paying attention, you little thug." The foal curled its lips around her thumb. Apparently it knew there was something it ought to be using its mouth for, but so far hadn't figured out quite what.

Mike sat on his haunches in the corner of the stall and watched her.

"What now?" he asked.

He had a silly grin on his face.

"You've got blood on your shirt."

"I also have a bruised foot and a lacerated knee-cap."

"How'd you do that?" Liz asked.

"The mare got my foot, and your little thug there got my knee the same way he just got your toe."

"Do you need first aid? The emergency room? God, you're not going to sue us, are you?"

"Hadn't planned on it. Do we go away now?"

"I wish," Liz said. The mare nickered and the foal struggled halfway to its feet before it collapsed. "Our babies are always so big it takes them a while to stand. And so tall they have to learn to duck to get under their mother's bellies to nurse. So until Angie and Kevin show up with the champagne, Vic and I will take turns doing the new baby waltz."

"What's that?"

The baby chose that moment to stand on all four feet for the first time. Badly. Mike found himself nose-to-nose with it. Its breath warmed his face. He laughed. The foal immediately collapsed in a heap.

"God, sorry, did I do that?"

"Not really." The little horse stood again on its four wobbly stilts. "It's a stud colt," Liz said. "Hard to tell when they're lying down."

Vic slipped in the stall door. "Kevin and Angie are on their way."

Suddenly Mike felt like a fifth wheel. "Then it's about time I went home."

"No! Stay," Vic said. "You've stuck it out this far. At least share the champagne."

He glanced at Liz who was studying the baby. "What the hell, why not?"

By the time Kevin and Angie arrived, shouting congratulations and waving bottles of chilled champagne, Mike had learned the new baby waltz. He was both taller and stronger than Liz and Vic and could hold the foal up as it staggered around the stall. He continually aimed it toward the proper end of its mother. After half an hour he was getting very frustrated. "Are they all this dumb?" he asked.

"Not dumb, just cumbersome," Kevin said. "Here, let me take over."

"No way. This little guy is going to nurse."

On command the foal finally managed to duck his head and latch on to one of his mother's teats. The sucking sound bounced off the walls of the stall.

"Look at that."

"Yeah," Kevin said. "Now go get some champagne. Thanks, old buddy." He clapped Mike on the shoulder.

Nobody had ever called Mike "old buddy." He wasn't certain he liked the familiarity. He tried on his ruthless face, but either he was too tired or too elated to pull it off. He climbed out of the stall, accepted a hug and a glass of champagne from Angie, and realized for the first time that he was completely wiped out. He glanced at his watch. Nearly four in the morning. How was he going to explain to Mrs. H. where he'd been all night?

He dropped beside Liz on the hay bale. She smiled. Her eyes were dark with exhaustion.

"How soon can you go to bed?" he asked.

She stiffened.

"Get some sleep, I mean."

"I could leave now. I'd kill for a hot shower."

Mike looked ruefully at his shirt. "Yeah."

"The vet's coming in less than an hour to check out Boop and the foal," Vic said. "I asked him to do a prepurchase on Traveller at the same time. Liz mentioned you planned to buy him. I think it's great, and you ought to stay for his check-up."

Mike checked his watch. "Of course."

"But not like that," Vic said, waving her champagne flute at him. She sounded a little tipsy. "You both smell terrible. You need a shower."

"Vic," Liz said in warning.

"Lord, yes," Angie turned up her nose. "Liz, take this poor man up to your house and stick him under a hot shower until he turns all pruny."

"And give him what to wear? He won't fit into my jeans."

"Oh, I'll find a jumpsuit he can put on." Vic looked him over. "We keep a stack of coveralls for occasions just like this, Mike. Don't think we've got one quite tall enough for you. Maybe it'll be a tad 'scace,' as we say down south, but you'll be decent and clean." She tripped off toward the office.

"It's all right, Mrs. Jamerson. I can..."

"We won't hear of it, will we, Kevin baby?" Angie said. She set down her glass, stood up and reached down both hands to pull Mike to his feet. "You are a disgrace, the pair of you. Liz, where's your manners, girl? Look after this fine gentleman."

"Oh, hell, all right," Liz answered. The look she gave Angie would have peeled paint. "Come on, Mike. You do smell like dried blood and horse manure. Melba would kill you if you walked into the house like that."

"She already thinks that something about this place destroys my clothes. Okay, thanks." He followed her, took the jumpsuit from Vic, who had just come back from the office, and barely managed to get into his car before Liz took off ahead of him in Vic's truck.

The sky had cleared now, the moon loomed large on the western horizon. The early birds were either calling to the worms or the sun. Or perhaps they were serenading their mates in hopes of a little matinee. In an hour, false dawn would give way to morning. Mike felt incredibly elated. All the big money deals in the world didn't give him this kind of buzz—but then, this was life, grubby, noisy…and miraculous.

CHAPTER TEN

"HERE'S SOME fresh towels," Liz said and handed Mike a stack of cherry-red towels. "Shampoo's on the ledge behind the shower. You want a razor? I've probably got one I haven't shaved my legs with yet." She heard the testiness in her voice.

He took the towels. "Thanks, I can shave at home." He made no move toward the bathroom.

She avoided his eyes. "What?" she asked.

"What's wrong?"

"Nothing's wrong. Everything's peachy. Why would you think anything's wrong?" She stood with hands on hips, her face turned away from him. "Just drop your clothes in the corner. I'll have everything cleaned for you."

He set the towels on the bed and reached for her. "Liz."

She backed up and raised her hands in front of her chest palms out as though to ward off a blow. "Thank you for all you did to help with the mare. I don't think we need a replay of the rest of the evening, do you?"

"Not a replay, no. Let's finish the game."

"Not a good idea."

"Why not?"

"Because, because—oh, hell, I'm tired and dirty and confused and dammit, just take your shower and go home! I've got to feed the dogs." With that, she turned and stalked toward the kitchen.

Liz fed the dogs and let them out while Jacko took time from his sunflower seeds to tell her in no uncertain terms what a jerk she was. "So maybe I am," she snapped.

She decided to make coffee—at least Mike wouldn't fall asleep on the way home.

She closed her eyes, listened to the rush of water from the shower and tried not to visualize Mike naked. It didn't work.

She smacked down an urge to strip and join him. His back had felt so strong. His hands... She longed to run her hands down his slim flanks, across his chest, and below. It wasn't what was *inside* him that heated her blood. It was what she damned well wanted inside *her* that was giving her heart failure.

A fatal mistake, that's what it would be. She couldn't simply sleep with Mike occasionally until he got bored enough or smart enough to move on to a more suitable partner. She did not commit her heart easily, and once she gave it, it stuck to the give-ee like superglue until it got ripped off. She'd tear a strip out of herself and wind up bleeding all over the carpet.

She'd never perfected the knack of the casual affair the way so many of the horse-show wives did.

Not that she'd had all that much experience. Only twice had she given her heart completely. The first time she'd been in college, and Jack Ransome was a graduate student who had never been on a horse in his life. They met in the stacks at the library when she dropped a copy of Stubb's book on horse anatomy on his foot and damn near broke it.

He took her to poetry readings, faculty teas and chic

little dinners where everyone talked about deconstructing Shakespeare. He was gentle, patient and adoring. With him she felt beautiful. He told her she was smart, just naive and untutored.

He said she made him feel alive, that she was a wild, elemental spirit, whatever the heck that was. She adored his dark beard and his quirky mind and his slim, pale body.

He took her virginity on a badly made single bed in his tiny apartment while October sleet slashed the windows outside.

The sex was pleasant and inventive. She enjoyed it, but she felt nothing like the cataclysms of pleasure her roommates went on and on about. Obviously she wasn't much good at sex, either. Jack never knew the way she felt. She couldn't bear to hurt him. Besides, it was her fault. Had to be.

They lasted until spring when she began once more to ride every day. He accused her of not making enough time for him. She realized they'd always done what Jack wanted to do, so she tried to introduce him to her world. Jack was as mystified by hoof dressings as she had been by Rothko and de Kooning. She wanted to learn. He didn't.

She cried for weeks after they broke up.

Funny the way things turned out. She'd met him ringside at Harrisburg a couple of years earlier. He was older, grayer, but still slim and handsome, with patches on the elbows of his jacket. He'd kissed her and said, "You got your revenge, you know." He'd pointed toward a willowy dark girl trotting a bay mare around in an equitation class with several other girls her age. "That's my daughter, Heather, out there. She's horse mad. I spend every weekend in the mud and grime cheering her on and half of my salary keeping her in handmade boots and stable fees.''

Liz had been glad to see him. They'd met that evening for a drink. He was twice divorced. He'd made a pass, but they'd both known they could never rekindle what they'd had.

Years after Jack, she'd fallen in love with Randy Esterhaze, a trainer from Florida. Everyone said they were the perfect couple. For Liz he was the perfect combination—a truly male man who understood what she did and never raised his voice at her. Until the end. That particular breakup had been public, noisy and humiliating. She caught him ''doing a line'' in her tack room. He accused her of being a puritan, told her that everybody did cocaine and that he had no intention of giving it up.

Vic helped her pick up the pieces that time. The last she heard, he was living in Vancouver and training for a wealthy Saudi businessman.

There'd been a few brief romances since, but she had to admit, she'd never given her heart again. Lately there'd been no one. Platonic meant safe. No scars, no blood. It was as though she'd been waiting for someone to break down her defenses.

If she admitted the depth of her feelings for Mike, even to herself, she wouldn't be able to have a fling and casually walk away. No doubt Mike was an expert at casual. He'd probably had plenty of practice.

Better not to take the risk in the first place. Back off now while she still had a chance for a dignified retreat. Besides, he was a client and the father of one of her students. The power was all on his side. That frightened her, especially when he still hadn't signed the Edenvale contract.

The sound of the shower stopped. Liz jumped and dumped a scoop of coffee grounds onto the kitchen counter. "Oh, bother!" she said and filled the hopper quickly, then poured water in and heard it sizzle.

As she cleaned up the spilled grounds, she listened for the opening door. She turned when she heard the slap of his bare feet against the floorboards.

He stood in the doorway naked except for the towel around his waist. "Left that overall thing out here," he said.

He followed her gaze to his chest and laughed ruefully. "All this hair on my chest used to be on my head. It migrated down around my fortieth birthday." He shrugged. "At least it didn't wind up on my back."

"Uh-huh." She knew her face was the color of that towel he was holding.

"Shower's free. I saved you some hot water."

"Uh—thanks."

"Coffee smells wonderful."

"How do you like it?" Her voice was a croak.

He raised an eyebrow. "Of course, you make it very hot, don't you?"

"Cream? Sugar?"

"Neither. Hot's fine. I like to savor the true flavor of everything I taste."

"Cups are in that cupboard," she said, her face heating at the innuendo. "You can dress out here. Excuse me." She bolted past him and felt his eyes boring into the back of her head. Sweet Patience on a monument, she was acting like a fourteen-year-old virgin! And he was enjoying the hell out of every bit of discomfort she experienced. Damn and blast the man.

She pointedly locked the bathroom door behind her. Mike's clothes lay in a heap in the corner. She bent to pick them up and stopped with her hand twelve inches away.

Later. When he was safely gone and she'd gotten back her nerve. Until then she didn't want to touch anything that had touched his skin. Maybe she'd send Vic up for the soiled clothing.

The room was misty, the mirror still coated with moisture. It smelled of soap, shampoo and Mike Whitten. The hair on her arms stood up. She didn't need to touch his clothes. He'd marked his territory as effectively as a bull elk in rut. All those male pheromones were bouncing off her skin like Ping-Pong balls. She yanked open the small window and stood on the toilet seat so that she could stick her head out and gulp air that was not crammed full of male musk and testosterone.

After a moment she shut the window and began to yank off her clothes. She glanced in the mirror as she stepped into the shower. Her nipples stood at attention, her breasts felt engorged and she knew her hair wasn't the only portion of her anatomy that was damp. If he were to break that lock right this minute, she'd probably throw herself at him, and they'd both wind up with broken legs on the slippery bathroom floor.

This could not go on. She needed to put some distance between them. From now on, it would be strictly business and in full view of half a dozen other people.

She picked up the bar of soap and realized that it was still covered with bubbles from his shower. She rubbed it down her belly and across her breasts and moaned softly.

She spoke to her foreshortened reflection in the showerhead. "I am totally insane and he'd better be the hell gone before I come out of this bathroom or I am in very big trouble.''

MIKE HAD NO INTENTION of leaving before Liz came back, even though she'd probably be wearing a full set of armor complete with chastity belt.

He'd been a class-A idiot. He had forced her along at the pace he wanted. She'd kept up with him until Vic showed up, but once she'd had time to think about the man she was about to invite into her bed...

He wasn't used to taking his time, wooing, courting. Oh, sure, flowers, the occasional diamond tennis bracelet. His secretary took care of that sort of stuff.

This was different. Women were a diversion, and he made certain he was nothing more than a diversion for them as well. They both knew the rules. Nobody got hurt. Fun and games.

Unfortunately, being with Liz was no game. Didn't feel like a whole hell of a lot of fun, either. Aside from the physical injuries he'd sustained, he found all this longing and pining a damned nuisance. Interfered with his concentration.

He wanted her in his arms and in his bed because somehow she'd worked her way into his heart. Maybe if he made love to her, he'd be less obsessed with her. Now that was a thought worth considering.

He found that the jumpsuit was definitely a couple of sizes too small. Since he was not wearing underwear, he was extremely careful when he pulled up the zipper. Even so, it stuck at the level of his sternum and refused to go higher. He shoved the sleeves up to his elbows, and ran his hand through his damp hair and down the stubble on his face. It rasped like sandpaper.

He leaned carefully on the edge of the kitchen

counter and sipped his coffee. He was afraid to sit down for fear he'd split his pants.

"You're still here," Liz said as she came out of her bedroom. It sounded like an accusation. She wore a navy T-shirt and jeans. She was barefoot and her damp hair curled in wild abandon around her face.

"You offered me coffee."

"So I did." She ran her gaze down the jumpsuit and immediately began to concentrate on his face.

"Vic was right," he said. "It is tight, but it'll do to get me home."

"Yeah, well, do you want breakfast or anything?" It was not an invitation. One step short of surly.

"No thanks."

"It's after five. The vet's probably already down at the barn looking over the baby. As soon as he's finished, he'll vet Traveller out. That shouldn't take much more than thirty minutes. You really need to stay."

"I intend to."

"What I mean is, we ought to get back to the barn right now."

"Ah." He shoved off from the counter. "I see. Of course. I'll get my clothes..."

"I told you I'd have them cleaned."

"Don't bother. Mrs. H. can see to everything. I'll have the jumpsuit laundered and returned to you ASAP."

Liz climbed into the front seat of her truck, and watched Mike edge into the driver's seat of his Volvo. Well, she'd wanted to see him naked. If anything, in that jumpsuit he looked beyond naked. He looked like what country folks called "nekkid." Her grandmother, who had adored men, used to call a man who was built like Mike "the ladies' kind friend." She wondered whether he had any idea just how obvious his sex was. If Angie was still at the barn, she'd be enchanted. She slipped the truck into gear and began to laugh. Serve him right to have a bunch of women gape at his crotch.

Paul Braithewaite, the veterinarian, had arrived and pronounced both mother and foal in perfect shape. Kevin had already left for the hospital and a pair of twins who were due to arrive any minute.

As Mike followed Liz into the stable, Angie was trotting Traveller down the aisle so that Dr. Braithe-waite could check its gaits.

"Morning," the vet said. "We've already got X rays of his legs and knees." He stuck out his hand at Mike. "Good little pony. Unless I find something wonky when I check the X rays, and I see no reason I should, he passes with flying colors."

"So I buy him?"

"I don't make that kind of recommendation. All I can say is he's sound and likely to stay that way."

"Thanks." Mike pulled out a card. "Send the bill to me."

Dr. Braithewaite stuck the card into the pocket of his jumpsuit, which fit considerably looser than Mike's, and went away whistling.

"We have a deal," Mike said, offering his hand to Vic. "Can you get me a complete list by this evening of the things I'll need to buy for Pat? And I'd like to hold a birthday party for her here with the campers at lunch on Friday. I can give her the pony then. If Mrs. Hannaford brings the food, can that be arranged?"

"Great idea," Vic said.

"I've got to get home before Mrs. H. calls the police to report me missing," Mike said. "Liz, would you walk out with me?"

"Uh..."

Vic shoved her. "Of course she will."

"I'll have the cashier's check cut this morning, and Mrs. Hannaford will bring it out this afternoon."

"Wonderful," Liz said.

"I'm relying on you to see that Pat doesn't get hurt on that pony."

"I'll do my best," Liz answered. All business.

"And, as your newest boarder, I have a favor to ask."

"Sure." Liz said, then realized she'd just given him carte blanche. "What sort of favor?" she asked suspiciously.

"I have a thing to go to tonight. A buffet on the terrace at the club. I don't want to go, but I'm meeting a couple of business associates there, so I have to show up. Will you be my date?"

"Me? Lord, no. I don't have anything to wear, and besides, I'm so busy here..."

"Of course she'll go," Vic said. "How dressy?"

Liz gave her a look that would curdle milk.

"Very informal. Slacks, shorts, that sort of thing." Mike turned to Liz. "We don't have to stay long, then I'll buy you dinner and we can go over the plans for the party and the list of stuff for Pat. Strictly business."

"Business?"

"Absolutely."

"She'd love to," Vic said and beamed at him. She poked Liz in the back. "What time will you pick her up?"

Five minutes later, Mike gingerly crawled into his car and drove off with Vic's promise that Liz would be ready by seven. Vic waved at him as he drove off down the driveway.

"I'm going to kill you," Liz said to Vic. "Don't you realize what you got me into?"

"What?"

"The commission on Traveller will clear our outstanding feed bill, and that Edenvale contract spells the difference between keeping ValleyCrest solvent this fall or going to work in a discount store. Mike makes the final recommendation about whether it gets signed or not. He's one customer we can't afford to offend. I've got no business dating him."

"Oh, come on!" Vic snorted. "He didn't twirl his mustache and demand that you pay the rent with your body."

"That's not the point. He *could*."

"All I saw was that he likes you and you're obviously attracted to him. He didn't hang around tonight because he wanted to see a foal born. He stayed because you stayed. I think you're looking for any excuse to duck out on him because you're scared of *your* feelings, not his." Vic shook her head. "And the way that jumpsuit fits him…" She sighed. "If I were twenty— no, ten years younger I'd go after him myself, contract or no contract."

At that moment Angie strolled out of the barn with her hands in her pockets. "My, my. Talk about your stud-muffins. I must remember to buy Kevin one of those jumpsuits."

"Buy it a couple of sizes too small," Vic advised. "That is, if you want the full effect."

"You two are disgusting," Liz said and shouldered past them.

"Only celibate," Vic called after her.

"Angie doesn't even have that excuse," Liz said.

"I'm into art appreciation," Angie said with dignity.

"My aunt Fanny," Liz said.

"His is much more interesting."

CHAPTER ELEVEN

ONLY ONE WOMAN at the supposedly informal patio party wore shorts, and those were a wildly patterned Hawaiian linen with a matching jacket that probably cost as much as the ValleyCrest commission on Traveller. Most of the other women were decked out in cool linen and cotton shirtdresses cut high on the thigh and low at the neck. Several dresses had no backs at all.

In Vic's beige linen slacks and top, Liz felt as though she was wearing a camouflage suit that was guaranteed to blend right in with the woodwork. Right now that did not seem like a bad thing. The party was already in full swing. The voices were shrill, the six-piece orchestra was gearing up to play dance music and a line of men in sport shirts and Dockers stood three feet deep around both of the bars. The ice sculpture around which acres of shrimp were piled had already lost its contours. Liz thought it might once have been a tennis racket. At the moment it looked like an especially bawdy phallic symbol.

She was aware of Mike's hand spanning her back. He probably regretted bringing her. She certainly regretted coming. At fancy horse-show parties, she knew most of the people, and no one paid attention to who had the most money or the highest position. At those moments they were all horse people. Period. With plenty to discuss. What on earth did these people talk about? Children? Servants? The stock market?

"Well, I'll be damned! If it ain't Liz Matthews!" a bass voice boomed behind her. "Come here right this minute and give ole Big Scooter some sugar!"

At the sound of the voice Liz broke into delighted laughter and whirled in time to meet the man behind her, head-on. He bent her back and kissed her passionately on the lips. "Lordy, if you ain't the prettiest thing!" He wore a rumpled white linen suit that strained across his thick shoulders and broad belly. He wrapped an arm the size of a country ham around her waist and crushed her to him. In his other hand he held a tall frosty glass filled to the brim with what looked like straight bourbon. "Where in hell you been?"

"Jumping horses, where else?" Liz patted his shoulder. "How've you been? And how's Little Scooter?"

"Living in a damned mansion outside of Osceola and running my gins. Still married to that Parker Dupree. Woman's got red claws on her a foot long. One of these days she's gonna do Little Scooter an injury when he's screwing her." He leaned over and kissed her noisily on the cheek. "He shoulda married you."

"Come on, Big Scooter, I don't clean up well enough to suit Little Scooter. You got a Grandson Scooter yet?"

"One's on the way. Give that woman one thing— she can breed like a hound bitch. Got me a two-year-old grandbaby and a ten-year-old granddaughter near as big as you."

"She ride?"

"Wants to."

"Tell you what. You bring her out to ValleyCrest. I'll find her a horse she'll win on."

"Once ginning season's over I'll do that little thing." He took a deep swig of his bourbon. "Now what say you and me go find us a motel room someplace close and get reacquainted?"

"Miss Mamie would cut your heart out and scalp me. Is she here?" Liz looked around.

"Shoot. Miss Mamie's down in N'Orleans spending my money on more of them damned antiques. Can't sit on a single chair in the house without her screaming I'm gonna break it." For the first time the big man looked directly at Mike. "This your beau?"

"Big Scooter Pardee, meet Michael Whitten."

Mike stuck out his hand. Scooter grinned, but refused to release either Liz or the bourbon. "I know who you are, son. Seen you at a couple of them chamber of commerce luncheons eating pig slop along with the rest of us."

"Mr. Pardee," Mike said coolly and dropped his hand.

"Say, I got me some extra money burning a hole in my pocket. What say you and me have us breakfast one day next week and you see if you can talk me out of it?" Scooter planted another kiss on Liz's cheek. "Got to take care of your beau, sugar." He looked away. "Ooh, looky there. I got to get myself some of that shrimp." He let Liz go, arched his eyebrows at Mike and staggered toward the buffet table and a tall, elegant redhead. He pinched her bottom. The woman yipped, turned, saw who he was and gave him a wet kiss.

"My God!" Mike whispered. "Somebody ought to deck that guy."

"He's a darling." Liz laughed. "I used to have a terrible crush on Little Scooter. We rode large juniors together. Last time I saw him, he was leaving to play linebacker with the Arkansas Razorbacks. He was six-six, two-eighty and drop-dead gorgeous.''

''You were engaged?''

''Us? Good grief, no. He's been aimed at Parker Dupree since she was born. Big Scooter owns half the counties in eastern Arkansas and Godfrey Dupree owns the other half. That was an alliance, not a marriage.''

''He's an oaf.''

''He's a rich southern good ol' boy. They all talk like that—the rich ones, at any rate. You ought to have figured that out by now.''

''I seldom see them with women around. So he's only playing games? About that motel, I mean?''

''He'd take a sow to bed in a pinch, but he's perfectly agreeable even if he doesn't score. I don't know how Miss Mamie's put up with him all these years.'' Liz grinned at him. ''Of course, she does have enough diamonds and sables to support a small specialty shop.''

''Liz Matthews!'' This time the voice was shrill and female. ''I haven't seen you since graduation.''

''Dixie Delaney!'' Liz caroled. The two women hugged each other. Then Dixie held Liz at arm's length.

''It's Dixie Harkness now. My second.'' She turned to Mike. ''Liz and I rode junior jumper together and then we were sorority sisters at college.''

''You still ride?''

''I stopped riding when Daddy stopped paying for it,'' Dixie said. ''But I've got a thirteen-year-old daughter who is dying to have a horse. Since I married Buddy Harkness last year, I can finally afford it.''

''Sign her up for lessons. And you, too.'' Liz looked down at Dixie's taut body. ''It's great exercise.''

Dixie slapped her firm tush. "Liposuction is easier." She grinned at Mike. "Buddy is a plastic surgeon. I met him when he did my boobs. It was love at first scalpel." She hugged Liz. "Let's us get together for lunch some day soon. I'm dying to talk over old times." She wriggled her fingers and wandered away.

Before Mike could react, a dozen other people, both men and women, had clustered around Liz. He found himself being introduced to people who said they knew him, but whom he didn't quite place. They all seemed to know Liz and to be delighted to see her. He tried to keep them straight. Their children either rode, so they saw Liz at horse shows, or they themselves had ridden as children, and knew Liz as a competitor from their early years, or they were the aunts, cousins, uncles, fathers, mothers or courtesy kin of people she'd known all her life. He felt as though he were trapped on the edge of a tornado. Liz was completely happy, glowing. She was purely beautiful. He wanted to bring that glow to her cheeks without all these other people around. From time to time she grinned at him before someone else swept her away.

"Mr. Whitten?" The voice at his shoulder had a slight German accent.

Mike turned and smiled sleepily. "Mr. Kreuger. How nice to see you." Mike shook Kreuger's hand.

"Mr. Yamata waits in the limousine. I will escort him inside. He does not speak English," Mr. Kreuger continued. "I will interpret. We are to be private, no? As you are aware, neither Mr. Yamata nor I want it known that we are here."

"It's all arranged." Mike tried to catch Liz's eye as he walked away, but she didn't see his gesture. Well, he'd warned her he had a business meeting set up, and she was much too comfortable among these people to feel abandoned. He felt a stab of annoyance that he had planned this thing in the first place, but he'd done it before Liz had agreed to join him. He followed Kreuger to the long black limousine that waited under the porte cochere.

Kreuger opened the rear door with a flourish and a small elderly Oriental gentleman climbed out.

He and Mike greeted one another in elaborately polite Japanese, exchanged bows and cards, and Mike led the way to the private meeting room he had arranged.

Mike knew he'd need every bit of his concentration and expertise as a business broker to bring this meeting to an advantageous end. He considered himself a matchmaker. He matched businesses that had potential with companies that had money to invest. His commission on this deal could be over half a million. If the deal went through.

Kreuger was a relative lightweight, but for all his grandfatherly demeanor, Yamata was a devious adversary. Mike had to offer him a win-win deal so that both he and Mike's clients could profit. This might be only a preliminary meeting, but it would set the tone for future negotiations.

As he stepped aside to allow the two men to precede him through the door to the club, he heard Liz's laugh. It took all his willpower not to turn around and return to her before she was spirited away by a more appealing version of Big Scooter. Damn the woman! Didn't she have any sense of decorum at all?

God help him, he was jealous of an aging alcoholic fat man named Scooter. He must be losing his marbles.

"WHY, if it isn't Liz Matthews."

Liz froze. Even after all these years, that voice was chillingly familiar.

"It is still Matthews, isn't it? You never married, did you?"

Liz felt her jaw set. She pasted a suitably social smile on her face. In such a large group of old friends, it stood to reason there'd be a few old enemies. Liz hadn't expected this one, however. She turned and held out her hand. "Hello, Rachelle."

Rachelle ignored the proffered hand. "It's Rachelle Claridge now." Rachelle smiled and Liz thought of *Jaws.* "I kept the name after my divorce. You still riding?"

"Yes. You're not, I take it."

"Lord, no. That was Daddy's thing. He's the one who wanted all those trophies." Rachelle flashed her left hand. Her nails were long and varnished in an iridescent hot pink. A large emerald solitaire caught a ray of evening sunlight.

Looks like the bottom of one of those old-fashioned pop bottles, Liz thought. "You certainly seemed to want them at the time."

For a moment Rachelle's composed smile slipped, but only for a moment. "So you're the latest of Whitten's Wenches? I wouldn't have thought you were his type."

"Whitten's Wenches?"

Rachelle laughed and picked up a glass of champagne from a tray held in a passing waiter's hand. "Since he moved to town full-time, he goes through women like a knife through hot butter."

"Really."

Rachelle dropped her voice conspiratorially. "He

courts 'em, beds 'em and passes on to greener pastures.'' She laughed that musical laugh again.

Liz longed to slap her silly.

"Not too particular about their marital status, either, so I've been told. He usually leaves 'em with a diamond pendant or tennis bracelet or something. Unless, of course, that sort of bauble would alert their husbands."

"Uh-huh." What was she supposed to say to that? And why was she surprised? Wasn't that just what she'd been telling Vic and Angie? Liz felt her stomach tighten. Too much champagne, too much party. Suddenly she wanted nothing more than to bolt to the safety of her cottage and her dogs.

"It would seem he's lookin' for fresh stock. Maybe doin' a little slumming."

"I beg your pardon?"

"Oh, darling, I didn't mean you. I think you look marvelous, although beige isn't really your color, is it? But your hair? Must take your hairdresser hours to get that tousled look. Who do you go to?"

"Go to?"

"For your hair, dear. My Andre says sleek is in this fall. But then you never were a slave to fashion, were you?"

"No, you were slavish enough for both of us. And I don't go to anyone."

"Then do let me recommend my Andre. He could work miracles with those split ends." Liz tried to draw away, but Rachelle laid a hand on her arm and leaned close to whisper. "Shall I point out some of your predecessors?" She nodded toward a lovely dark woman smiling up at a tall, graying man. "They were having marital problems a while back. Mike sympathized them right into marriage counseling.''

''I don't believe you. Mike's not that kind of man.''

''Darling, they are *all* that kind of man. Mike simply has a shorter attention span than most.''

''Or higher standards.''

''Of course, darling. Whatever you say. Let's change the subject. You know I'm a real-estate agent now?''

''How nice for you.'' Liz began to look around desperately for someone, anyone, to rescue her. Mike had disappeared. She knew he'd had a meeting, but he might at least have told her he was going off to attend to it. Rachelle continued to cling, and considering their past history, that was distinctly odd.

''You and Vic are sitting on the largest piece of prime property in the county. I'm sure you've been approached about selling it.''

''Often.''

''Well, promise me you won't make any deals until I come out and talk to you.''

''We won't make any deals, period. We're not selling.''

''Not even twenty acres? You could make enough to live on quite comfortably and upgrade that stable. It's the sensible thing to do.''

Liz closed her eyes. The woman was satanic, but she was right. She and Vic might sentiment themselves into bankruptcy, then where would they be? Still, the thought of having Rachelle's long pink nails anywhere near her land made her want to gag. She should talk to someone about the land. But not Rachelle. Maybe Mike could recommend someone.

She looked at Rachelle curiously. The woman never said anything without a reason. Maybe she was one of the Whitten Wenches and was still smarting over being dumped. Liz sucked in a smile. For anyone to dump Rachelle for Liz Matthews would be Rachelle's ultimate humiliation. Good. She deserved a little humiliation to pay her back for all those championships she'd stolen from other riders when they were teenagers.

Liz could have endured Rachelle's wins if they'd been honestly earned. But Rachelle won dirty.

Her daddy sweetened the pot for judges who could be bought, and "persuaded" trainers to scratch horses that Rachelle felt were too tough to compete against. And Rachelle had a complete menu of ways to upset young horses or inexperienced riders in the practice ring. Her competitors missed classes because they couldn't find one of a pair of spurs five minutes after Rachelle visited their tack rooms.

Bridles broke mysteriously while hanging on tackroom walls after Rachelle passed by. Somehow the professional braiders who spent long nights braiding the manes and tails of the hunters "ran out of time" to braid other people's horses after they finished Rachelle's. Rachelle always made it worth their while. So far as Rachelle was concerned, the rules of sportsmanship did not apply to her. Apparently she hadn't changed.

"I'll come out and talk to you and Vic sometime next week. After all, we have history." She wiggled her fingers and slid away.

The history they had, Liz thought, was like the destruction of Pompeii or the London blitz. The woman moved like a copperhead in those hot orange palazzo pants. No doubt looking for another throat to sink her fangs into.

But she'd confirmed Liz's view of Mike. Liz's eyes

swept through the crowd of beautiful, curried and expensive women on the terrace. Thanks to Rachelle, she considered every one of them as a possible ex-mistress of Mike's. Every tennis bracelet—and there were many—seemed to carry Mike Whitten's brand. She'd expect his leftover loves to greet him coldly or cut him dead, but a dozen had given him smiles and air kisses. Maybe he was so good, they were happy with the experience even after he broke their hearts.

Well, not this girl, Liz thought. *I don't mind breaking the occasional rib, but my heart? Forget it. Ribs heal fast. Hearts never heal completely.*

Forty-five minutes later Mike bowed Kreuger and Mr. Yamata into the limousine. Before the driver started, Yamata lowered the window and inclined his head toward Mike. "It will be a pleasure working with a man of your perspicacity," Yamata said in completely unaccented English. "I look forward to seeing you in Osaka." He sat back, and the window slid up soundlessly. Mike grinned. The old fox! Not speak English? He didn't think Kreuger was too happy, but Yamata was the man who counted, and Mike felt he'd made a good impression. He'd fax the report to his clients this evening after dinner.

Unless he had better things to do before morning. He went to find Liz.

LIZ WAS BEING SQUIRED around the dance floor by an oral surgeon who Mike knew only by sight and occupation. He had a reputation as a womanizer, but Mike had to admit the man was a hell of a dancer. Liz might not know how to samba, but the surgeon, whose name Mike could not recall, had done a more than adequate job of teaching her to tango in the time Mike had been gone. He leaned against the brick wall of the club, where the lights couldn't reach him, and watched her. Her athlete's body moved with incredible grace.

"Michael, dahlin,' how nice to see you." Rachelle rubbed her arm against his shoulder and offered her cheek to be kissed. "I must have been missin' your calls."

"I've been out of town a good deal," Mike said without taking his eyes off Liz.

"Interesting idea to bring your Pitti-Pat's riding teacher to this party. Very egalitarian, even for you."

The music ended, Liz spotted him, smiled and wove her way through the crowd to him while the surgeon pattered along behind speaking urgently in her ear. She smiled at him and shook her head. He turned away sadly.

Her upper lip glistened with perspiration and the hair around her face was damp and curling more than usual. The freckles across her crooked nose stood out. She looked stunning.

Mike stepped out of the shadows, but before he could reach Liz, Rachelle moved in front of him.

She slid her hand under his arm and smiled up at him. "Liz and I were just renewing old acquaintance. I'll just bet you don't know that we used to ride horses together back in the old days before we grew up."

"Never together," Liz said quietly.

"Oh, Liz, of course we competed against one another, but it was all friendly, wasn't it?"

"Sure. Friendly."

Mike carefully disengaged his arm. He should have talked to Rachelle before tonight, but he simply hadn't thought about her. His bad manners were obviously going to come back to haunt him. He made a note to send her flowers in the morning. At the moment, all he could think about was extricating himself and Liz from the party, because there was something going on between these two women that he didn't understand. And he didn't think it had much to do with him.

"Uh, sorry, Rachelle, but Liz and I have to go or we'll lose our dinner reservations. Nice to have seen you."

"Of course, sugar, I understand." Rachelle leaned over and kissed his cheek. "Give me a call next week sometime, why don't you? We can do lunch." She wiggled her fingers at Liz once more. "Good to see you again. And don't forget. Andre can do miracles even with hair like yours." She undulated away and was swallowed up by the crowd.

"Come on," Liz said, and walked down the patio steps without waiting for him. He wished with all his heart he had Mrs. H. with him to interpret what had just happened. Then he glanced back at the party. Amazing. He felt he knew less about these people than he did about the people he'd spent only a couple of hours with at Liz's party.

As HE PULLED out of the parking space, Liz turned to him and said casually, "Has Rachelle been your mistress long?"

Mike swung the wheel and narrowly missed the brick column that held up the wrought-iron gate. "What the hell kind of question is that?"

"A simple one."

"Simple? It's right up there with 'When did you stop beating your wife?' No, Rachelle is not my mistress. We were seeing each other but I have not slept with her. I don't intend to."

"Why on earth not? It's not as though either of you was attached or anything."

"How the hell did my love life become a topic of conversation?"

"Sorry. You're right. It is none of my business. I'm sorry I disappointed you."

"What do you mean, disappointed me?" He turned right onto the road.

Liz looked down at herself and sighed. "Rachelle's right. I look like a farmhand—which is what I am—next to all those women with their designer shorts and their diamond tennis bracelets."

He slammed on his brakes. A yellow Toyota swerved to avoid his back fender. He ignored the driver's glare, but he did swing over to the no-parking zone at the curb.

"We're going to clear this up before you get us both killed," he said. "If anybody was a disappointment, it was me. Hell, you knew all those people, and the ones you didn't know when you got there you knew when you left. You speak their language, which might as well be ancient Assyrian so far as I'm concerned. I would have busted that Big Scooter—what the hell kind of name is that for a grown man anyway?—in the jaw if you hadn't stopped me. And if the tango hadn't stopped when it did, that oral surgeon what's-his-name would be in dire need of his own services to put his damned teeth back in his head. Do I make myself clear?"

"Rachelle's right. My hair is awful."

"Hell's bells, woman. I like your hair. And I don't give a damn what you wear. As a matter of fact, I'd prefer you didn't wear a damned thing but your skin." He reached for her. She was securely locked into her seat belt. "Unhitch that thing," he snarled and unsnapped his own.

"This was supposed to be business. You promised."

"I lied." He punched the buckle on her seat belt so hard she coughed.

"Mike, I can't!" She put her arms up in front of her to fend him off. He crushed her against him in spite of them. He kissed her hard. For a moment she fought him, and then she opened her lips to him.

A steer bellowed beside them. Startled, Mike broke the kiss and stared out his window. Big Scooter sat beside them in a canary-yellow Mercedes 600 convertible with a large horn made from a steer's horn mounted beneath his side-view mirror.

"Y'all too old to mess around in the front seat of a car," Scooter shouted. "Buy the gal a motel room, why don't you?" He shouted with laughter and banged his big hands on the wheel.

Liz leaned across Mike's body and spoke out the window. "Scooter, you're drunk. Get out of that car this second."

"Shoot, sugar, you saying Big Scooter can't hold his bourbon?"

"Mike?" Liz asked. "Do something."

Mike climbed out of the car and stood in front of Scooter's radiator with his hands in his pockets. "This is one hell of a car. I'd sure like to drive it."

Scooter laughed and shook a sausage finger at Mike. "I know what you're doing."

Mike smiled lazily. "You're upsetting Liz. I've been told that no true southern gentleman would do that."

Scooter's face fell, and he glanced at Liz, who was climbing out of Mike's side of the car. "This Yankee of yours hits a man where it hurts."

"Women, too," Liz said as she climbed into the car beside Scooter. She leaned over as though to stroke his shoulder, grabbed the keys from the ignition then tossed them to Mike. He fielded them neatly in one hand.

"Hey, no fair!" Scooter bellowed.

Liz was already out of the car and out of reach. "Shove over, Scooter, and let the nice man drive you home before you wind up in the hoosegow with a suspended driver's license."

"Or worse." Mike said.

Scooter grumbled, but he moved.

Liz mouthed a silent "thanks" to Mike.

"My keys are in the ignition. Where does Scooter live?"

"I'll lead, you follow." She climbed into the driver's seat. "Is there anything I should know about driving this car?"

"Works the same as your truck only quieter."

"Lovely." She drove off sedately. Mike followed. Scooter slumped in the passenger seat with his arms folded across his chest.

"I like Liz," he said. "Not sure I like you much. You're sneaky."

"I try."

"You be good to that girl. Sober, I can still take on men half my age."

"No doubt," Mike said with a wry grin.

Scooter let out a roar of laughter. "Drunk, I can whup my weight in alligators." He leaned over toward Mike, who nearly choked on the smell of bourbon. "Think I'll take a little nap." He leaned back, passed out and began to snore.

Mike concentrated on the silhouette of Liz's curly head in the car in front of him. At this rate, he'd never get her alone. "Damn!" he said aloud. "It's a conspiracy."

CHAPTER TWELVE

"THANKS FOR DRIVING Scooter home," Liz said nearly an hour later as Mike turned off Poplar Drive and headed for the road that led to ValleyCrest. "That was quite a performance. All you needed was the red cape and the tight pants. Ho-ho, *toro!*"

They had left Scooter waving a cheerful if unsteady goodbye from the front steps of his Chickasaw Gardens mansion. His butler stood apprehensively behind him ready to catch him if he fell. The butler dangled the car keys over his head where Scooter couldn't see them as a sign that Scooter, whether he wanted to be or not, was home for the evening.

"Man needs Betty Ford," Mike said in annoyance.

"He's gone way down since I knew him. He always drank, but I've never seen him really drunk before. Not like this, at any rate. And he never used to drive when he'd had even a beer. He generally has a driver. I don't know what's gotten into him. Of course, I haven't seen him in years and Miss Mamie *is* out of town. Everybody was always ready to forgive Scooter anything because he was rich and funny and good-hearted. Tonight wasn't funny. It was pitiful. Poor Miss Mamie."

Mike dropped a hand on her knee. "Nothing you can do about it."

She didn't remove the hand, but she didn't acknowledge it, either. "I know. It's the most helpless feeling when you care about somebody who's hell-bent on self-destruction. Except that my daddy wasn't rich or good-hearted. He never laid a hand on me. He used to tear me up with words.''

Mike glanced over at her. Her chin was propped on her fist. She stared out the window of the car, but he doubted she saw the traffic. "Sorry. I didn't know.''

"No reason you should. Uncle Frank used to do the same things, said he was doing it for my own good, making me a better horsewoman. My father just wanted me to hurt as bad as he did.''

"Words can hurt worse than blows.''

"Always. Uncle Frank said I had to toughen up, learn how to be a professional. He tried to show me that no matter how much power he seemed to have over his customers, they could walk away, take their money and their horses with them, and there was not a thing he could do about it except suck it up. I didn't understand that fully until after he died. All of a sudden, customers I considered close friends left Vic and me. Even Angie left us. Didn't matter that we needed them, and they knew it. We were just the hired hands. To people like Rachelle and, yes, even Scooter, that's all I'll ever be.''

"Nonsense. Scooter's nuts about you. Besides, you don't suck up a damned thing.''

"Sure I do. How about when you accused me of trying to trick you into buying Traveller?''

"That was business. I'm always hard-nosed about business.''

"Buying Pat a pony was business?''

"Of course. Did you sell Traveller out of the goodness of your heart or because you needed the commission?''

"Listen, I sweated bullets getting another horse for Janey so Pat could have Traveller. Damned straight it was the goodness of my heart." Liz had no idea where the anger she felt bubbling up was coming from. Not true. It was coming from Rachelle and her comments about tennis bracelets and split ends and slumming. Liz was still the kid in the dusty chaps braiding other people's manes at four in the morning. That's all she'd ever be. All she'd ever be to Mike. "And this little favor I did you tonight? Was coming to that blasted party business too?"

"Of course not."

"You said it was when you asked me."

"I meant that we'd talk business, not that I invited you as a business proposition. I didn't think you'd go if I simply asked you on a date."

"I'm hardly in a position to refuse, not so long as that Edenvale contract isn't signed."

The moment the words were out of her mouth she regretted them. She wanted to turn to Mike and beg him to forgive her, but the words wouldn't come.

When Mike spoke, his voice sounded deadly quiet. "You think I'd hold the Edenvale contract over your head that way?"

"How could I possibly know? If we go strictly by your reputation, then yes, you could."

"The hell with my reputation."

"None of this makes sense otherwise. What can you possibly see in me except a change of pace from the Rachelles of this world?"

"The hell with Rachelle. Are you going to tell me that when I held you in my arms, danced with you, that I was merely a client? That you didn't want me as badly as I wanted you that night on the porch? Because I won't believe you.''

"Yes, I respond to you. But I keep seeing the consequences if I give in to my desires. There aren't any consequences for you. You walk away to the next woman and never look back. Toss us the Edenvale contract as a going-away present.''

"Who said anything about going away? I just bought a pony that is going to remain at ValleyCrest.''

"For the time being. But until when? You go to bed with me? Kiss me again and tell me you don't want me.''

"I want you desperately, but I am not going to let that interfere with my judgment. I can't simply sleep with you and walk away. All I want is to get out of this heart-whole. My best chance for that is not to let you within a yard of me because I can't breathe and I can't think and I can't be rational when you are.''

"I want you heart-whole too.'' He made the turn into the ValleyCrest gates and drove up the driveway faster than he should have. Ice water in his veins, huh? At the moment he felt as though he were burning alive. And angry. He hadn't been angry, not truly angry, since Pat went into the hospital. "The man you're describing is a monster.''

"No, just a man used to getting what he wants any way he can.''

He stopped the car, popped his seat belt and turned to her. "I'm not talking about a one-night stand here.''

"Good, because I don't do one-night stands.''

"There has to be a first time even for people who spend a lifetime together. Sometime every couple has a one-night stand. If they don't, they have no future. I'm willing to risk that, why aren't you?''

"Because I know the outcome. We don't fit, Mike. Tonight proved that. You belong with those beautiful women back there. We might fit sexually, but that's limited and limiting. We don't see the world the same way, we don't have the same goals or ambitions, the same needs and wants. We can't even have a decent conversation over dinner. All we have is chemistry. That's not enough.''

"It's a start.''

"No, it's an end. Go call Rachelle if you want to get your rocks off.'' She opened the car door, slid out and ran up her front steps before he had time to react.

"Liz!'' He ran after her. "Don't run away from me. Stay and fight this out.''

"I don't want to fight. I can't bear fighting. Don't you get it yet? Please, please, if you care anything about me at all, let me go.'' She opened the screen door, walked in and slammed it behind her.

He wanted to hit something, anything. Instead, he turned on his heel, climbed into the car and drove off. He didn't slow down until he hit the first red light.

The moment his taillights disappeared, Liz came out, sat down on the steps and hugged the dogs to her. She spent an hour justifying her words, trying to blame Mike for the disastrous way the evening had ended.

Finally, she had to admit she'd been wrong, stupidly wrong. For a woman who hated confrontation, she could certainly engineer a doozy when she put her mind to it. Talk about catering to the clients! Mike would have every right to move Traveller to another barn after the things she'd said to him. She prayed that he wouldn't. She'd have to find some way to apologize.

The skin on her arms crawled at the prospect. He'd be distant, businesslike, and back to the cold fish he'd been the first day he came to ValleyCrest.

She wouldn't have to decide whether to take her relationship with Mike to the next level—or to any level, for that matter.

So what were her feelings? She could be falling in love with the man. And she'd sent him away before she had time to find out? That made about as much sense as galloping a green horse down on a five-foot fence. She'd never considered herself self-destructive. She was into self-preservation. Always had been.

Maybe that's what she'd been trying to do tonight. Preserve herself before she could find out for sure that the only thing worse than having him in her life and her bed was to have him for a little while then watch as he walked away.

He'd still be heart-whole. Hers might never mend.

LIZ NEITHER SAW nor heard from Mike the next couple of days. He wasn't out of town, so he must be avoiding her. Wasn't that what she'd asked him to do?

Vic noticed how mopey she was, but Liz refused to discuss the party she'd been to with Mike, except to say that if she won that grand prix she was going to get the most expensive haircut she could find and then buy herself a dress—maybe two.

Vic tried to sound Mike out when she discussed the tack Pat needed to ride Traveller. He was back to his cold, unresponsive self. Eventually she gave up, ordered Pat's things to be delivered to Mike's office Friday morning and concentrated on keeping Liz from breaking her neck on Trust Fund.

The morning of Pat's party dawned hazy. The September fogs were early this year, but the heat continued.

"We'll probably have tornadoes for the Labor Day show," Liz said, looking at the thick yellow haze on the horizon. "Just our luck."

"The first cold front to break up this mess is going to be a corker," Vic said, wiping the back of her neck. "At least the heat should keep Traveller from misbehaving. He won't have the energy." She tossed a shovelful of fresh shavings into Boop's stall. The foal reared and pawed at her. Vic laughed. "Better knock off that stuff, Thug. It may be cute now, but we are not putting up with bad manners from a seventeen-hand two-year-old. Guess who will lose whose *cojónes* early?"

Melba Hannaford arrived at eleven, but not alone. Walter Simpson had driven her out in his Bronco. "Thought Melba might need a tad of help setting up all this stuff," he said to Vic. "Besides, I didn't have a dang thing better to do today."

"Admit it, you wanted the free food," Melba added with a touch of pride. "He's got more than enough to do. He's got the most wonderful workshop. And the wood? He's better than any craftsman I've ever seen."

"It was that or shoot myself," Walter said. "Retirement sucks." He whispered to Vic, "I'm building Pat a special saddle rack. Wanted to have it ready for her birthday, but Melba kept me busy doing other things. Still need to finish sanding and staining."

Melba bristled. "I work full-time, Mr. Simpson. You're retired. Not my fault if you're incapable of organizing your time properly."

Walter grinned at her. "Always did like feisty women."

"Get over here and help me tote this stuff. That's

what you came for, isn't it?" Melba sounded angry, but Vic could see that she was blushing.

"Is this a surprise party?" Walter asked as he carried in a large cardboard box bearing the logo of the finest baker in town.

"No way we could manage that," Vic said. "The party's not a surprise, but I think the presents may be. Can you manage? I need to get to the ring. The kids are practicing jumping small courses. The Labor Day show will be here before we know it."

"How's my grandnephew doing?" Walter asked.

"Fine. Eddy keeps talking about getting a horse for Christmas."

"Oh, Lord," Walter said. "I'll have to help out with the expenses."

"What else do you have to spend your money on?" Melba asked tartly.

He wiggled his eyebrows at her. "Strong drink and wild, wild women like you."

She slapped his arm.

MIKE ARRIVED a little before noon. Liz glimpsed his car as it drove up the driveway from the road, and half expected him to come out to the ring to watch Pat. She was riding Wishbone. Liz didn't think she was ready to try Traveller over even the lowest fences. She'd ride Wishbone in the Labor Day horse show.

Liz kept glancing at the stable door, but Mike did not appear.

If her object had been to get rid of him, she'd certainly succeeded beyond her wildest dreams. She wouldn't be surprised if he moved Traveller and Pat to Mark's barn. Then she'd never see him except at ringside.

Finally the class was over and the party started. The kids didn't want to wait, so Liz and Albert rinsed down the horses, and Liz began to turn them out into the paddock. It gave her an excuse to stay away from the party a while longer.

"Git your tail in there to that party," Albert said finally. He sounded exasperated.

"You go. I'll finish putting the horses out."

"I don't know what's going on between you and that man, but you better fix it, girl. You look like one of my walker hounds after he's let a possum get away."

She handed Albert her lead line and walked to the office as though it were the last mile. She could hear the kids whooping and shouting. Must be a huge success.

The first person she saw when she opened the lounge door was Mike, one foot propped against the wall behind him and his hands in his pockets, not really a part of the merriment. When he saw her, his jaw tightened, he pushed off and edged around the children to meet her at the door.

He had not changed from his business suit. Granted he wore beautiful clothes tailored to his broad shoulders and narrow waist, but every time she saw him dressed this way she felt a mingled flare of sexual heat and emotional chill. She backed out of the door.

"Wait. I have something for you," he said.

"Oh?" She tried to sound as neutral as possible.

He pulled a thick envelope from his breast pocket "Here. It's the signed contract between Edenvale and ValleyCrest." He slapped it against her open palm.

Liz gulped.

He turned to go back into the party. "It's notarized. I originally planned to give it to you this afternoon after the party. Check the date I signed it." He shut the door behind him.

With trembling hands, Liz opened the envelope and riffled through the sheaf of papers to the last sheet. Mike had signed and notarized the contract a week ago. She closed her eyes and sat on the nearest tack trunk. Why hadn't he given it to her or to Vic right then? She'd made a fool of herself, accused him of holding the contract over her head, and all the time it was a done deal.

"Why you sitting out here blubberin'?" Albert said. "Didn't I tell you to get your tail in that party?"

"I can't." She handed him the contract.

"Uh-huh. Good. We can eat a while longer."

"Oh, Albert. I've really screwed up." She launched herself at him and threw her arms around his neck.

He patted her awkwardly. "Yeah. Thought so. Don't know what you did, but tell the man you're sorry."

"That won't matter to him."

"Matters to you." He removed her arms and held her away from him. "You do wrong, you fix it. I been teaching you that since you were riding a small pony. Now you go admire Pat's new pony, and then you find a way to tell that man you're sorry. You hear?"

She nodded. "Yes, Albert." She took his hand. "Come with me, please."

"Shoot, might as well. I got to eat."

Twenty minutes later the single half sandwich and sliver of birthday cake sat in Liz's stomach like ballast. Mike studiously ignored her, while Albert watched her as though she were going to take off like a rocket.

Vic had edged out of the party moments before.

"When do I get my presents, Daddy?" Pat asked.

"We'll do presents at home tonight with just you, me and Mrs. H.," Mike said.

"Oh." Pat sounded deflated.

Liz suspected that two months ago that announcement might have set off a major tantrum. Now Pat merely shrugged. "Okay. It was a nice party, Daddy."

"Yeah!" The kids cheered.

All that sugar kicking in, Liz thought. *Won't they be fun to teach this afternoon?* And the farrier was coming to redo the horses' shoes before the show. Perfect timing. She glanced at Mike and decided she'd apologize by letter. Easier for both of them if she didn't have to face him while she did it.

"Now, you children get out of here so we can clean up," Melba said. "I'll leave the leftovers in the refrigerator so you can all have some more birthday cake later. All right?"

More choruses and shouts. "Can we help?" Janey asked.

"No, you go on, scat." Melba smiled at Mike and winked. She'd clean up later after Pat's surprise.

"Come on, Daddy," Pat said.

"I have to go back to work."

"You can stay a little while, can't you?" She held his hand in hers. "It's my birthday."

He sighed. "If you insist. But I only have a few minutes."

Pat dragged him out; the other children followed. Albert, Liz, Melba and Walter trailed along behind.

"Forgot to tell you," Mike said. "You do have one small present here." He shoved Pat around the corner of the barn. Halfway down the aisle, Vic held a shiny new leather lead line attached to an equally shiny new leather halter clasped around the head of a gray pony who seemed deeply offended by the wide pink ribbon tied around his neck.

"Happy birthday, Pitti-Pat," Mike said.

Pat stood stock-still, an expression of shocked disbelief on her face.

"Go on," Mike said.

Pat caught her breath and took a hesitant step forward. The children behind her made sounds that were a combination of joy and envy.

Liz glanced at them. She remembered a string of these moments from her own life—watching from the sidelines while other children received their very own horses, to be ridden by no one else. She'd never owned a horse of her own until three months before her seventeenth birthday.

"You never forget your first horse," Vic told Pat. "Here." She held the end of the lead line out to her.

"No, you don't forget your first horse." Liz whispered. She'd plundered her meager savings to buy her first at an auction. A skinny bay Thoroughbred mare with bad rain rot on her skin and thrush in her hooves, but Liz had turned her into a champion. Liz tilted her head slightly. She could just make out First Love, her back hollow with age, but dappled and rotund, contentedly cropping her retirement grass in the far pasture.

"Oh, Daddy," Pat barely breathed. She ignored the lead line and wrapped her arms around the pony's neck. He shook his head in protest. "Oh, Traveller, my very own pony." She buried her face against the soft gray pelt. He nickered softly.

"He comes with restrictions," Mike said severely.

"Huh?" Pat looked up.

"Absolutely," Vic said. "First, you will not ride

him without supervision, and two, you will not do anything on him without express instructions from either me or Liz. You promise?''

''Sure.''

At that moment Pat would probably have agreed to cut the whole hundred acres at ValleyCrest with a paring knife. But both Vic and Liz saw the gleam in Pat's eyes.

''Uh-oh,'' Liz whispered.

''Uh-huh,'' Albert said. ''We all gonna have to watch her.''

CHAPTER THIRTEEN

MIKE LEFT soon after without saying goodbye to Liz. She heard him promise Pat he'd return about five to watch her ride Traveller. Liz watched him drive away, spewing gravel behind his Volvo like an angry rooster.

She'd finally gotten under that cool of his and found a whole lot of anger. Liz admitted he was entitled, even as she flushed with embarrassment at the memory of his face when he'd handed her that signed contract.

Vic took one look at Liz's stricken face and commanded, "You. Right now. Take Squirrel, and the two of you go for a trail ride."

"I can't do that. We've got students to teach until three."

"I'll handle the students. I don't want to see you back until four when Pete is due to start redoing all the horses' shoes. Are we clear on that?"

"But..."

"No buts. Git! A couple of hours racing around the pasture on Squirrel will help you both."

"You know I don't like that mare," Liz said sulkily.

"All the more reason. She hasn't had a good run in two weeks. She'll wear you out. Get your saddle and get out of here. That's an order."

Vic seldom gave orders. Liz grabbed a lead line and went to fetch Squirrel out of the side paddock.

Liz saddled the mare, and together they danced out

of the gate and into the big pasture. Squirrel was raring to go, nostrils flaring, scenting a race.

Twenty minutes later Liz was dripping with sweat and her legs were aching. "You're like riding a damned sewing machine after Trusty," Liz snapped and hauled the mare down to a walk.

That, unfortunately, gave Liz leisure to think.

She had never been so full of what her grandmother used to call "conflictions" in her life. How could she have fallen for a man like Mike? For one thing, the feelings were only on her side. The bruises he'd endured were to his ego, not his heart.

All the more reason to avoid becoming another of Mike's conquests. She'd been so sure she'd loved Jack Ransome in college, and later, Randy Esterhaze, but those were crushes beside what she felt for Mike. This was the biggie. An unfamiliar world where she didn't have the skills to survive, much less compete.

And if Mike wasn't enough of a problem, there was Pat. Couldn't separate one from the other.

She'd finally been forced to admit how attached she'd become to Pat yesterday when Pat plumped herself down on a hay bale beside Liz and stretched her legs out in perfect imitation of Liz's.

"You ever have a big sister?" Pat said with studied casualness.

"Nope. Only child. Like you."

"You had a mother. That's not like me."

"I had a mother until I was nine. Believe me, that's not nearly long enough."

"Better than never having a mother at all." Pat waggled her paddock boots and studied them carefully. "Not much father, either."

Liz started. "Your dad's crazy about you."

"Yeah. When he's home he is. Most of the time it's Mrs. H. and me. She's the latest, you know." Pat snickered. "Until she came along, I was pretty good at ditching them. Used to drive Daddy crazy."

"And that, I assume, was the point?"

Pat shrugged. "Sure. No nanny, no trips to Hong Kong. Doesn't work with Mrs. H. But it's okay. I like her. She lets me get away with stuff that would fry my daddy's eyes if he found out about it."

"For instance?"

Pat waved a hand at the barn. "This, for instance. Staying late. And reading in bed with a flashlight under the covers, and buying stuff that doesn't make me look like I'm two years old. And shaving my legs." She continued without missing a beat. "It's my fault, you know."

"I beg your pardon?"

"That my mother died." Pat's voice still sounded casual, as though she were talking about the latest Saturday-morning cartoon show. She kept her eyes on those waggling boots.

"I felt the same way about my mother," Liz confided. "Like I'd killed her. I was wrong."

"You did?" Pat said.

"Absolutely. So by definition everything that went wrong afterward was my fault as well. When Vic and Uncle Frank had to take me in, I felt as though I had to be perfect so they'd keep me around."

"I don't feel that way."

"How do you feel?"

"Like if I'm not making noise or acting up, I'll disappear and nobody will notice I'm gone."

Liz gulped. How well she could remember feeling the same way. She wanted to grab Pat and tell her how wrong she was. She couldn't. Liz knew how much it had cost the girl to confide in her. She only hoped she could help Pat change her view of herself.

Now, Liz walked the mare into the area beside the ring and swung out of the saddle.

"Feel better? Vic asked.

"Rubber-legged is more like it. Look at her." Liz waved a hand at Squirrel, who seemed as fresh as she had two hours earlier.

"She's an endurance horse, Liz."

"I am definitely not an endurance rider."

Albert took the reins from Liz's hands and shoved her in the direction of the office. "Pete's due in ten minutes to shoe them horses. Drink something before you pass out."

She passed Janey and Pat climbing into the hayloft, giggling as they went. Now that they were both in charge of their own horses, they no longer left with the other campers.

"Daddy says we have to put a railing in front of the loft," Pat said over her shoulder.

"Good idea," Liz replied. "In the meantime, you break your neck up there and I'll kill you."

"I'm going to ride Traveller for him this afternoon," Pat said. "I made him promise he'd be here by five."

As if I'd forgotten. "You will obey orders, young lady, and you will not do anything stupid or I will personally snatch you off that pony myself."

"Oh, Liz." Pat giggled.

Liz stopped and turned to Pat, hands on hips. "That is a promise. The pony is still green, and so are you. Remember that. You can't ride in the show next week with a broken neck."

Pat obviously started to make a smart-mouth remark,

saw Liz's face and quickly reconsidered. "Okay, I promise."

"Come on," Janey said peremptorily from behind her. "I'm going to ride my horse with you. You'll be fine."

"Don't help, Janey," Liz said as she walked to the office door.

And sank onto the ratty leather desk chair, propped her feet on the rolltop desk, and surprised herself utterly by bursting into tears.

AT LEAST THE HAT hid her blotched face and red-rimmed eyes, Liz thought as she watched Janey and Pat circle her along the rail at a sedate walk. She felt Mike arrive rather than saw or heard him. The air around her became charged with the electricity he invariably produced whenever he came within a country mile of where she stood. She pointedly kept her back to him, her face in shadows.

"Daddy! See! Traveller loves me."

"Just be careful," Mike's deep voice spoke from the ring.

Liz closed her eyes. *Go away!* she thought. *I can stand it when you're not here.*

"Trot," Liz said. Both children obeyed.

The lesson continued with more decorum than Liz had expected. She began to relax.

"Liz!" Vic stuck her head out of the stable door. "What kind of stud do you want?"

Liz's head whipped around. She caught Mike's eye and felt herself blushing fiercely. "What are you talking about?"

Vic raised her eyes. "Studs, Liz, studs. In Trusty's shoes. For the grand prix. Earth to Liz."

"I'm not sure," Liz replied.

"Well, you'd better get sure. Come in here this minute and discuss it."

"I'm busy."

"So is Pete. Farriers do not make money standing around waiting for clients to make up their minds."

"Oh, bother," Liz whispered, and walked over to Pat.

"This is the first and greatest commandment," she said quietly. "While I am out of this ring, you will do absolutely nothing but walk around the edge. No trot, no canter, no trotting rails on the ground, no little jumps. No nothing. Zip, zilch, nada. No showing off for dad. Promise?"

Pat's lower lip grew two inches. "We're doing great."

"Promise!"

"Phoo. Don't be long."

"Five minutes."

Pat shrugged.

As Liz turned away, she realized Pat had never actually promised.

MIKE SAW THAT Liz kept her face turned away as she walked past him. Fine. She deserved a little chagrin. What had gotten into the woman anyway? That damnable party at the club had been the kiss of doom. They'd started out amicably enough. She knew he was meeting Kreuger and Yamata. She'd been chatting happily to everyone there. He'd been surprised to discover that she and Rachelle were old competitors, but even Rachelle's attempt to put her brand on him shouldn't have caused the kind of reaction Liz had thrown his way. It was almost as though someone at the party had told Liz he was an ax murderer.

He willed Liz to turn around and look at him. One glance. Enough to reestablish contact. He'd tried staying away, but thinking about her drove him nuts.

He'd been mad as hell when she'd accused him of holding the Edenvale contract over her head, especially since he knew he'd already signed the damned thing.

So why hadn't he just told her that at the time? Okay, he was human. She made him mad. Maybe his little "gotcha" with the contract at Pat's party wasn't the smoothest tactic to get her back.

For a man who prided himself on reading every nuance of a conversation, he couldn't even tell for certain whether he and Liz had argued over what was really bothering her, or whether she'd just manufactured the whole thing to cover up the real reason she was upset. Sandi had done that occasionally. Drove him nuts then, too. How could he negotiate a truce with Liz when he didn't even know what he was supposed to be negotiating?

Whatever had happened between them he wanted her back. Had never stopped wanting her. That kiss in the rain had whetted his appetite for more. Much more than kisses.

"See, Daddy," Pat called. "We fit perfectly."

He smiled at his child, who walked sedately around the ring on her new pony. Give Liz credit, the pony did seem quiet enough.

"I'm going to canter," Janey called out from the other side of the ring. "We need to practice our flying changes." In a moment Janey's horse was flying around the ring.

Mike saw Pat take a grip on her reins, and as Janey

flew by, she set her pony to the rail and shoved him into a canter as well. Mike caught his breath. Child and pony seemed molded together, and he had to admit they were a beautiful sight. Even if they scared him half to death.

Both horses flew around the ring, then at the start of the second pass Janey turned her horse down the center toward a long white pole lying on the ground. As her horse crossed it, he seemed to hesitate in air for a microsecond and came down with his other forefront leading. It was like a dance step.

Ten seconds later Pat followed.

He held his breath for that moment of hesitation, that suspension in air. Instead, the pony's front hooves went straight up, he twisted and came down stiff-legged a full ninety degrees from where he'd started.

"Oh, no!" Pat yelped. The whole scene dropped into slow motion. Pat slipped sideways, her right foot slid out of her stirrup, her body disappeared over the pony's side only to reappear as it landed with a thump in the dirt. The pony bounced off in a series of bucks that took him halfway around the ring.

"Pat," Liz shouted from the doorway. Even though Mike was closer than she, for an instant he had been too stunned to move. She beat him to Pat, who now sat up in the dirt.

"I'm not hurt," Pat said and scrambled to her feet.

"You darned well ought to be!" Liz snapped.

"Get out of my way," Mike said and scooped his child up in his arms. "She's going to the emergency room now. You swore she wouldn't get hurt. Is that your idea of keeping a promise?" Mike turned a furious face to Liz. "God, this place is a death trap and you and Vic are the head executioners."

"But Daddy," Pat wailed.

"You've had that damned pony less than five hours," Mike said abruptly. He ran for his Volvo. "How long do you think it'll take him to kill you?"

He didn't look back. Something had happened to his eyes. The rage he felt had given him tunnel vision. He'd been right all along. This place was a death trap, these people were insane, and he for one was not going to subject his beloved child to this kind of danger ever again.

He slid Pat into the passenger seat of his Volvo carefully. She was sobbing hysterically. "Please be still, Pitti-Pat," he said softly. "You could have a concussion."

He didn't look in his rearview mirror as he drove away. He didn't dare see Liz. In his anger he might well do or say something that he'd regret later.

Two miles down the road, he felt Pat's hand on his arm. "It's okay, baby," he said soothingly.

"Daddy! Stop, please. We've got to go back."

"Not now. Not until you see a doctor. Maybe not then."

"Daddy!" Pat shrieked.

He slammed on his brakes. He'd never heard such an anguished sound from his daughter's lips, not even when she was in worse pain that he could even imagine. His blood froze. Behind him, a pickup truck jammed on its brakes and slid around him, its driver cursing loudly.

"Pat, baby! Pat." He reached for her.

"No!" Again that shriek. "Listen to me, please, please!"

He ran his hand over her hair. "Where does it hurt, baby?"

"Daddy!" She twisted away from him. Her chest was heaving. He wondered if she'd broken a rib and punctured a lung.

"We've got to get you checked out."

"No! For once, Daddy, just shut up and listen to me."

He was stunned. She'd never spoken to him that way in her life.

She was trying to control her breathing. "It isn't Liz's fault."

"Hell, yes, it's Liz's fault. Liz and that aunt of hers. Seeing a big fat commission..."

"Shut up!" Pat shrieked again, drumming her fists against the dashboard.

He gulped.

"You never listen! Never! You see what you want to see and hear what you want to hear. For once, listen to *me*."

"I always—"

"No, you don't. Never. Liz told me that while she was inside I couldn't do anything except walk around the edges of the ring on Traveller. I promised—well, sort of. I broke my promise, Daddy. I wanted to show off for you. I've never ever tried to change leads before, I didn't even know the signals. It's all my fault, Daddy, and you yelled at Liz."

He reached out to touch her arm.

"I hate you! Leave me alone!" She twisted away.

He couldn't move. He couldn't breathe. The rational part of his mind told him that she was nearly a teenager now, and that everyone said teenagers said things like that to their parents. But his Pitti-Pat? Never.

"You don't mean that," he whispered.

"I do! I do! I hate you because you hate Liz!"

Before he could move, she had unbuckled her seat belt and reached for the handle of the door. "I'm going back," she said. "I've got to apologize to Liz."

He grabbed the door and held it closed. "No, you don't. Whether it was your fault or Liz's, you're still going to get checked out. I don't give a darn whether you hate me or not." How he wished that were true. He felt as though someone were tearing into his guts with a hot poker.

"Liz…"

"I'll call the barn. Tell them you're sorry you broke the rules."

"Tell Liz you're sorry you yelled at her, Daddy, promise."

He nodded.

"Daddy?" Pat's voice suddenly sounded very small. "I didn't mean it."

He twisted in his seat and felt her wrap her arms around his neck. He cradled her against his chest and stroked her hair. "I know, baby, I know."

"I'M SORRY," Janey said. "If I hadn't cantered, Pat wouldn't have."

"Not your fault," Vic said. "Put the blame where it belongs."

"On me," Liz said. "I know what she's like. I should have realized she'd show off for Mike." She turned away. "I thought she'd changed, that I'd gotten through to her."

The cordless telephone on the wash rack beeped. Vic picked it up, and said with an edge of ice in her voice, "I'm delighted to hear that Pat's fine, Mr. Whitten." She listened for a moment, raised her eyebrows to Liz and said, "You want to speak to Liz?"

Liz made wild "no" motions with her hands.

"I'm so sorry, but she's not available at the moment." She held the phone away and smiled at it grimly. "Of course I'll tell her that Pat apologizes. And that you do? Anything else? No? Thank you for calling." She dropped the phone into its cradle. "Bastard! And to think I was trying to set you up with him."

"He panicked," Liz said tiredly. "I've heard you say worse to Uncle Frank when I got hurt."

"Yeah, but I knew I was right."

"So did he. The kind of man he is, Vic, it took a lot for him to say he was wrong. Give it up. I have." She walked away. "I'm going to the cottage and stand under a hot shower until I'm pruny, then I am going to eat as much triple-ripple fudge ice cream as I can dredge up from the freezer, and then I am going to bed—unless I decide to eat all the cookies I can find."

"You gonna be my size by Christmas you do that," Albert called after her. "You'll break Trusty's back, girl."

"Nobody cares what I look like," Liz said without turning around.

An hour later she dropped the empty gallon container of ice cream into her trash compactor, slapped her hands together and began to search her cupboards. Somewhere she had stashed a bag of chocolate-chip cookies. Probably stale by now. At least chocolate never broke your heart.

Thirty miles away Mike stood looking out on the lights of this adopted inland city, wishing he could see the ocean. He took a sip of the amber liquid in his glass, made a face at it and set it down on the glass end table beside him. What was Liz doing out there beyond the city lights? Probably sticking pins in his image.

He narrowed his eyes and set his chin. He had promised Pat to apologize to Liz and apologize he would. Secondhand over the telephone wasn't good enough. He had to see Liz face-to-face, try to explain, vindicate himself, discover what walls loomed between them.

Then he could start breaking down those barriers. Because they would come down sooner or later. Mike Whitten didn't lose often, and when he did, it was against greater odds and a much tougher adversary than one long-legged, opinionated and frequently grimy female with jade green eyes and a sexy crooked nose.

CHAPTER FOURTEEN

"I KNOW IT'S short notice, Liz," Melba Hannaford said over the telephone the next morning. "But Pat begged me to ask you to dinner tonight. She feels terrible about what happened yesterday."

"Physically?" Liz asked in alarm.

"Of course not, dear."

"I don't think…"

"If you're worried about running into Mr. Whitten, he's been called out of town suddenly. It will be just the three of us. Please come. Mr. Whitten made Pat promise not to visit the stable today even though she only has a couple of minor bruises. She does need to see you. She has to take responsibility for her actions."

"You're speaking as a nanny?"

"In loco parentis."

Liz sighed. "All right, what time?"

After she hung up the telephone, Melba turned to Pat, who stood beside her, still wearing the oversize gym shorts and T-shirt she slept in. Mike had long since left the house to play handball. "I'm not sure we're doing the right thing," she said.

"We are, we are. You'll see."

"Maybe I should cancel my date with Walter."

"No way! Serving is no big deal." Pat danced away. "I'm going to fix everything."

At five minutes after eight Liz rang the Whitten door-bell. She seldom came this far into the city and had never been in this fancy apartment building, much less visited the penthouse. She was glad she'd put on dress jeans and a silk shirt. Even with only Pat and Melba, this place was too high-class for her blood.

The door opened. "Liz! Come in!" Pat whispered and pulled Liz inside.

"Hi," Liz said.

Pat looked around guiltily.

"Put your purse down and come see my room," she said and all but dragged Liz around the corner and down a hall to a crisp white door.

Pat's room looked like a dormitory room in a very posh girls' school. Polished dark parquet floors, modern steel student's desk with matching steel chair and very expensive and equally modern double bed made of filigreed wrought iron. The few pictures on the wall were of horses cut from magazines and framed in simple black frames. No curtains at the window, no frills, no stuffed animals. Not a posh girls' school—more like a very chic prison. Liz shivered.

"This isn't where I keep my stuff," Pat said. "I just sleep here. My stuff's next door in the playroom." She went to a connecting door beside what looked like a large walk-in closet. She opened it, flicked a light switch and motioned Liz to follow her.

The floors were also polished dark wood without rugs or carpet. Under the soffit, track lighting had been installed so that the room glowed with warm light. The floor-to-ceiling white wood cabinets were lit from the inside as well. Arranged behind glass doors were shelves of books, horse models, beautiful dolls, stuffed toys, a fancy sound system with accompanying yards of CDs—everything a child or preteen could desire to play with. Immaculate, sterile, organized, shut away. Liz gulped.

"Isn't it great?" Pat said. "I've got every Breyer horse they make."

"And not a speck of dust on any of them," Liz said quietly.

"Huh? Oh, we have a central vac and filters. It never gets dirty." Pat said cheerfully.

Liz longed to open those glass doors and shove all the stuffed toys out onto the fancy polished floor. The place cried out for a little chaos, a couple of pets. Even a hamster or an aquarium would help.

"Pat? Who're you talking to?"

Liz froze, and so did Pat.

Mike stood in the doorway with his mouth open. "Liz?" he said uncertainly.

Liz turned to Pat. "Pat, Melba told me…"

"I know, I know." Pat hung her head in mock repentance. "Don't blame Mrs. H. I put her up to it." She turned to her father. "I invited Liz for dinner, Daddy. And you'd just better be civil."

"I am invariably civil to guests."

Liz followed him. "Look, maybe I'd better go. This isn't the world's greatest idea."

"No, of course you'll stay," Mike said. "I need to talk to you in any case." He raised his eyebrows at his daughter, who was attempting to sidle through the main living area toward what was probably the kitchen.

She grinned and slid around the corner and through the swinging doors.

For the first time Liz looked around her. "My, this is…uh…impressive."

"Yes, the view is incredible." He might have been

speaking to someone he'd met only minutes earlier. Talk about control. Liz glanced down. Even his hands were clenched. So the anger was still there, lurking just under that icy surface. She'd try not to set him off again. She wasn't certain she could take another dressing-down, deserved or not.

"Uh-huh." She gazed around her. The room looked to be about the size of the average soccer stadium, and considering the area, there wasn't much in it.

All the upholstered furniture was extremely modern, very spare and covered in black leather. An ebony concert grand piano stood in one corner. The floors were polished parquet. No rugs. The tables were glass tops on steel supports. Even the dining-room table was made of glass and steel.

The only color in the room came from a portrait of a woman hanging over the black onyx fireplace. Had to be Mike's wife, Pat's mother. The woman was stunningly beautiful with dark, lustrous eyes and a polished mane of blue-black hair. She wore a red dress and held a red rose in her clasped hands. Liz turned away before Mike could catch her staring.

Boy, had she been fooling herself. She probably wasn't even worth being considered for a position in Whitten's Wenches—not if this woman was the baseline against which all the others were measured. She felt a lump rise in her throat and reached up to smooth down her wild hair. It sprang right back up defiantly.

"Would you like a drink?" Mike asked. He sounded very cool.

Liz shook her head.

Mike pushed a button and a mirrored bar opened silently behind him. He turned away; Liz heard the clink of ice cubes. "Not even a soft drink?" he asked.

"Maybe some Perrier?" Liz asked. Her mouth was nearly too dry to speak.

He nodded and a moment later swung around to hand her a heavy crystal glass.

"Look," he said at the same moment she said, "Mike—"

Both stopped awkwardly.

"Me first," Mike said. "Pat told me what really happened yesterday. My behavior was inexcusable. I'm sorry I flew off the handle like that."

Liz hesitated before she said, "Apology accepted. You were being a parent. You didn't know."

"I know you, and I know my daughter. I should have realized."

"Yeah. Well, we mostly don't."

"No."

The silence felt heavy between them. Liz gulped her Perrier. Mike sipped his bourbon or scotch or whatever it was and stared at her.

Her eyes fell first.

"Liz, I don't know what really went wrong between us, but whatever it is, I want to fix it somehow."

"Nothing to fix," she said airily.

He started to speak, but the kitchen door opened, and Pat said, "Here's the salad, everybody. Liz, come sit here." She pointed to a chair midway between one end of the table and the other. Pat sat at the foot nearest the kitchen, Mike at the far end. There must have been acres between them. Liz thought it was like one of those old movies where Milord and Milady ate at opposite ends while servants hovered around them, and they used bullhorns to make conversation.

The food was good. Pat was a polished hostess—no doubt she'd acted as her father's hostess for years.

Mike said little, but every time Liz swung her eyes to his end of the table he seemed to be staring at her.

Pat kept up a running commentary on horses and the excitement of the upcoming horse show.

"May I help you in the kitchen?" Liz asked after the crème brûlée.

"No way. Mrs. H. will clean it all up tomorrow morning," Pat said.

"Pat," Mike said with a note of warning.

"Get real, Daddy," Pat answered. "I'll clean it up. I was just kidding. Cop a sense of humor, why don't you?"

Mike sighed. Despite her vow to stay uninvolved, Liz grinned at him. "Told you she was growing up."

"I may not survive until she's twenty-one," Mike said. "I don't have the hang of adolescents."

"Nobody else does, either. You're in good company."

"Would you like a brandy or a liqueur?" he asked as he stood.

"No—yes. A B&B. I won't be over the alcohol limit if I drink one, will I?"

"Hardly. I'll make it light."

She watched his broad back in his black silk shirt. Someone watching them would never realize they'd shared a kiss so passionate it had nearly knocked Liz's shoes off. They were strangers now. Except that she felt the glow whenever he came into a room.

What the hell, she'd get over it.

"I'm going to take a bath and go to bed early," Pat said. She came out of the kitchen, wiping her hands on her jeans.

"Oh, then I'd better go," Liz said and started to stand.

"Finish your B&B first," Mike said, and handed her the tiny glass. "It's also known as a pony. Pat, did you know that?" He smiled at his daughter.

"Yes, Daddy, I knew that." She clucked. "I've known that since I was a child." She kissed her father's cheek and turned to Liz. "You stay, Liz. I'll come out and say good-night. Please, please, please?"

Liz grinned. Sandbagged again. "Sure."

"Great."

"Alone at last," Liz breathed, and then wished she could take back the words.

Mike raised his eyebrows. "I'm hoping you think that's a good thing."

"I didn't mean..."

He sat in the leather chair opposite her. "I've apologized for overreacting. I don't know what else to apologize for."

"How about deliberately holding back the Edenvale contract even though you knew it was signed?"

"I had no idea it was an issue with you."

Liz could tell he was starting to get angry. "You'd never understand." She couldn't possibly tell him about Whitten's Wenches. She'd die first.

"Try me."

"Let's just say that you are the person you are and I am the person I am and we don't fit. Let's deal with it and move on."

He leaned forward. "Crap."

She raised her eyebrows at him. "Oh, is it?" She waved a hand around. "One look at this place ought to tell you we're in different worlds—make that competing universes."

"I live the way I live because of Pat."

"Why, Mike? Why because of Pat? You keep telling

me you know you're overprotective, but you don't do anything to change. You say she doesn't have allergies, she's not sick, yet you treat her as though she had AIDS or tuberculosis or…hell, I don't know…ebola or something equally dire.''

"Not AIDS," Mike said quietly. "Leukemia."

"What?" Liz gasped.

"I suppose I should have told you before, but I promised Pat. Nobody at her school knows, not her friends, not my friends." He stood and walked to the bar where Liz heard him pour another drink. He stood with his back to her while he continued, "Why do you think I picked up my business lock, stock and barrel and moved to Memphis? I tried commuting for a year, but two years ago, I cut all my ties with Seattle. I wanted to be here permanently. Just to be safe.''

"I thought…I didn't…"

"She was eight. She came down with a cold," he said bitterly. "A few swollen glands. No big deal. Kids come down with stuff like that all the time, don't they? Not this time. It's even got a cute acronym—ALL—*all*, acute lymphocytic leukemia. The big L, every parent's nightmare.''

"Oh, God, Mike." Liz felt as though her heart were being ripped from her body.

"When they told me," Mike continued as though she hadn't spoken, "I got us on the next plane from Seattle to Memphis. Saint Jude is the best research hospital in the world for leukemia. Not a death sentence, they said. A seventy-three percent cure rate. Sometimes no worse than a bad cold. Right." He sounded bitter.

He whirled, and his eyes bored into Liz's. "Within a month she had no symptoms. For all intents and purposes she *was* cured at that point. What they don't tell you is about the follow-up care. Two and a half years of chemotherapy. And then you wait six months. If all the tests come back normal, the child is finally considered cured, and only then. The longest six months of any parent's life.''

"Oh, Mike.''

"No, I'm wrong. Those two and a half years of IVs dripping poison into her veins, of watching her drop pound after pound, throw up. See her feverish and miserable day after day. Her hair all fell out.'' His voice trembled. He looked up at the portrait above the fireplace. "Pat's hair was down to her waist. She had lovely hair, just like her mother's.'' He turned away and set his glass down on the bar with studied care.

He didn't turn around, but continued speaking with both hands on top of the bar and his back to Liz. "When it was at its worst, when I was afraid we'd lose her, that she'd never see her twelfth birthday, that's when I promised her. If she'd just live, I'd buy her a damned pony. God help me.''

"And now?'' Liz stood, took a single step toward him and stopped, longing to touch him, to hold him, but not daring to move.

He shrugged. "It's been a year since her last test. She's cured.'' He raised his shoulders, sighed and turned to face Liz.

Liz began to breathe again. "She's completely cured?''

"Define cured. Is anyone ever cured of anything? Do we know why she got sick in the first place?''

"Mike, children who were cured of ALL are now in their forties and perfectly healthy. If they say she's cured, why don't you trust them?''

"I don't dare take that chance!" His voice sounded anguished. "I can't lose her again."

"So that's why you live like...this?" Liz waved a hand at the room.

"I knew you'd hate this place."

Liz eased herself carefully onto the leather arm of one of the sofas. "Come on, Mike. Look around. No wonder Pat wants a kitten."

He frowned at her. "I can see why you'd think that dust and allergens make a house a home."

"That was below the belt. But have you looked at Pat's room, really looked?"

"I think it's a beautiful bedroom—and she's got another room for her horse toys and her books."

"Right. On neat shelves behind glass doors. Very inviting for a kid. I love parquet floors, and these are beautiful. But couldn't you even spring for a rug to go in front of the fireplace?"

"Wooden floors stay clean."

"So Pat sleeps on disposable sheets?"

Mike turned away. "Don't be ridiculous."

His ears were flaming. Liz had learned that meant he was getting angry. They'd had all of five minutes of wary politeness, but now they were back to daggers at five paces. Figured.

"Of course you worry. I'd probably be in a mental institution by now under the same circumstances, but sometime you have to cut her loose. She can't continue to live under a glass dome like one of those fancy china dolls in her room."

"Look what happens when I try to break the pattern."

"She falls in love with a pony?"

"She falls *off* him."

"Did the doctors say her bones were extra brittle? Is she allowed to play sports?"

"Certainly. That's not the point."

"Of course it is. I'm surprised you let her go to school. Why not a tutor? And double locks on the doors."

"She's had enough tutors. How do you suppose she's managed to keep up to her grade level? She kept up with her schoolwork. It wasn't easy for her. I know you see a manipulative, bad-tempered brat, but after what she's been through she deserves the occasional tantrum. I don't keep her a prisoner."

"Her tantrums make her miserable. If she's not a prisoner, why didn't you want her to ride to the camp in the van with the other children?"

"When she was two years old I sent her to preschool because all the experts said I should. She was sick practically nonstop for the next two years with every virus and cold known to man."

"And by the time she got to first grade she was immune. All my friends with kids tell me that."

"All your friends." His voice was cold. "More experts. What experience do you have as a parent? Who's to say those colds didn't set her up for the leukemia? You? Hardly."

She felt the familiar churning sensation under her sternum. "Right. I'm not a mother. But I have deep personal experience with horse manure, and that's what you're giving me. All kids get sick, Mike. They don't get half the things they used to, but they still get temperatures and bugs."

"And deadly diseases."

"Has she been sick one day since she's been at ValleyCrest?"

He shook his head. "Not yet."

"And she's laughing and running around and making friends. She's not the odd man out any longer."

"No, and for that I'm grateful."

"So why don't you get her a kitten to sleep on those plastic sheets?"

"Back off." He sounded annoyed and maybe a little embarrassed. "We sleep on cotton sheets, not plastic. Washed and disinfected every morning along with the towels."

"No frilly comforters, no fancy curtains."

He flipped a hand toward the glorious view outside the windows. "Who needs curtains up here? Pat and I have blinds in our bedroom."

"Real dust catchers."

"Mrs. H. vacuums them every day with the central vacuum. A cleaning crew comes in twice a week."

"Does she put disinfectant in her bathwater too? Hell of a way to raise a teenager."

"She's not a teenager yet. And I'm the one raising her. You seem to forget that. All this is for Pat."

"What does Pat think about it?"

"She's never known anything else."

Liz laughed shortly. "She does now. She comes up to my house in the afternoons plenty of times, and it's chock-full of animal hair, dust kittens and plant spores. The air in the stable is saturated with horse dander and hay dust. Doesn't seem to have done her any harm."

"Not yet."

"And it won't. Why won't you believe her doctors?"

"Because this damned world runs on irony. Get too happy, too complacent, too sure you know what you're doing, and you get zapped."

"That's not true."

"The hell it's not."

"Just because it happened once..."

He laughed mirthlessly. "Once? Try three times."

Liz caught her breath. "Pat's had leukemia three times?"

"Hey, that was disaster number three. First, my wife died of a brain hemorrhage the afternoon Pat was born. Then, Pat wasn't expected to live twenty-four hours. She was in an incubator for three months before I could touch her except through rubber gloves. I thought after all that, Pat and I would have clear sailing for the rest of our lives—hell, I was bound to be over my limit for tragedy, right?"

His eyes sought those of the vibrant, lovely woman over the mantelpiece. "So now I just concentrate on preserving the only love I'm ever likely to have. And if that means Pat lives with bare floors, it's a small price to pay."

"My God." Liz came off the sofa in a rush. "*You* preserve? For whom are you doing all this preserving, Mike? This isn't about Pat. It's about you. You're not protecting Pat, you're guarding yourself."

"It's about risk and death. What the hell do you know about those? The only person you were close to who ever died on you was your uncle, and from what you've told me, you grieved more over your bank balance than for him."

"How dare you say something like that? I didn't want Frank dead."

"You didn't feel as though your lungs had been ripped out of your body, either, did you?"

"I did when my mother died in my arms from a heart attack at thirty-six." She stood. "God, you really do fight dirty." She strode to the door and picked up her purse. "Kevin warned me."

He flushed. "I'm sorry, I forgot about your mother, but you were only a child when she died."

She had to get out of there. She was going to cry any minute, and if she didn't, she was going to hit Mike over the head with the nearest blunt instrument.

"Where are you going? Scared to finish it?"

She opened the front door and stood with her hand on the knob. "If this isn't about you, then what do you want for Pat?"

"I want her alive."

"Define alive."

"Breathing, talking, thinking, moving..."

"Happy?"

"How can she be happy if she's dead?"

MIKE WATCHED as Liz ran down the hall and punched the down button. The doors opened and then slid shut. And she was gone.

"Daddy?" Pat stood behind him in a pair of hugely baggy pink cotton shorts and a black T-shirt made for a giant.

He turned, dropped to his knees to put his arms around her and carry her back into the living room. She buried her head on his shoulder and threw her arms around his neck. She felt heavier in his arms, longer, leaner. Not his baby anymore. "Liz had to go home."

He felt her back heave, heard her sobs. His anger dissolved in an instant. He hugged her, wishing he could keep all the pain and sorrow and suffering of this world outside the door away from his daughter.

"Daddy, you and Liz were yelling at each other again."

He patted her. "Not yelling, baby, a little disagreement."

"I heard, Daddy. It was about me." She hugged him tighter. "Please, please, Daddy, don't sell my pony."

His heart lurched. He set her down in the living room and once more dropped to his knees before her. "Pat, Pitti-Pat, I won't sell your pony."

"You've got to make up with Liz, please, Daddy. You promised. After tonight she'll never let me come back. You shouldn't have told her about me, Daddy. You promised you wouldn't tell."

"Of course she wants you back, Pat, she likes you. I may not agree with her, but she sure as hell likes you enough to fight me like a tiger over you." He tried to laugh. It came out more like a groan.

Pat sniffed and pulled away from him. "Why don't you like her?"

He let out all the breath in his lungs. He knew now exactly how Liz had felt that afternoon a while ago when she'd knocked her breath out. "I do like her." Much more than he could admit to his child.

"Then make up with her. She's right, Daddy. She and the other kids and Janey and the barn and Traveller all make me happy." She touched her father's rough jaw. "I know you mean well, Daddy, but like I told you, I'm not your Pitti-Pat anymore. You've got to let me grow up."

"You've barely turned twelve years old."

The eyes with which Pat regarded him were old. "In some ways I'm a lot older than you."

Mike gulped. He got to his feet. He felt completely drained and at a loss for words or action.

"I think you better go apologize." She tried a smile. "Again."

"This time I don't think she'll let me," he said, sighing.

"Then try harder. Please, Daddy, for me. I love Liz."

He opened his mouth to say the same words. He stopped. He couldn't love her. Not possible.

He kissed the top of Pat's head. "For you, I'll try." He started toward the door. "Pat, I can't. Mrs. H. isn't back from her date yet."

"She'll be back any minute. It's not as though we didn't have a doorman downstairs and the best security system in the world. I am twelve years old. Janey's already baby-sitting. She's the same age I am. I can stay at home by myself for an hour."

"You've never stayed alone."

"I'll call you on your cell phone the minute Mrs. H. gets back. You're stalling. Liz is going to be way ahead of you."

"Pat…"

"Daddy! Get out of here. Now!" She shoved him toward the front door. Reluctantly, he let her shove.

At the door he turned. "Call Mrs. H. at Mr. Simpson's. Tell her I've had to go out and she needs to come home. Promise?"

"Yeah, yeah, yeah. Go!"

By the time he reached Walter Simpson's house from his car phone, Mrs. Hannaford was already on her way home. "Sorry to break up your evening, Walter," Mike said.

"You owe me one. Woman trouble?"

"You might say that."

"I was married for forty-one years, Mr. Whitten, and as much as I loved Cary, I never understood her."

"That's comforting."

"It's the truth. I got to tell you, Mr. Whitten, I like you, but if you're planning to turn Liz Matthews into another one of your Whitten's Wenches..."

"I beg your pardon?" Mike said.

"Melba says she heard from Angie that one of the ladies at your club was giving Liz chapter and verse on all the women you been sleeping with since you moved to town."

"What the hell? Walter, has the whole world gone nuts? What with Pat's hospital stays and moving my business, when did I have time to do all this tom-catting?"

"I'm just telling you what I heard, Mr. Whitten."

"What Liz heard."

"She's the one told Angie."

"No wonder Liz has been treating me like a pariah." Mike sighed. "Thanks, Walter. You may have single-handedly uncomplicated my life."

"Glad to oblige."

CHAPTER FIFTEEN

LIZ FOUND Aunt Vic waiting for her on the front-porch swing with all the dogs clustered around her feet.

"Did you know Mike would be there tonight?" Liz asked.

"Melba mentioned it."

"Why won't people butt out of my life and stop all this matchmaking? Mike and I are not going to happen. Ever."

"What's the worst thing that could happen to you?"

"He breaks my heart."

"And?"

"Isn't that enough? He breaks my heart, I'm miserable, I feel like a gullible fool while he struts around like a turkey cock with the next enlistee in Whitten's Wenches."

"What a vicious bastard."

"He's not vicious."

"Sure he is. He makes love to you and leaves you and tells all his buddies about it and laughs at you behind your back. Vicious."

"He wouldn't do that. But everybody would find out anyway."

"So it's not your heart that would get broken, it's your pride?"

"I don't want to get laid and left because I'm in love with the son of a bitch."

"Um. So, let me get this straight. You love him, you want to spend the rest of your life with him—am I right on that? But you think if you go to bed with him he'll walk out and you'll never see him again?"

"You're doing this on purpose."

"Hey, I'm following your logic. Now, if you don't go to bed with him, he will get fed up and walk away, so you'll be right. He will have left you, but you won't have had the pleasure of making love with him. You'll go back to your dogs and parrot. How about your heart? If you don't go to bed with him and he walks away, your heart will feel marvelous?"

"Of course not. I'll be in agony."

"Seems to me you're definitely damned if you don't and you have a good chance of being damned if you do, but at least if you do you'll find out what kind of a lover he is."

"I'm afraid to risk it."

"Finally. Truth at last. Liz Matthews, who has been riding lunatic horses over impossible fences since she could walk, who doesn't have a nerve in her body, who's had at least a dozen broken ribs, a broken leg, a broken nose, a half-dozen busted collarbones, not to mention bruises and scrapes too numerous to mention, is running scared when faced with the possibility of a broken heart? And I thought I was a coward."

"Damn you, Vic. I thought you'd understand."

"Understanding and supporting are two different things. Here is an incredible man who for some reason that totally escapes me, wants you passionately..."

"Not after tonight he doesn't."

"I doubt that. The point is, you think he wants a one-night stand, a conquest to add to his collection.

You want a lifetime. But even life-long love starts with a one-night stand.''

''My God! Have you two been working on the same script? That's what Mike said.''

''He's right. And if he loves you and leaves you, is your heart going to be any less broken because you didn't have the gumption to risk loving him? What if he stays? Or worse, would have stayed if he'd had any encouragement.''

''He wouldn't.''

''Oh, and I'm supposed to believe that you understand what goes on in Mike's mind. Hell, you don't even know what goes on in your own mind. Leave consequences aside for the moment. What do you want?''

''I want to make love to him until my bones crack.'' Liz thought for a moment. ''And then I probably want to cut his head off.''

''Then I'd suggest you do it, and quickly, because frankly, if I were Mike, I'd be getting pretty damned fed up with your all-seeing, all-knowing judgment. You're not worth all the angst.'' Vic walked away without another word.

Liz sat down in her place. Why was sex so important anyway? Why did it seem as though she were burning her bridges, crossing her Rubicon, passing the point of no return? She was not a virgin. Sex had never meant a whole heck of a lot in the past. She didn't think she had much aptitude for it, if her relationship with Jack was anything to go by. But whenever she thought of going to bed with Mike, the whole thing took on an entirely new dimension. It wasn't fair. She ought to be able to rip off her clothes, jump his bones, enjoy the hell out of the experience and walk away unscathed. He would.

At least she was smart enough to realize she couldn't manage that. She pulled herself up. Didn't matter now. She'd effectively shut him out of her life forever.

THIRTY MINUTES later, when he pulled the Volvo alongside Liz's truck, the lights were still on in her living room. The dogs began a cacophony of barks and yips. He sat for a moment before he opened the car door. He had no idea what he was going to say to Liz— assuming she'd let him in.

The porch light came on and the front door opened. The four dogs tumbled across the porch and down the stairs to his car. He stepped out and waded through them.

"Come to finish me off?" Liz said. She stood in the doorway. Her hair was even wilder than usual as though she'd been tearing at it in frustration or fury. She was barefoot but still dressed in her silk shirt and jeans. With her hands on her hips she didn't look as though she was interested in peace. She did, however, look sexy as hell. "I'm the one who's bleeding, not you," he said.

"So you want your rematch."

"I want to come in."

"It's late."

"I know. Can I come in?"

She shrugged and walked inside. The dogs accompanied him.

"Go to bed," she told them. Obediently they went into the darkened kitchen.

Mike glanced into the corner of the room, expecting

that damned parrot to tell him what a jerk he was. The cage was covered and silent.

"Want a drink?" she asked.

"I've had plenty, thank you."

"So? Why did you come?"

"Pat heard us. She's pretty upset."

"Oh, Mike, I'm so sorry. The last thing I wanted was to involve Pat in all this. None of this is her doing."

"So upsetting me was okay?"

"Yes."

"Look. I may not agree with you about Pat, but I don't interfere with you."

"Only every other day or anytime something goes a little wrong."

"She's still here. I'm still here. Can we agree to disagree on this one? I won't interfere with her life out here if you don't stick your nose into our life at home."

"Can I hold you to that?"

"I may be a son of a bitch, but my word is my bond." He stuck out his hand.

"Deal." She took his hand.

He held on a moment too long. Their eyes met, locked.

"You've been crying," he said and ran his thumb along her cheekbone.

"Rage does that to me."

"Listen, can I have that drink after all? This has been a hell of an evening."

"Yeah, I feel as though I've been rode hard and put away wet myself." She went to the cabinet in the corner, hunkered down and scanned the bottles inside. "I'm not much of a drinker, but I've got scotch and bourbon and the usual stuff."

"Scotch, neat, no ice."

She brought him two fingers in a tall glass that she probably used for iced tea. He took a sip. It burned all the way down to what was probably the start of an ulcer. If anybody could give him ulcers, it was Liz. "You're not having anything."

"Maybe in a minute. Sit."

He sat on the shabby sofa, and this time he drank deep. He tasted aged oak and a hint of iodine as the alcohol hit his stomach like a blast furnace. Another gulp like that and he wouldn't be sober enough to drive home. He rolled the glass between his palms and stared down into the swirls of amber liquid. "Pat was afraid I was going to sell her pony."

"Oh, Mike, no! You wouldn't."

"Of course I wouldn't. Apparently you're not the only one who thinks I'm a monster."

"Not a monster." Liz sank onto the rug and tucked her bare feet under her. "Kevin says you drink antifreeze for breakfast to keep your blood from freezing. I used to believe him."

"Does he now. Clever Kevin."

"He says you are utterly ruthless and completely fearless."

Mike shrugged. "Only with money." He spoke into his glass. His heart was pounding. He couldn't take another screwup tonight. Fearless? Right.

He stared at the scotch then set the glass carefully on the table beside him. He leaned forward, forearms on his thighs, hands loose between his knees. "Look at me."

After a moment's hesitation, she raised her head. Her eyes were brimming with tears. The freckles across her crooked nose stood out. He held her gaze and said softly, "You know I want to make love to you. I've wanted you since the first moment I saw you on that plow horse of yours."

Slowly, almost imperceptibly, she nodded her head.

Now was the time to tell her all that stuff about Whitten's Wenches was bunk. Before he could move or speak, however, she came smoothly to her knees in front of him. He sighed. He didn't know where to start. He didn't want to talk. "You act as though I want to roast you over a slow fire."

"You do that every time you touch me. Try kissing me again instead," she said softly.

He stared at her a moment, uncertain he had understood her words. Something had definitely changed in her attitude. He didn't question it longer than a nanosecond. His right arm slid around her waist and pulled her forward. Gently, he ran his other hand along her jaw and bent to brush her lips with his. She made a soft sound, but didn't pull away. He deepened the kiss. Her lips opened to him and he probed her mouth, tasting her. Her tongue met his, and her arms closed around his neck. His heart lifted. Maybe there was hope after all.

He ran his hands down her arms, caught her under the elbows and stood, pulling her up with him so that their bodies met from thigh to breast. He broke the kiss. "Listen," he said urgently. "I'm a man, I play by men's rules. It's been twenty years or more since I necked on somebody's couch and went home afterward. It'll be hell, but if that's what you want, by heaven I'll try."

"You mean that."

He nodded. "Yes. Whatever you're afraid of, I won't force the issue."

She shook her head. "No," she whispered.

His heart plummeted. He released her.

"No, I've never wanted that—necking on the couch." Her eyes searched his face. "Vic's right."

"Vic? What has she got to do with this?"

"Nothing. Everything. Don't ask."

He felt her fingers lace through his. She turned toward the bedroom.

Dear God, he prayed silently, *Don't let me blow this one.*

Liz walked ahead of him. Her back was straight, her shoulders nearly as broad as his. She was so incredibly sexy. She couldn't possibly feel the same burning hunger for him that he felt for her, but he could teach her passion if only she'd give him the chance.

In the dark bedroom Liz turned to him. Her fingers fumbled at the buttons of his shirt.

"I'm not very good at this," she said softly.

He captured her hands. "Let me."

She stared unblinking into his eyes as though he were guiding her through some terrible ordeal. Great. She was scared to death.

He unbuttoned her shirt and slid it off her shoulders. He heard the soft rustle of silk as it floated to the floor behind her. He concentrated on the pulse throbbing at the base of her throat, almost afraid to let his gaze wander to her breasts, as though he might break the spell and send her running away from him once more.

She stood immobile as his hands slid from her ears to her throat and lower, to cup the breasts that strained against her bra. She whimpered once as he reached around to unhook it one-handed.

Her breasts were high and golden. He cupped them in his palms and ran his thumbs across her erect nipples. She gasped as he bent to encircle one with his tongue.

He raised his head, pulled his shirt over his head and flung it behind him. "Do you want me to stop?"

"No," she whispered. "Hold on to me if I lose my nerve."

She arched her back against him and cradled his head in her arms. It was the first time she'd touched him since she took his hand. He felt as though her arms were the one place he'd been seeking all his life—the one safe place.

He tried to keep his touch gentle, his pace slow. But when she slid her hands down over his flanks and pressed him against her, he suddenly had enough of slow.

He picked her up and carried her to the bed.

He kicked off his loafers. Her eyes in the moonlight from the window looked dreamy. He bent over her, hooked his fingers into the zipper of her jeans, opened it, slid the jeans down her legs, then tossed them into the darkness. All the while her eyes never left his face.

"You're so lovely," he whispered as he unzipped his jeans.

Once they were both naked, he lay beside her. Her rib cage strained with taut muscle, and yet her breasts were warm and soft. He bent to kiss her and she answered him.

The kiss was long and deep and full of ineffable longing. As he caressed her, her hands slid over his shoulders, his chest, his stomach, and finally encircled him.

He nearly lost control right there. "Not yet," he breathed, and moved his tongue down her body, across her midriff, the softness of her belly.

As he bent his head between her thighs, she gasped. He probed her and encircled her with his tongue and smiled at her reaction.

"Oh, please," she groaned. She screamed and he felt her spasm against his lips. As she lay whimpering, she dug her fingers into his shoulders. He raised himself to enter her. She came again almost at once and clutched him as though she were drowning.

But he was the one who was going down for the third time. Drowning in the richness of her. "Tell me," he whispered. "Tell me what you want."

"You, just you."

She abandoned herself to him fully in that moment. A great sob tore from her throat. She arched her body against him. A wave of elation swept over him. She was his, at last and completely.

He rolled her over on top of him. He wanted to see her face and her body in the moonlight, probe the sweet secret hollows of her body.

Damn! He was too close. He shut his eyes against the sight of her. He wanted to hold off forever—hear more of those sounds of passion from her throat. He wasn't certain how soon he could do this again, and he wanted to, wanted to make love to her all night, all day, all year, for the next couple of millennia.

In desperation, he rolled her beneath him, but she clamped her legs around his waist and drew him more deeply into her.

The pleasure was beyond enduring—way the hell past his at any rate. She climaxed one more time before he exploded. A moment later he folded into her arms.

They were both slick with sweat. She cradled his head against her breast and stroked his back. He longed to stay locked in her arms and her body forever, but that wasn't possible.

"The French call that the little death," he whispered into her hair. "We do much more of that, my lovely kelpie, and you're going to wind up with The Big Murder on your hands."

"What did you call me?" she asked drowsily.

"My lovely kelpie."

"That some kind of doll?"

He kissed her crooked nose. "Actually, it's a water sprite. Takes the form of a beautiful black mare to entice men. Then it drowns them."

"I don't want to drown you."

"I like your weapons better, but the effect is the same. Poor bastard dies of a surfeit of love."

He felt her muscles stiffen. "What did I say?"

She relaxed again. "Nothing."

He held her until she drifted off to sleep. Her hair tickled his nose, he was afraid if he sneezed he'd wake her, and he was losing all feeling in his left arm. He reached down to the foot of the bed and pulled a quilt over them both, then laced his fingers behind his head and closed his eyes.

He'd never expected Pat's disastrous impromptu dinner party to end this way. He knew from that first kiss that he could release all that pent-up passion in her if only she'd let him, but she was a tough adversary.

That first day he'd lusted for her, wanted to satisfy his curiosity about her. What he felt now went way beyond lust. Liz fitted into his heart the way he fitted into her body—like the missing piece of a jigsaw puzzle. She had no idea how important she'd become to him...

SHE WOKE HIM with a kiss. He opened his eyes and stretched. It was still dark outside. He returned her kiss and was instantly aroused. She bit his shoulder gently. He stroked her belly and below. She gasped. He wasn't the only one aroused.

There would be no turning back, Liz thought, whatever the consequences. And no regrets either, even if she never saw him again after this night—this incredible night. Amazing that at her age she'd never known what it was to have a man, a real man, make love to her. It was as though she'd been blind and deaf all her life and had suddenly begun to see shooting stars and hear symphonies.

"Seducer," she whispered as her lips sought the hollow at the base of his throat and felt it pulse more rapidly against the tip of her tongue. "Ogre," she continued as she slid down to take his nipple in her lips. He groaned as she flicked it with her tongue and moved to the other. "Monster."

He reached for her shoulders as her tongue slid to the hollow at his waist and circled his navel. "You are a pirate and a cutthroat." She nibbled the thick black curls of hair on his belly. His eyes were closed, his back arched against her. He groaned with pleasure.

Her tongue followed the taut triangle of muscle that ran from the apex of his hips to his groin. He had a body like one of those Greek statues, only bigger. She slid her hand down to his groin.

His groans intensified. He tried to pull her up, but she resisted. "Not this time." she whispered. "My treat. It's payback time."

She pushed him back onto the bed and took him in her mouth. She loved the sounds she evoked from him.

Lovely to have him completely in her power at last, if only for a few moments.

Finally, in desperation, he grabbed her under the arms and hauled her up his chest, then rolled her under him. She was laughing at him.

"So I'm a torturer?" he snarled and kissed her.

Neither of them wanted or needed the slow buildup, the sweet sensuality of the first time. This was battle—body-to-body combat with no quarter asked or given.

At some point they slid off the bed and never noticed.

This time they exploded together.

Finally, he leaned back against the mattress. She straddled his lap and laid her head on his shoulder. He stroked her hair, her back, her bottom. His big hands spanned her rib cage.

"Oh, my," she said against his shoulder.

He chuckled. "Something like that."

Her voice held an edge of wonder. "I never knew making love could be like this." She raised up on one elbow to peer into his face. "You make me feel like a virgin."

"That's the greatest compliment any man can receive." He grinned at her and brushed her damp hair away from her face. "I'm glad you don't have close neighbors. They'd probably have called the police on us by now."

"Why on earth? What we did isn't illegal."

"It is in some parts of the world."

She chuckled. "Worth going to jail for. But why would the neighbors care?"

"A couple of times there you yelled pretty loud."

She drew back. "I did not." She bit her lip. "Did I?"

"Oh, yeah."

"Well, you did a little shouting yourself right at the end."

"Guilty as charged. We Celts tend to ululate in triumph when we win a big battle."

She froze. "Is that what you call it? Ululating? Triumph? Win the big battle? Oh, great warrior, is that what this was? A triumph?" She moved off his lap to sit beside him. She hugged her knees.

The moonlight etched her spine, and he ran his fingers down it. "The greatest damn triumph of my life."

The instant the words left his mouth he felt her back stiffen under his fingers. She scrambled to her feet and went to stare out the window.

"What?" he asked. He went to her, wrapped his arms around her, cradled her breasts in his hands and kissed that sweet place at the nape of her neck.

She leaned back against him and covered his hands with hers. "It's nearly dawn." She glanced at the clock. "Almost five in the morning. Hadn't you better go home?"

"Damn! I need to be there when Pat and Mrs. Hannaford get up. I'm already going to be buried under questions from Pat and insinuations from Mrs. H." He turned her to him and took her face in his hands. "I don't want to go. Please believe me."

She nodded. "I do."

"Go back to bed."

"I have to start work."

"I see." He released her and began to hunt for his clothes. There were all over the room. So were hers.

She stood at the window and watched him dress. He

knew there was something wrong, but he had no idea what he'd said or done to upset her and had no idea how to find out.

She came with him to the front door. The dogs raised their heads, but apparently last night's screams had not convinced them he was a serial killer. He took her in his arms once more, kissed her deeply and tenderly, then he was gone.

She watched until she could no longer see his taillights.

A triumph. The greatest triumph of his life, he said, but still a battle won, an enemy conquered, a trophy to drag behind his chariot wheels in the triumphal parade.

Last night they had been wonderful together, but for a man like Mike, making love must have little to do with love.

She had no one but herself to blame. How many other nights would there be before he wanted to make love to someone else?

She felt as though loving him had thrown her into an entirely new universe that she had never known existed. Could she ever endure returning to the real world without him?

CHAPTER SIXTEEN

LIZ WONDERED what Mike's usual thank-you routine was for his lovers—red roses, dinner invitations? She hoped it was too soon to expect the diamond tennis bracelet. That was probably his kiss-off present.

None of the above, apparently. By one in the afternoon she hadn't heard from him.

What would she say when he picked Pat up, assuming he didn't send Melba? She knew he wasn't out of town. She couldn't eat a bite of lunch and her stomach was killing her. She had nobody to blame but herself. She tried blaming Vic, but it didn't work. The decision to make love with Mike had been hers. She'd thought she understood the consequences, but then, she hadn't expected the experience to be so damned cataclysmic.

She decided to work out her nervousness by grooming every horse in the place. Her head was stuck under a chestnut gelding's rotund belly when she heard a voice behind her.

"Do you have any idea how tough it is to keep my hands off you?"

Liz banged her head into the gelding and turned to face him. Her heart was pounding. "Mr. Whitten. At two o'clock in the afternoon? And in jeans? What's gotten into you?"

"The answer would definitely incriminate me." He smiled at her.

Not much crocodile left in that smile these days. Liz's heart melted. So did the rest of her body. She clasped the currycomb tightly so that her hands would stop shaking.

"Everybody needs some time off occasionally," Mike continued. "I've been working too hard." He reached for her across the closed stall door. She sidestepped him neatly and ducked behind the horse.

"If you do get your hands on me, they're going to be very dirty." Liz glanced down at her grubby jeans and resumed grooming. She thought her voice sounded almost normal.

"Dirt has its good side. It's closer to you than I am."

"And more recently."

"That can be remedied. Come here."

"Mike, we can't," Liz whispered, and pointed to the wash rack where Angie and Vic watched them with surreptitious interest. "Not unless you want the bush telegraph to swing into action."

"What bush telegraph?"

"The horse bush telegraph. Can't you hear the drums beating already? The horse-show world lives on gossip."

"I don't care if the damned bush telegraph spreads the word about you and me coast to coast."

"I do."

"Then I suggest you find some way to get us a bit of privacy or I'm going to start faxing the news to everyone I know."

"And what news is that? That I slept with you?"

"That you are mine."

"Really."

"Come on, Liz, put down that brush before I use it on your bottom."

"It's called a currycomb."

"Looks like a brush to me."

She looked him up and down and narrowed her eyes. "Fine, you want privacy, privacy you'll get. Come with me."

"Where?" He raised an eyebrow. "The hayloft?"

"Too hot and much too prickly. Despite all the novels that say differently, doing anything in a hayloft that requires removing any portion of your clothing is a truly unpleasant experience."

"Speak from experience, do you?"

She threw the currycomb at him. He fielded it in midair and tapped the back of it suggestively against his palm.

"No, my friend, it's time you learned to ride a horse," she said. She opened the stall gate and snatched the currycomb out of his hand as she went by.

"A horse?" he bellowed.

Albert stuck his head out of the mare's stall. "Something wrong?"

"The woman's trying to kill me," Mike replied.

"Oh, in that case." The head disappeared again.

"Thanks for the help," Mike called.

"Anytime," came the reply.

"Come on," Liz said. "I'll put you on the horse-size equivalent of Wishbone. It won't hurt." She grinned at him. "Much."

It did, however, become a joint effort. Janey, Pat, Eddy and Kimberly began to groom the big chestnut gelding the moment Liz cross-tied him on the wash rack.

"Mike needs to learn to do that for himself," Liz said severely.

"Maybe tomorrow," Janey said from beneath the horse's belly. "This is too good to miss."

"Yeah, we're gonna watch him fall off," Eddy said with ill-disguised glee.

"I do not intend to fall off," Mike answered.

Pat cocked her head at Mike. "Maybe we could put a burr under Cinnamon's saddle. Even the odds. He's real quiet."

"I'm cutting you out of my will tonight," Mike told her. "If I live that long. And what do you know about odds, young lady?"

Pat merely arched her eyebrows at him and picked up one of Cinnamon's hooves to clean.

Liz came out of the tack room carrying an aged hard hat, which she set on Mike's head.

"This is silly," he told her.

She shoved it down. "It's a tad too tight, but it's not silly. Come on, time for your first lesson."

Mike felt like the loser in a fraternity hazing incident, but he listened to Liz and gamely climbed onto Cinnamon. The horse snorted once and then began to crop the sparse grass by the ring.

"Don't let him do that, Daddy! Pull his head up."

Mike pulled. The horse resisted for a moment, then stood quietly chomping his stolen grass like a cow. A moment later Liz rode out on Trust Fund. "Vic agrees that Trusty could use a little trail ride. He's been working too hard lately. Come on, pard, stretch your heels down, pick up your hands and walk. That's all we're going to do." She headed out into the pasture.

"Hey, no fair!" Eddy called. "We want to see him fall off."

"Another time," Liz said, and turned her horse toward a dirt path that wound into a clump of tall pines.

"Good luck, Daddy," Pat said, and then, "please be careful. Don't do anything silly!" She trotted after him, giving him instructions on his seat and his hands as she ran. As he turned into the trees to follow Liz, he saw Pat standing halfway down the trail with her hands on her hips and an anxious expression on her face. He waved and turned away.

Under the trees the path widened. Liz waited atop Trust Fund, who seemed not to mind standing around doing nothing.

"He's quiet today," Mike said.

"For him, this is recess," Liz patted his neck. "So how do you like the feeling?"

"Great. But can we find a place where I can make love to you for the rest of the afternoon?"

"Whoa! Is that the only reason you agreed to this?"

"Well, there weren't any hot coals handy to walk over to prove how much I want you. Riding a horse seemed a pretty good substitute."

He moved his horse up beside her, took his reins in one hand, reached for her hand and brought it to his lips.

"Relax. We've got all afternoon. This is *my* world. Let me show it to you."

The late-afternoon breeze barely ruffled the pine needles. Mike heard no sound except the creak of leather, the soft footfalls of the horses. He began to catch the horse's rhythm. Peaceful. Smoothed out the soul.

"I can't believe you've never ridden a horse before," Liz said. "Not even at your fancy prep school?"

"I played lacrosse until I got my nose broken for the second time in six months and had to have twelve stitches in my forehead. I wasn't quite this ugly before."

"You're not ugly."

"Sinister."

"Not even that—okay, maybe. When I first met you, I thought you had horns and a tail."

"I do."

"Right." She turned the horse toward another meadow dappled with late-afternoon sunlight. "But afterward? At college? I mean, you play all those business sports—golf, handball, tennis. Power games."

"Sailing was my thing. I spent three summers as a deck ape on a coffee grinder."

"What on earth is that?"

"A deck ape is a kid who's hired because he's over-grown, muscular and can turn the crank on one of the big winches on the deck of an ocean racer when he's told to. The job requires strength, not brains."

"Ocean racing! Sounds incredibly romantic."

"Oh, it is. If your idea of romance is working around the clock at a forty-five-degree angle covered in salt spray and sleeping in a six-foot bunk that never dries, in clothes that mildew on your body. Between the sweat and the snores, it's usually more pleasant on deck, except that people keep falling over you and praying devoutly you'll fall overboard and get the hell out of the way."

She laughed. "Substitute dust and mud for the salt water and you've pretty much got the world of horse shows. Why did you do it?"

"I've always loved boats. Besides, it was a great way to meet rich and powerful men. I crewed in the San Francisco to Honolulu race two months before I graduated and came home with a job at the biggest international business brokerage house on the West Coast."

"And thus began a meteoric rise?"

"I'm the best at what I do."

"And you don't sweat."

"It's only money. If you're smart enough, what you lose today you win with interest tomorrow."

"The trick to thinking in terms of 'only money' is to have enough of it not to care. I've never had that luxury."

"The major bucks go to my clients. Whitten's law states that bills accumulate in inverse ratio to the amount of money available to pay them. My portion of the bill to get Pat home from the hospital when she was three months old was over eighty thousand dollars."

"Good grief!" She laughed. "I agree with Whitten's law. My bills seem to grow by leaps and bounds whenever I'm really hurting for cash."

"Plus I have to make enough money so that if something happens to me, Pat will be taken care of."

"By whom? Your parents?"

He snorted. "Hardly. Melba Hannaford is her guardian and there's a battery of top investment counselors keeping the money in her trust fund growing. My parents are retired from Berkeley. They're certified geniuses, but they don't have enough common sense to raise radishes. Look at me."

"You're not so bad."

"Yes, I am," he said seriously. "I scared the hell out of my professors at Yale. They used to whisper that I was certainly single-minded. What they meant was that I had tunnel vision. I wanted success and money and power. Period."

"How empty."

"Took me four years in Seattle to realize that. By the time I met Sandi it was damn near too late."

"She changed all that?"

"Yeah. For a while."

A large meadow opened up before them. Across the way a pair of horses raised their heads and nickered. Mike's horse replied and shifted its weight.

"Do you mind standing here while I give Trusty a little exercise?" Liz asked.

"As long as all I do is stand."

"Be back in a minute." She clicked her tongue and walked Trusty ten or fifteen feet into the meadow, then she lifted herself so that her hands bridged the reins and the only portion of her body touching the saddle were the soles of her feet against the stirrups. Pat had told him this was called two-point position. He called it damned sexy, but only when Liz was in the saddle.

Trusty trotted forward, slowed, seemed to sit low on his haunches. Liz shouted "Yah" and he seemed to explode. Horse and rider galloped as though they'd been shot from a starting gate at a racetrack. Mike's horse snorted, seemed to want to follow them for a moment, then relaxed as Mike tightened his reins and patted the gelding's neck.

The two other horses in the pasture raised their heads and joined in the race.

Liz had forgotten her own hard hat so her hair flew around her head in a nimbus caught by the rays of the sun. He longed to join the race. Crazy. He'd get himself killed. Then he grinned. Okay, maybe not today, but some day he would. He'd talk to Vic about giving him lessons—maybe he'd go to another barn so that he could learn to ride without letting Liz know and then surprise her in a couple of months.

A couple of months. Six months. Five years. A lifetime. He could no longer imagine life without her. She'd vanquished him. He'd been ambushed, bushwhacked, sandbagged and hog-tied.

At the far end of the pasture Liz hauled Trusty up, turned him and came back to Mike. She was laughing and Trusty trotted as though he were on springs. "Fun! I'll bring the kids out tomorrow morning."

"Not for anything like that," Mike said, suddenly seeing Pat on the ground under Traveller's feet.

"Lord no. But they need a break too." She slapped Trusty's neck. He snorted happily. "Come on." Liz turned her horse to the right and clicked. She ducked her head to avoid an overhanging branch. Mike saw no sign of a trail until he followed. The path was narrow, boxed in on both sides with large trees. Twice he nearly took a branch across the bridge of his nose. He didn't need to break the damned thing a third time. "This way," Liz called from up ahead.

Suddenly his horse stepped out of the trees into a tiny meadow completely hidden by a copse of trees. Liz halted her horse at the top of a small rise and rested her hands on her thighs. At the foot of the meadow ran a small stream that chuckled softly across a bed of stones. Black-eyed Susans nodded beside the stream. The place smelled of wet loam, rain-washed grass and wildflowers.

"This is my hideout. I used to come here to get away from the barn when I couldn't take all the noise and the people any longer. Then, we used it to camp out when I was a teenager. I still come out here when I'm really pissed at the world or just need to chill out. Ought to bring the campers here for a sleepover. Maybe one weekend after school starts."

"Beautiful," he answered, but he was looking at Liz.

She swung her leg over Trusty's back, dropped to the ground and walked over to a rain-smudged plastic tack trunk that sat almost concealed under the trees. "I keep some stuff out here for emergencies."

She opened it, pulled out a couple of halters and lead lines, draped them over her arm, then picked up a bundle of something and threw it on the ground behind her.

"If you get down off that horse, you think you can get back up? I don't know whether I'm strong enough to hoist you."

"Possibly," he answered.

"Okay, but if you can't, you walk. And wouldn't the kids just love that." She fastened the halter over Trusty's bridle and looped the end of the lead line over a stout branch. "So get down." She handed him the other halter and lead line. "Tie Cinnamon over there. Here, I'll give you a hand."

She walked him through the process. "Quick release knot. You ought to know how to tie one of those, being an old sailor and all."

He did. He turned in time to watch her pick up the bundle, untie it and fling it out.

"You wanted privacy, you got privacy," she said, and sat down on the open sleeping bag.

He needed no further invitation.

This time the lovemaking was ineffably sweet. Mike felt the breeze against his naked back, looked down into her unfocused jade eyes, kissed her sweet lips and made love to her slowly, gently, moving with her as though to the rhythm of the earth beneath them.

Afterward he lay with her head in the hollow of his shoulder. "I could stay here forever," he whispered.

"The water moccasins and the raccoons might resent our intrusion."

He blinked. "Water moccasins? You're kidding, right?"

"Look over your shoulder at that stream. Down here in our fine South, suh, you got water, you got accompanying moccasins." Then she laughed. "But they generally avoid people when they can. The raccoons—they'd probably watch."

He laughed. "Voyeur raccoons, that's something one doesn't get in the average motel."

"If we want to avoid some very knowing looks from Vic and Albert, we'd better get ourselves organized and get out of here."

He groaned. "I'm not sure I can walk, much less ride a horse."

AN HOUR LATER the horses walked back into the barn to the combined catcalls and applause of the children who had finished their lesson and were now lying in wait for them. Mike gave them all—but especially Pat—a boxer's clasped overhead handshake and nearly fell off when he let go of the reins.

"Hey, get a load of you!" Angie said from the barn door. She glanced over her shoulder. "Uh, Liz, Vic's talking to someone inside."

"Oh, who?" Liz jumped off Trusty, handed his reins to Angie and came over to hold Mike's stirrup as he dismounted.

"Me." Rachelle answered. "Mike, darling, as I live and breathe, I never expected to see you on a horse."

Rachelle sounded pleasant enough, but Mike caught

the glint of a shard of ice beneath her words. He glanced at Liz and saw her jaw set like granite.

"I promised I'd come talk to you and Vic about selling some of this property," Rachelle said. "I probably should have called first, but I simply assumed you'd be available." She laughed sweetly, leaned over and kissed Mike's cheek. "I didn't realize you'd be giving a private session—lesson."

Mike didn't miss the flash of anger in Liz's eyes. Uh-oh, this might get a little hairy. "You go ahead, Liz," he said, and led his horse around Rachelle to the wash rack. "I'm sure Angie will help me with these horses, won't you, Ange?"

"Sure, Mike." The grin Angie gave Rachelle was downright malicious.

"Vic's waiting in the office. We've been talking for a few minutes already." Rachelle wiggled her fingers at Mike and led Liz away.

Mike kept his eye on the closed door of the office. Beside him Angie did the same thing. He realized he didn't want Liz to sell even one acre of this place. The two old houses needed work, money was tight, but he had plenty to rescue them. And this place—the openness, simplicity of it took the knots of his muscles. This had become Pat's special place. After this afternoon it seemed to be turning into his as well. For everyone's sake, it must not change.

Five minutes later the office door opened, and Rachelle emerged, still smiling. Vic and Liz didn't seem quite so happy. His heart bumped.

"Just think about it, that's all I'm saying," Rachelle said. "You have my card. You'd never know you'd sold off even one acre. Except in your bank balance."

She smiled at Mike and called, "Walk me to my car, darling."

He heard Angie's sniff. "I'll come too. Time I got home to Kevin," She said. He heard her booted footsteps behind him.

"So nice to see you. I've missed you," Rachelle said throatily. She linked her arm through his. Mike realized Angie stood behind his right shoulder. Rachelle smiled at her, "So nice to see you, too, Angie," she said, and when Angie didn't move, she sighed and waited while Mike opened the door of her fire-engine-red Chrysler convertible and helped her in. She didn't kiss him goodbye, but started the car, backed up, turned around and drove sedately down the driveway with her red hair streaming in the wind.

Mike turned to go back and face Liz. Instead, he caught Angie with her tongue out and her fingers stuck in her ears.

She started guiltily the moment she caught Mike's eye.

He laughed. "I get the feeling you're not fond of her."

"I thought you had better taste. Sorry if she's a friend of yours."

"What's Rachelle ever done to you?"

"Me? Practically nothing except cheat me out of blue ribbons and try to break up my marriage." Angie stalked toward the barn. Mike caught her arm.

"Whoa. You can't make a statement like that and just walk away."

"The hell I can't. Let me go."

"Angie?" he said threateningly. "I'll ask Liz."

Angie laughed. "Liz and Vic wouldn't tell you squat."

"That leaves you. Sit down now. Talk to me."

Angie sighed. "Take your big mitt off my arm."

Mike released her.

"Okay. She had incredible horses."

"I assumed that from a couple of statements Liz made."

"She was about as good a sportsman as a wolverine. She always entered easy classes, classes where she knew her horse outclassed everybody else. That's not cheating exactly, but it's a cheap trick. One of many. Hiding people's tack, upsetting riders and horses in the practice area. Even buying the occasional judge, although Daddy made the actual purchase. She hated anybody who ever beat her, but she really hated Liz, because Liz could take a wild young horse that knew absolutely nothing around a hunter course and make him look like the biggest packer in the world, while Rachelle could turn her hundred-thousand-dollar packers into bad-mannered stoppers in a year."

"How?"

"Bad temper. Bad riding. She looked pretty in the saddle, but she was never consistent. Horses didn't trust her. Their last two years as junior riders, Liz started beating her in a lot of classes."

"She didn't take it well?"

"Well?" Angie laughed shortly. "She began a personal vendetta against Liz. In one competition, she leaned over the in-gate just as Liz rode past her, and flicked her crop against the hocks of Liz's horse. He bucked and kicked into the ring. Of course Liz lost and Rachelle won the championship. Liz was ready to kill Rachelle, but Uncle Frank stopped her. He wouldn't let her protest to the steward. He probably wanted to sell Rachelle's father a fancy new horse. Besides, he said, professionals don't cry. They take their lumps and get on with the job.''

"So Liz said nothing?''

"I've never seen Liz that mad before or since." She grinned at him. "Uncle Frank didn't own me. I took care of the problem.''

"I'm almost afraid to ask what you did.''

"Not as much as Rachelle deserved." Angie snickered and stuck her thumbs into the belt of her jeans.

"I can't believe you'd hold a grudge for twenty years.''

"For my friends I'll hold a grudge until Judgment Day. Remember that, Mr. Michael Whitten. Rachelle broke up Dr. Claridge's marriage so she could marry him, and when he caught her cheating and asked for a divorce, the settlement she demanded practically broke him.''

"She told me he ran around on her.''

"Peter Claridge? He was one of Kevin's mentors. Gentlest man I've ever met. Next she went after Kevin. I knew what was going on, but Kevin is so deaf, dumb and blind he never even noticed.''

"How come I never heard any of this?''

"Mike, Mike. You haven't been in town that long, and you only joined the club what, six months ago? Guys don't tell each other this stuff. They may boast about the number of women they've had in the last week, but you never get any details. You saw what Rachelle wanted you to see. You're not the first and you won't be the last.''

"I consider myself a more than adequate judge of character. It's my job.''

"In business, maybe. As long as it's men. So far as women go, you don't have one more clue than Kevin.''

THAT EVENING Mike took Liz, Pat and Vic out for pizza. Albert had turned up his nose.

Liz began to relax. Maybe Rachelle had been exaggerating at that party. Mike didn't seem like a man used to flying from woman to woman.

Later, after they made love, and as they lay sated in one another's arms, Mike said suddenly, "I want to learn to ride a horse. Really ride. The way you do."

"Oh, you do, do you?" Liz laughed. "I'd no more teach you to ride than play bridge with you—talk about your instant disaster."

"Then recommend somebody else. Or maybe Vic can give me lessons."

"And the danger?"

"I'm not about to do anything foolhardy. But this is your world, yours and Pat's. So long as I can't do more than stroll around the pasture on the equine equivalent of Sleepy, I don't feel the challenge."

"You're serious, aren't you?"

"Yes." He ran his fingers through her wild hair and stroked the nape of her neck. "Very serious." He hesitated.

He didn't merely want to understand her world, he wanted to share it, to smooth it out and clean it up for her. He knew money was tight, but he knew better than to offer her a loan.

He'd find some way to talk to Vic. Maybe ask her to find him a suitable horse he could overpay for.

Liz curled against him and slept. He looked up at the ceiling of her bedroom. It badly needed a coat of paint. He had never seen the inside of Vic's house, but he knew it had been built before the turn of the century. There were things that needed to be done around here, things he wanted to do to make Liz's life more comfortable. To take care of her.

He slid into sleep realizing he had never felt that way about anyone in his life except Pat. Sandi had made more money than he did and had been fiercely independent. But Liz, for all her outer toughness, had the tender inside of a kitten. He wanted to hear her purr.

CHAPTER SEVENTEEN

EARLY THE FOLLOWING Friday morning Liz, Vic and Albert moved all the horses that were participating in the show to stalls in the showgrounds. Albert's nephew Kenny, a junior in preveterinary medicine at the local university, had been hired to feed, water, clean stalls and generally baby-sit the few horses that would remain at ValleyCrest.

An exasperated Mike found he could not avoid flying to Cleveland for an emergency business meeting Friday morning, but swore he'd be ringside by early Saturday afternoon to watch Pat ride even if he had to hire a private plane to bring him home. Liz assured him that he'd be there in plenty of time to watch Pat's two beginner classes, and to cheer Liz on in the grand prix that took place immediately afterward.

Mike checked and rechecked the weather reports, which swore that Labor Day weekend should stay hot and as humid as midsummer. The weather forecasters merely mentioned a strong cold front just over the border in Canada. So far it was slated to come through late Monday night. If the front moved earlier, air travel could be delayed. To be on the safe side, Mike reserved a car in Cleveland and notified his business associates that if there was any chance of his getting stuck in Ohio, he'd walk out on their meeting and drive all Friday night to get home.

"Looks as though the show will squeak through in good weather," Liz said when he called her from his hotel late on Friday night. "I'll take sunshine and heat over tornadoes and lightning any day of the week."

"I remember," he said with a low chuckle. He could almost see Liz blush at the remembrance of that wet, wild kiss on her front steps.

Then with a tenderness Liz didn't recognize, he said, "I miss you."

Liz caught her breath. Mike usually made love passionately, as though he were storming a fortress. She was amazed to find she matched him passion for passion. He could be gentle, tender, but even that night when he had come to her the first time, she had never heard such naked longing in his voice. Why did it frighten her?

This was what she said she wanted, yet suddenly she missed the easy banter that allowed her to keep a bit of herself hidden and safe from him. So she said, "I have been too darn busy to miss even you." Liar.

"Ouch. That's my ego you hear imploding. How's Pat doing? Mrs. H. says she's snarling at everyone like a bobcat."

"Not quite that bad, but she's like me—the more nervous she gets, the meaner she turns."

"Are you certain it's not too soon for her to show Traveller? Will he behave?"

"Mike, she's got to start sometime, and this is a real baby-beginner division she's in. Stop worrying. She'll be fine."

"And you? Will you be fine too?"

"I have to be," Liz said grimly. "Our people need to win for the publicity."

"I meant you in the grand prix."

"Who knows? I hope so, not only for the prize, but so I can sell Trusty for a bunch of money."

"If it'll keep you out of trouble, I'll buy him for a bunch of money."

"No thank you, Daddy Warbucks. I win or I don't, but I will compete to the best of my ability."

"I didn't mean…"

"Sure you did." She relented. "It was a kind thought, but I don't take real well to pats on the head, remember?"

"I wasn't…"

"Let me do my thing, Mike. Let Pat do hers. I don't try to keep you from flying off to Cleveland, do I?"

"It's not the same thing."

"Yes, Mike, it is. Exactly the same thing. If I were a plumber, I would plumb. I am a rider. I intend to ride."

"Don't take chances, that's all I ask."

She bit back a retort. "No crazy chances. Trusty wants to survive as much as I do. He'll look after me."

"Oh, right. I wish I were there to argue with you. We seem to make up in remarkably interesting ways."

Liz giggled. "Maybe one of these days we won't need the arguing part first."

"Please take care. I…" He hesitated, then, "I'll see you tomorrow," he finished lamely.

THE MOMENT HE SAW the jumps being set up for the grand prix, he felt his heart stop for a moment. They looked as tall as the Washington Monument.

Mrs. Hannaford and Walter Simpson had brought Pat along with a gigantic picnic basket full of munchies. Mrs. H. waved when she saw Mike climb out of his car, still in his navy business suit.

She came over to him shaking her head. "I don't think I've ever seen Pat quite so uptight," she said. "She's bitten my head off half a dozen times. I finally had to get Liz to tie her stock. She wouldn't let me touch her. She even snapped at Walter. I told him it was just first-show nerves."

"I'll get her to apologize later. Where is she?"

"Up at the practice ring with Vic and Liz."

Mike started up the hill when Mrs. H.'s voice stopped him. "Mr. Whitten? Pat said please stay down here by the ring until her class."

"Why?"

"She said you'd upset her." She shrugged apologetically.

"Oh." He sighed. "I see. And what did Liz say?"

"She agrees. She's pretty uptight as well. She won't have but fifteen minutes after the beginner's class to tune Trusty up one more time before she has to ride in the grand prix. It's a very tight schedule and they don't make allowances for conflicts."

Mike took a deep breath. "So what did Pat and Liz suggest I do? Hide behind a tree?"

Mrs. H. laughed. "Don't be silly. Come with Walter and me. We're going to stand beside the ring and watch all the ValleyCrest beginners go." She took his arm and began to lead him across the path between the two rings. "Don't you remember your first football match? I'm sure you treated your father like pond slime when he showed up."

"It would never occur to my father to show up to watch me win the Nobel Prize, much less play in a football match," Mike said.

"Oh." She patted his arm gently. "Well, if he had,

you would have. My boys all did, and I think girls are worse. Stay with us.''

He craned to see whether he could spot Pat or Liz, but there were so many horses, so many riders, organized mass confusion. Ring announcements blared, jump crews raced around resetting the jump courses, parents and dogs and baby strollers and spectators all crowded the grounds and the stands.

Mike gave up and followed Mrs. H. and Walter docilely. He didn't feel docile. He felt uncomfortable about this whole day. The sky blazed blue, but there was an unmistakable hint of menace in the air. That cold front had begun to move. He knew Liz dreaded riding in thunderstorms. Horses and riders would be sitting ducks for any stray lightning bolt. A big enough front would spawn tornadoes, and this ring was no place to be in a tornado.

Mike felt the heavy still air in his bones. Years of ocean racing had schooled him well in weather signs. Mother Nature was definitely gearing up to pitch a temper tantrum. No wonder human tempers were frayed. He turned his head as a horse whinnied and stamped in annoyance behind him. The horses knew. What would the still, heat-laden air do to Traveller's already uncertain temper? Mike clenched his fists. He wanted to find Pat, drag her down off that pony and take her home.

She'd never forgive him. Nor would Liz. He could only stand by and watch. And pray. For both of them.

A heavy hand descended on his shoulder at the same moment a deep voice cheerfully bellowed into his ear, ''Hey, son.''

Big Scooter. Mike turned, expecting to receive a blast of bourbon-scented breath in his face.

He was surprised. Scooter's eyes were clear, and the hand that shook Mike's felt rock steady.

Scooter must have registered Mike's expression, because he snickered and said, "Hell, son, I been on the wagon ever since that night y'all took me home." He leaned close to Mike. "My butler called Miss Mamie, told her what I'd done after the party. Miss Mamie said if I didn't get aholt of myself she was staying in N'Orleans. Can't afford to have Miss Mamie too close to those antique stores on Royal. So I quit." He snapped his fingers. "Just like that."

"Glad to hear it, uh…Scooter."

Scooter leaned closer. "Confidentially, it's been hell." He sighed deeply. "I been seeing the world through bourbon-colored glasses for a long time, son. But Miss Mamie and my doctors tell me if I expect to see my grandson bag his first deer I better shape up."

"You getting any help?" Mike was amazed to hear himself ask the question. Certainly Big Scooter's sobriety was none of his business, and a couple of months earlier he would never have dreamed of asking such a personal question.

Scooter pulled himself up and stuck his thumbs into his flaming red suspenders. "Course I am, son. Meetings most every day. Miss Mamie's got me going to a shrink." He seemed proud. "Guess I been crazy all my life. Maybe it's time to get myself sane." He waggled his eyebrows. "Gettin' up to some things with Miss Mamie I haven't been able to for some years now."

Mike had no idea how to reply to that so he said nothing.

"Come to see if any of the old crowd I used to know is still alive," Scooter said. "Now I'm not drinking I got to find something else to occupy my time."

"And did you?"

"Hell, yeah. I'm gonna give my granddaughter a horse for Christmas, see if I don't." He slapped Mike on the shoulder again. "Got to go find Miss Mamie. She's around here somewhere." He peered around vaguely, and drew a hand along his jaw. "You know, son, when all's said and done, only two things matter in this life. Having a good woman who loves you in your bed at night—I got that, though Lord knows why Miss Mamie's stuck with me all these years—and children who don't hate you. I'm working on that part."

"You'll make it," Mike said, again amazed to find that he cared.

"My liver and my doctor appreciate your good words." Scooter wandered off, then turned back and pointed a finger at Mike. "Next week breakfast. I'll call you."

Mike watched him amble up the hill toward the concession stands. He'd felt nothing for the man but distaste the first time he met him. Now he saw Scooter through Liz's eyes and wished him well. Scooter was right. Mike felt his heart expand with sheer joy. He had a good woman in his bed, a woman who loved him when he'd never thought any woman ever could again. And a child who didn't hate him. Well, most of the time, at any rate.

He spotted Liz standing at the side of the practice ring with her back to him. He'd never before seen her in full riding kit—skintight beige britches, shiny boots to her knee. God, what a body! She wore only a short-sleeved white cotton shirt, back damp with sweat, and no hard hat, although she'd corralled her wild hair tight against the back of her neck and covered it with some sort of net thing that left it looking like a half-eaten bagel. He longed to sneak up behind her and drag it down so that he could lock his fingers in it, turn her to face him and plant a wet sloppy kiss full on her lips.

He started toward her and saw Pat trot down to a small cross-rail fence set up in front of her in the practice ring. Both pony and child had been obscured behind other horses and riders. Pat wore the same uniform as Liz but with the addition of a black riding jacket and her shiny new velvet hard hat.

He watched Pat guide Traveller at a trot over the tiny jump with the same trepidation he'd felt when he watched Liz maneuver Trust Fund over huge fences. He realized he'd stopped breathing only when he started once again.

"Stay here, Mr. Whitten," Mrs. H. said, her hand on his arm.

"Yeah. Sorry." He leaned against the trunk of a handy tree.

"They're calling Pat's first class," Walter said.

"All they do is trot around the little fences once. No cantering," Mrs. H. whispered. "Pat'll do fine."

Pat trotted into the ring on Traveller and he felt his heart swell with pride. Whatever happened, she'd come a very long way. Liz had been right all along.

The first three fences were creditable. Then even at this distance Mike saw that Pat began fussing with Traveller's reins. The pony decided he'd had enough and stopped dead a pace from the fence.

Mike's heart stopped the instant the pony did. This time, however, Pat stayed on. She backed him up hard, yanking on his mouth and kicking his sides. Her jaw was set, her face furious. She whacked the pony with her crop and he lunged forward. He took the jump raggedly. The rest of the course was even more ragged, and they finished ingloriously. Mike started for the paddock before she left the in-gate and was six paces away by the time Pat rode out. Liz was waiting for her, her hands on her hips, anger in every line of her shoulders.

The instant Pat cleared the ring she threw her leg over the saddle, jumped down and flung her reins at Liz. "He's a horrible pony! I'm never going to show again." She turned and ran full tilt away from her father, from Liz, from the pony, and up the hill toward the stables where the ValleyCrest horses were installed.

"Pat!" Liz called after her. "Come back here." She turned and saw Mike.

He tried to say something, but Liz held up a hand. "Not now. Hold this pony!"

"Look, maybe it was too soon to let Pat do this…"

"No rider of mine is going to blame mistakes on a green pony, and no ValleyCrest rider is ever going to be a lousy sport. This is my problem. Get out of the way and let me handle it."

He felt a flare of anger and started after her, then realized he still held the pony and called instead, "I'm her father, dammit."

Without turning, she snapped, "And I'm her trainer. In this situation, Mr. Whitten, I rule."

"She does, you know," Vic said and took the pony's reins. "We promised you we wouldn't train brats. We won't."

"She's forcing Pat to do something she's not ready for."

"Like behave herself when she encounters a disappointment? Oh, I think she's ready for that, Mike."

"That's not what I meant."

Vic laid a hand on his arm. "Come on, we have to walk this pony anyway to keep him cool. Talk to me."

She led him off up the hill. "Did anybody ever make allowances for you?"

"I didn't need any allowances."

"Sure you did. We all do. But most of us don't have parents running interference. Liz told me about Pat..." She glanced up at Mike's face. "Sorry, Mike, but she thought I ought to know and she was right. Pat has every reason in the world for her bad behavior. But reasons aren't excuses. She's come a long way. Let her learn to win on her own. She needs to win."

Mike started to snap at her, then took a deep breath. "You're right. She hasn't had much success in her life, has she?"

"No. And we all need it. Liz will tear about six inches of skin off her from the top of her head to the soles of her feet, and they'll probably both wind up in tears, but in the end, if Pat is the tough cookie I think she is, she'll come back down to this ring, get on this pony and take her lumps. She's got to have the experience. There's no other way."

Mike glanced over his shoulder at the barn area, then patted the pony's silver neck. "Yeah. You're right. God, am I such a bad father?"

Vic laughed. "You're a wonderful father, and I suspect you were an equally wonderful husband." She fell silent. "Mike..."

Mike saw Vic's face and chortled. "What are my intentions? Honorable. Well, semihonorable."

Vic looked into his eyes for a moment, then she said, "We need to stay close to the ring." She turned around and walked the pony back down the hill. "Pat has another class to ride this afternoon. And Liz will barely have enough time to warm up Trusty before the grand prix starts."

"Does Liz have to ride?"

"Absolutely. We need the money."

"About that…"

"No. Don't even talk about money," Vic said. "Talk about Liz. You know she's more like a combined sister and daughter to me than a niece. I'm not that much older than she is. I don't want her hurt."

"I don't plan to hurt her."

"Does anybody ever plan to hurt anybody?"

"I suppose not." He stopped and took the reins from Vic. Traveller leaned his gray head against Mike's chest and seemed to go to sleep. "No doubt between Mrs. H. and Liz and Angie you are fully conversant with my entire history."

Vic nodded. "Women are like that, you know."

"I'm beginning to realize. Men don't have a chance."

"We try to keep that quiet."

"First off, all that nonsense about Whitten's Wenches is just that—nonsense."

Vic stopped and raised her eyebrows. "How'd you find out about that?"

"An ally. A male one."

Vic nodded. "Walter."

"Thank God he told me. Why didn't you or Liz or Angie, or for that matter Mrs. H.?"

"We didn't choose to dignify the rumor by asking."

Mike laughed. "Come on, Vic."

"Oh, all right. We considered the source, if you must know. Liz would never have believed Rachelle in the first place if she hadn't already been feeling vulnerable."

"Why, for God's sake? A beautiful, talented woman like Liz…"

"Take a look at yourself, at your world, Mike, and tell me Liz had no reason to feel vulnerable after that party you landed her with."

"Yeah. Maybe you're right." He patted Traveller, who seemed to have relaxed considerably.

"Now, you said your intentions were semihonorable," Vic said. "Would you care to explain that?"

Mike took a deep breath. "I had what I thought was the great—the only—love of my life with my wife, Sandi."

Vic nodded.

"We thought we were adults—we were old enough, certainly—but I can see now we were Romeo and Juliet. We created a glorious fantasy world in which reality could never touch us. The first time we ran headlong into reality, reality won."

"I know, and I'm sorry."

"My point is that Liz is real—she's about the realest thing I've ever met. She doesn't only have her feet on the dirt, half the time she's covered with it. She infuriates me, she makes me laugh, she fights me, and her capacity for loving is wide enough to encompass the whole damned world, animal, vegetable and mineral. How could I not—want—her?"

"So I'm supposed to stand back and see where this leads?" Vic said.

"Isn't that what you're telling me to do about Pat?"

"Touché. But remember, you hurt her, you're dog meat."

LIZ PULLED the heavy dark green canvas back from the ValleyCrest tack-room door. "Get back on that pony this instant."

"I won't." Pat was curled into a ball on a hay bale in the corner.

Liz saw the same child she'd seen that first day, after that first disappointment. "You're scared to ride?" she said softly.

Pat whirled. Her tears had cut furrows down her cheeks. Her face was flushed, her eyes unnaturally bright and hard. "I am not! Traveller's awful. You saw him!"

"I saw you start messing with his mouth and driving him crazy with your legs is what I saw. And then I saw you smack him for your mistake, fall all over the rest of the jumps and act like a jerk afterward." She clicked her tongue. "So, unfortunately, did everybody else."

Pat wailed.

Liz wanted to reach out, to take Pat in her arms, but she held her distance. This time she had to be all trainer. "You ride against yourself, not anybody else. The trick is to deserve to win. And learn to lose gracefully even if you think the judge is an idiot with bran mash instead of brains."

Pat sniffled. "I hate it."

Liz laughed. "No, you don't. You're as big a competitor as your daddy ever was. As I am. Takes one to know one. You hate losing. Learn to lose. Even baseball players never hit five hundred. They always mess up more often than they score."

"Everybody'll laugh if I go back down there."

"No, they won't. But they sure as hell will if you don't. Now, grab a piece of ice out of the ice chest, wipe off your face, get yourself down to that ring and get back on your pony. Don't plan to win, just try not to make a total nincompoop of yourself. Your daddy and I will be cheering ringside.'' Liz turned on her heel and walked out. She listened for the sound of Pat's footsteps behind her, but heard nothing.

She walked down the hill. Vic was busy schooling the other ValleyCrest riders. Mike stood beside the ring holding Traveller, Albert stood under the trees holding Trust Fund. Oh, well, at least that would give her longer to school Trusty.

She heard footfalls behind her and shortened her stride. Pat came up beside her. She was setting her hard hat solidly back on her head and buckling her chin strap. Liz kept walking.

When Mike saw them he opened his mouth, but Liz shook her head. He smiled at Pat and handed her the reins. ''Leg up?'' he offered.

Pat took the reins and bent her knee. He tossed her into the saddle and she turned the pony away without acknowledging his existence. Instead, she turned to Liz. ''Winning's better.'' She trotted off toward the in-gate.

''Keep your fingers crossed,'' Liz whispered.

Suddenly they were surrounded by the other ValleyCrest riders, all mounted on their ponies and horses, all watching Pat start for the in-gate.

''And our last rider is Patricia Whitten on Traveller,'' the announcer said.

She met the first fence perfectly. ''Yeah,'' Janey whispered.

Liz's hand reached for Mike's and held it hard. ''Sorry I snarled.''

''Sorry I interfered,'' he whispered back.

''Don't breathe until it's over.''

He didn't.

Pat cleared the final fence, trotted in a circle and

trotted out the gate with perfect aplomb. The other riders parted for her.

"And the winner of baby-beginner class number fifteen is Patricia Whitten on Traveller," the ring announcer said.

A cheer went up from the ValleyCrest riders.

Pat wheeled and rode back in to accept her blue ribbon as the other riders who had won ribbons followed behind her.

Mike wrapped his arms around Liz's waist, swung her around in an arc and kissed her. "I love you!" he shouted over the din.

Pat walked Traveller toward them.

Her face was the color of Thanksgiving cranberry sauce. She rode straight to her father and held out her ribbon. He took it from her fingers, saw that they were trembling.

"Daddy," she said so softly he nearly missed it. "I don't feel so good." Then she slid out of the saddle and into his arms.

CHAPTER EIGHTEEN

"Hey, Pat get hurt?" Angie walked up, holding Trusty's reins. "I just saw Mike carrying her to his car."

Liz turned a distracted face toward her. "Was he taking her home?"

"Said he was taking her to the hospital."

Liz brushed by her.

"Hey, Liz, you've got barely enough time to get Trusty warmed up."

Liz kept running.

"And they're about to let the jumper riders walk the course. You can't leave now. Where are you going?"

Liz barely broke stride. "To follow Mike. Tell Vic I'm so sorry. I'll make it up to her somehow. I can't ride in the grand prix. I've got to find out how Pat is."

"Liz? Liz?" Angie kept calling as Liz disappeared over the brow of the hill at a dead run.

"Give him here," Vic said as she materialized at Angie's shoulder. "God, this is dreadful."

"Pat got hurt?"

Vic continued to stare after Liz. "What? No. Actually, she won."

"Then what's the problem?"

"Mike says she's burning with fever. She fainted in his arms."

"Geez, that's terrible. Probably some damned virus. Lousy timing."

"More than that, maybe much more."

The announcer's voice sounded. "Grand prix riders, you may now walk the course." He repeated his instructions.

"I've never known Liz to walk out," Angie said. "Not on something this important. Who's going to ride Trusty?"

"Nobody." Vic turned stricken eyes. "This late there aren't any catch riders available. We'll just have to forfeit the five-hundred-dollar entry fee."

"No way, Vic, I know you need that prize money."

"Can't be helped."

"Couldn't she have waited an hour to go haring off after Mike? It's not as though the kid's going to die or anything."

"Oh, Angie," Vic said and turned away.

"Vic? Vic, what did I say? Vic?" she called plaintively. "Please, come back here and talk to me."

Vic turned back. Her eyes were bleak. "It's a long story. Right now I have to go tell the office we're forfeiting."

Angie took a hard look at Vic's face and then glanced up at Trusty. She took a deep breath. "Let's hope heaven really does protect fools," she whispered. "You're not scratching. I'll ride Trusty."

"You've never even been on him."

"Tell the office there's been an emergency change of rider. Where's Albert? We need him to hold this animal while you and I walk the course."

LIZ DASHED into the emergency-room entrance at Baptist East and began to search the anguished and stunned faces for Mike's. He wasn't there.

"Excuse me," she asked the bored-looking woman behind the desk, "Could you tell me where I could find Patricia Whitten or her father, Michael?"

The woman turned to her computer keyboard. "You a relative?"

Liz hesitated only an instant. "Yes. I'm Pat's aunt." She crossed her fingers and hoped they wouldn't ask for identification.

"Let's see." The woman clicked some keys. "Not here."

"What do you mean, not here?" Liz heard the edge of hysteria in her voice. "She's got to be here. He was no more than five minutes ahead of me."

The woman shrugged. "You check the waiting room? Sure this is the right hospital?"

Liz caught her breath. She'd assumed he'd taken Pat to the closest hospital, but he might have spent the extra time to drive her downtown to the children's hospital. "I—uh—I don't know. Could you check and see if *anyone* by that name has been admitted?"

The woman clicked the keys once more. "Not yet. Listen, if she just got here, the paperwork wouldn't be on the computer yet. Why don't you call her doctor?"

Because I don't know her doctor, Liz thought. "Where's the nearest pay phone?"

The woman pointed. Liz found a stray quarter in the bottom of her britches pocket. Her purse lay on the front seat of her truck. She tried to remember whether she'd locked the doors.

For a moment she felt faint and realized she was starting to hyperventilate. She leaned her head against the wall beside the pay phone for a moment until the nausea subsided.

The first place she called was Saint Jude, but they had no record of a Patricia Whitten being admitted. Next she tried the children's hospital, and after five minutes of being shunted from office to office, she finally got in touch with someone at the admitting desk. Yes, Patricia Whitten was being admitted. When Liz asked her status, her room number—anything—she got no information. She slammed down the telephone and raced for her truck.

Twenty minutes later she stepped out of the elevator on the fourth floor of the children's hospital. Ahead of her was a nurses' station. Two nurses chatted idly, one leaning against the desk, the other sitting in front of a computer keyboard. Liz tried to figure out how she could slip past them without being stopped. She had to know if Pat was all right.

All right? Hell, no, of course she wasn't all right! She was probably dying thanks to Liz Matthews and her all-seeing, all-knowing judgment.

And Mike would die as well. Maybe his body would live on, but his soul would blink out. Even if they were able to save Pat once more, even if he faced the terrible long haul of another illness, maybe even bone marrow transplants, he'd do it alone. After this, he'd never allow Liz to be a part of their lives again.

He'd be right. How could she have worried about a little personal heartbreak? This was truly loss, much worse than anything she could have imagined that day he and Pat marched into the stable like an invading army. Liz knew now that her own pain, no matter how terrible, was finite. She felt where it began and ended.

Because she couldn't feel Mike's pain or Pat's, it became infinite, endless, monolithic and impossibly cruel.

For a moment she considered simply turning around and driving home. She was the last person Mike would want to see. If she thought she'd seen his anger before, that was nothing compared to the abuse he'd heap on her tonight.

If it would save Pat, protect Mike from suffering, she'd trudge the world barefoot over broken glass.

One of the nurses saw her and smiled. "Can we help you?"

"Uh, I'm looking for Patricia Whitten? Or her father?"

"I think he's in the parents' waiting room." One of the nurses pointed down a hall.

Liz spotted him at once. He stood at the window with his back to her, staring up at the encroaching darkness outside with his hands in his pockets.

Her nerve nearly failed. But she had to know. She had to show him that she loved him, loved Pat. She went to him.

"Mike?" she said softly.

He didn't react.

"Mike?" she said a little louder.

He turned and stared at her as though he weren't quite certain who she was. "Yes?" he said.

"Mike, how is she? How is Pat?"

"On phenobarbital at the moment. Her fever was a hundred and five. They were afraid of convulsions."

He sounded calm, rational, almost relaxed.

Liz felt her heart begin to pound. She'd expected fury. This was much, much worse.

"What does her doctor say?" She had to get through to him somehow. She walked closer. "Mike? Are you all right?" She knew how idiotic her words were the moment they left her mouth.

"Fine."

She began to open her arms, looked deep into his dead eyes and dropped her hands to her side. She had never felt so cold.

"The doctors?"

Mike shook his head. "Her doctor says he has no idea what it is. They're doing tests, but it's the weekend. They won't get the results until Monday. In the meantime they're getting her fever down."

"You've talked to him? Did he say...I mean, is it...?"

Mike shrugged. "What else could it be?" He turned back to the window.

"Oh, Mike." She felt as though the words were torn from her soul. "Please, please, I'm so sorry. If only I'd listened to you."

He swiveled and looked at her in genuine puzzlement. "You bear no responsibility for this."

"Of course I do. You tried to tell me..." He was shaking his head at her doggedly.

"Liz, this has nothing to do with you. This is something I have to deal with alone."

Just like that. Polite. Final. He wasn't even cold, he seemed merely empty. He couldn't be touched by anyone or anything. Certainly not by her. How could she have ever thought she'd become a part of his life? His and Pat's?

Defeated, Liz turned and left the room. In the hall, she leaned against the wall and buried her face in her hands. She'd been scared plenty of times, but not like this. She had to try to reach Pat even if she couldn't reach Mike.

She walked over to the nurses' station. "Could you tell me which room Patricia Whitten is in, please?"

The nurse glanced up from her desk. "Sorry, unless you're a parent we can't give out that information. She's been isolated."

"Then, please, can you give me her doctor's name. Surely that's not confidential."

"What's your interest?" The kindly tone belied the words.

"I am...I am someone who loves her."

This time the nurse looked at her more closely. "You'd better sit down." She turned to an LPN standing behind her. "Bring this lady a cup of orange juice, stat."

For a moment the world spun. Liz leaned her palms against the desk and pressed down hard. A moment later a cup was thrust at her. She drank it down and the nausea receded slightly.

"Okay," the nurse said. "I can't tell you much unless you're her mother."

"Please tell me what you can."

"Right. She's not exactly in intensive care, but we're keeping a close watch on her until we can break that fever." She glanced at a chart in her hands. "It hasn't begun to drop yet, but we're hoping it will soon. Kids her age don't usually get temperatures that high."

"No."

"But no convulsions, so that's a good sign. We're pretty sure it's not meningitis. Could be some crazy virus she picked up. Could be anything. Kids." The woman shook her head.

"You know she's had ALL?"

"We know." The nurse put her hand over Liz's. "It's worrisome, but it doesn't have to be a recurrence, although she does have a couple of enlarged lymph nodes.''

''Is that bad?''

''Could be. Could just be her body trying to isolate the infection. Keep the faith. And even if it is ALL, we can do miracles today. Long-term remission—years of healthy life.''

''I'm worried about Mr. Whitten.'' Liz gestured toward the waiting room.

''Yeah. So's Pat's doctor.''

''Please, if I could just speak to him?''

''Sorry, he's left the hospital. He's on call if there's any change, but there's nothing we can do tonight except wait.''

Wait. Do nothing. Sit, pray, bargain with God.

''If I leave you my name and telephone number, will you call me if there's any change?''

''Sorry, honey, we've got all we can do to keep up.''

''Then may I call you?''

''I get off at eleven, but you can call before then.''

''And will you check on him?'' Liz pointed toward the waiting room once more. ''Her father?''

''Sure.'' The nurse turned away.

Liz was certain the woman meant what she said at that moment, but would she remember to check on Mike if there was a rush of new patients? She started to go down the hall to see if she could locate Pat's room, but when she turned her head, the nurse was watching her. Liz smiled and walked to the elevators.

Kevin was the only doctor she knew. She had no idea whether he had admitting privileges at the children's hospital, but surely she could get him to find out the name of Pat's doctor, get a doctor-to-doctor update.

She walked to her truck, and only as she heard the snickers and saw the stares did she realize she still wore her complete riding kit. Tough. Pat still wore hers as well. Mike had brought her into the hospital in her boots and britches and riding coat. No doubt, at the moment, she wore a hospital gown. With tubes. Maybe an oxygen tent. Liz thought of her as so big and tough, but she was really just a sick twelve-year-old girl.

"Liz?"

Liz raised her head. "Oh, Melba, thank God you're here. And Walter."

She reached both hands to them. "They're on the fourth floor. I couldn't see Pat. She's under sedation. Isolated. Mike's in the waiting room." She took a deep breath. "Melba, he's—"

"Oh, dear, he yelled at you. I'm so sorry. You must realize…"

Liz shook her head. "I was ready for anger. He's perfectly calm. And too quiet."

"You look about to fall down yourself," Walter said. "Melba, honey, you go on up. I'll take Liz to the cafeteria to get something to eat."

"No thank you, Walter," Liz said with a small smile. "Both of you stay with Mike. He needs you."

"Oh, my dear, it's you he needs," Melba said. Her eyes swam in tears.

"He'll never need me again," Liz whispered. She pushed past them and nearly ran to her truck as they called her name behind her.

She remembered suddenly that she'd left Angie holding Trust Fund outside the practice ring. With four horses to load into the trailer afterward and bring home and only Albert to help load them. Traveller would be one of the horses to be brought home tonight. Now Pat wouldn't be riding him in the morning. Maybe she'd never ride him again.

Liz bumped into the hood of somebody's shiny new Honda parked three spaces down from her truck. For a moment she leaned on the hood with both hands to steady herself. No, she refused to consider the possibility that Pat might never ride again. This was some crazy virus. Something that would go away in twenty-four hours.

She couldn't remember driving to the hospital. She had no idea where she'd parked her truck. After ten minutes wandering through the parking area she located it and discovered she'd left the keys in the ignition and locked the truck behind her. She'd never done that in her life.

She went around to the passenger side and located the magnetic key box. After she opened her door, she carefully put the key back. She might need it again the next time her mind deserted her.

The effort had cleared her brain. She had to go back to the horse show. Vic would be frantic to know how Pat was. She glanced at her watch. The grand prix would be over by now.

And all that entry money down the tubes. Not Vic's fault. Have to make it up to her some way. Stop hurting people. What gave her the right to risk Vic's livelihood any more than to risk Pat's life? So sure, so casual, so certain that everything would turn out fine because Liz Matthews said it would.

She drove through the parking lot at the horse show without spotting the ValleyCrest trailer. She'd missed Vic and Albert completely. She didn't bother to find out who had won the grand prix.

OUTSIDE VALLEYCREST the four-horse trailer stood open and empty, but still hooked to Vic's big truck. All the barn lights were on. Liz wanted to drive right on by without stopping, go hide in her house with her dogs and her parrot, but she couldn't do that. Hadn't she done enough damage for one lifetime?

She climbed out of the truck as bone-weary as though she'd ridden a hundred-mile cross-country race. A large figure loomed in the doorway. "You all right?" Albert said.

"Never again." Liz said. She folded her arms across her chest and leaned against his broad body. She felt his arms drop around her shoulders.

He patted her gently. "You cry if you want to," he whispered.

"I can't do that, either."

"How is she?"

"Sedated. Fever over a hundred and five."

"That's bad."

"Yes."

"Mike?"

"Dead inside. Like me."

"Uh-oh." He stood there and held her until she felt strong enough to move away.

"Where's Vic?"

"Up to your house. Waiting for you."

"Go home, Albert. You've been here from kin to cain't."

"Yeah. Maybe I will. You call me you need me. Kenny's coming by the barn about noon to clean the stalls. I'll feed and water first thing before I go to the show. So if you got to go to the hospital, don't you worry about the horses. Vic'll do all the coaching."

"Thanks." She turned toward her truck.

As she climbed in, Albert said, "We'll get through this."

"No, no, we won't. Not this time."

"Child'll be fine, you'll see. I got faith."

"I hope you're right, but even if she's fine tomorrow the damage is done. Mike'll never trust her here again and he'll never be able to look me in the face again without seeing the woman who damn near killed his kid."

"He's not that kind of man, child. He loves you."

"He did. Not anymore."

CHAPTER NINETEEN

VIC MET LIZ at the door of her cottage. Liz hugged the dogs to avoid Vic's questions. Their welcome nearly broke her.

"Come in here and talk," Vic said.

Liz told her everything, including a description of Mike's strange despair.

"Not your fault," Vic told her.

"Of course it is!" Liz wailed. "What do I know about life-threatening diseases and the havoc they leave behind? I should have trusted Mike to know how to look after his own daughter." She raised a stricken face to her aunt. "But she was so miserably unhappy before. I wanted to fix things. Oh, boy, did I fix things."

"Stop that. You'll get hysterical. You're out on your feet. Lord knows what your blood sugar level is."

Liz shook her off and began to pace. As she walked by the cage in the corner, Jacko said sleepily, "What a jerk."

Liz began to laugh. She tried to stop, but she couldn't get her breath.

"Liz, stop it this instant before I smack you across the face like in one of those old B-movies."

Liz gulped and began to heave.

"And if you're going to throw up, at least make it to the bathroom."

She did, but barely. Fifteen minutes later she half

staggered out of the bathroom, her face clear of the last
vestiges of makeup and looking gray despite her tan.

Vic handed her a steaming cup of hot chocolate. "I
know it's hot outside, but the air-conditioning's on in
here and you need the warmth. And the sugar. Sit
down."

Liz sat, blew on the chocolate and obediently took
a sip. It tasted bitter. She leaned her head back against
the sofa, closed her eyes and propped her booted feet
on the coffee table. A moment later she felt Vic's fingers tugging at the heel of her left boot. "Don't bother
with those," she said. "I'll do it later."

"You've had these things on since five this morning.
Shut up."

Liz's feet did feel considerably better released from
prison. It was as though her restored circulation finally
reached her brain. "Vic, I'm so sorry about the grand
prix."

"You are, are you?" Vic said, sinking into the worn
club chair on the other side of the coffee table.

"And about leaving you with the horses. I just
couldn't…"

"It's okay," Vic said softly.

Something in her voice brought Liz's head up.
"What?" she said.

"I know you're in no mood to hear good news."

"I would kill for some good news right now."

Vic grinned. "Then how's this?" She reached into
her jeans pocket and pulled out a slip of paper, un-
folded it and waved it in front of Liz's astonished eyes.
"We won!"

"Huh?" Liz leaned forward and read a five and
three zeros, a period and two more. "How? Who?"

"It was the damnedest thing. You ran off, and Angie

said she'd ride Trusty. Just so we wouldn't lose the entry fee, you know. I mean even sixth place paid six hundred and fifty dollars, so we wouldn't have lost any money unless we went seventh or worse. It was a good gamble.''

"Angie's never ridden a horse like Trusty in her life.''

"She has now. Those two acted as though they'd been a team since Trusty was foaled. I've never seen a horse look after somebody like that. It was amazing.''

"I'll say. He never looked after anybody but himself when I was riding him.''

"That's the other thing.'' Vic spread her hands. "Promise you won't be jealous?''

"Jealous? Of Angie's winning us five thousand big ones? Are you crazy?''

"And wouldn't take a penny of it. Called it payment for running off and leaving us.''

"She's truly a sweetheart. I'm not jealous.''

"Even when I tell you she offered us seventy-five thousand dollars for Trusty? Made Kevin write me another check—'' Vic pulled a second slip of paper out of her jeans ''—for another five thou as earnest money. Didn't even want a vet check. Said she trusted us.''

"She'll have a vet check and like it,'' Liz said. "Complete physical, X rays, the works. And if anything shows up, she gets her money back.''

"Of course. But it won't, Liz. You and I both know Trusty is one hundred percent perfect.'' Vic's eyes were shining. "Do we take it? I mean, he's not just my horse, we're partners.''

"Do we take it? Are you crazy? Of course we take it.'' Liz grabbed Vic's hands. "Take that, Rachelle, with your offers of selling off just a few acres here and a few acres there.'' Then her face crumbled. ''Oh, God, Vic, how could I forget even for a second? I may have killed that child.''

MIKE ADJUSTED his shoulders and legs on the hard benches of the waiting room as he'd adjusted them far too many times in that other waiting room. He pillowed his head on his folded jacket. He tried to feel something, anything. Nothing would come.

Irony at work. His daughter wins her first class, he publicly admits his love for Liz Matthews, and less than five minutes later he's racing to the hospital with his sick child. Did this sort of thing happen to everyone, or had he been singled out? He felt as though he were trapped in a computer game with unknown and unseen players manipulating his fate based on the throws of their computerized dice.

And he had no idea what his character—this character that he was portraying—was supposed to do next. If he made the wrong decision, he'd no doubt land himself and the other players in even greater disaster. Every rational decision he made seemed to lead to disaster. For that matter, so did every decision that arose out of his gut feelings. He couldn't seem to do anything right.

Dr. Mortenson said Pat's fever was worrisome, but it could be anything. Not necessarily life-threatening. Not necessarily a relapse.

He didn't think he could live with any more ''not necessarily's.'' He needed some certainty for a change.

So what was certain? He loved his child. Once again she was isolated from him and under sedation. He loved Liz Matthews.

Liz. He had a vague recollection that she'd come to

the hospital, but he couldn't remember what they'd said. She'd left. Had he sent her away? Had he said something hurtful to her out of his own anger at himself? He considered calling her.

No. She was better off out of this mess. Besides, he didn't know anything new about Pat's condition. When he knew, he'd call. He hoped he'd be able to reassure her, but he doubted it.

And if he could not reassure her? If Pat wound up going back to Saint Jude? What then? He would never be able to risk Pat's health at ValleyCrest again. He would be the monster he swore he wouldn't be. Another child would ride Traveller.

He could never ask Liz to share his sterile world. She'd die in that hideous apartment. He didn't blame her for Pat's illness. She hadn't any true conception of the possible consequences.

But he knew. Had known all along. He'd ignored his instincts.

Whatever happened, he would not allow Liz to be hurt any more deeply than she had been. He didn't know how he'd fix any of this. And at the moment he was too tired to try. He didn't think he'd ever be able to sleep again. As if denying him even that small control, his body dropped him deeply into sleep at almost that exact moment.

"FEVER'S DOWN," Dr. Mortenson said. He peered down at Mike with a slight smile on his face.

Mike heart leaped. He dragged his hand down his face, sat up and rubbed his eyes. His bones ached. His neck felt as though it had been wrenched in a vise. But if Pat's fever really was down, he felt like a million bucks.

Mortenson's next words disabused him. "Not all the way down, you understand. But manageable now, one hundred and two."

"Can I see her?"

The doctor shook his head. "She's still isolated. Just a precaution. Don't want her catching anything else, and hospitals are notoriously bad places to be sick in." He grinned.

Mike didn't respond. "When can I see her?"

"Maybe this afternoon. At the moment she's knocked out like a flounder. We've got her on some stuff. Broad-spectrum antibiotic to be on the safe side."

"Blood tests?" Mike held his breath.

The doctor shook his head. "Mike, you know the medical establishment better than that. Lab work on Sunday? Get real."

"Push it through."

"No can do. Hey, another twenty-four hours is going to make no difference. In the meantime, the fever may go away of its own accord."

"And the lymph nodes?"

"Could be anything. They're dust catchers for every germ around."

"You know the anything it could be."

"I know." The doctor sobered. "Look, I'm not taking this lightly, Mike. But I'm not getting bent out of shape, either."

"Should I get a private duty nurse?"

"Not necessary. All she's going to do is sleep. Hey, I'm an optimist. Pat's a tough little girl. She's gotten this far. She'll get the rest of the way. Trust me."

"What choice do I have?"

"Yeah. Well. In the meantime, you look like hell. Go home, shave, clean up, get a few hours' sleep and some food in you and come back. By then maybe you'll be able to see her.''

"I'll stay."

"The hell you will. You're a scary sight even for me. Think how you'll look to her. I don't want her upset. Go home. Doctor's orders." He moved away and said over his shoulder, "Oh, and don't get picked up for vagrancy on the way to your car."

Mike considered trying to sneak by the nurses. Pat was not in an ICU environment where there were glass windows across her room and where she was monitored by machine and human beings every moment. There was no way to stand outside her room and look in.

If he couldn't get into her room, he might as well be at home. The last thing he wanted her to see was a father who looked the way he did at the moment. The doctor was right. He'd come back looking fresh and upbeat, as though Pat had some little nothing virus that would be over quickly and leave no ill effects. He didn't believe that for a minute, but somehow he had to make her believe it.

He spoke to the nurses briefly, asked them to check on Pat, turned and left. In his car his hand lingered on the car phone. Liz would be at the horse show by now, unreachable by phone, and he didn't think he could face all those solicitous and curious people he knew from the barn. She had a job to do. It would be kinder if he simply backed off and let her do it. He'd call her this evening to give her an update after he'd seen Pat.

Or maybe ask Mrs. H. to do it. He didn't think he could bear to hear Liz's voice. He'd had such a short time to glory in loving her before it all turned sour. Now he could never get it back. His fault. All his. As if to punctuate his thoughts, he heard the first rumble of thunder from across the river to the west. He glanced up, surprised that he'd paid no attention to the weather.

He should have. He'd been told again and again that although the city was not in an actual tornado alley, weather fronts did spawn tornadoes and massive destructive thunderstorms. The longer the hot, dry spell, the worse the break in it. The city had been without a major cold front for nearly six weeks. Liz had told him the show should end early this afternoon. Surely the steward would have sense enough to shut down and send everyone to cover should the weather get really bad.

He nearly drove through a red light and almost hit the car to his left. He raised his hand in apology. Clearly, he was more exhausted and distracted than he thought.

Mrs. H. opened the apartment door to him before he could turn the key in the lock.

"How is she?" Mrs. H. asked. She looked terrible. Walter stood up and came toward him to stand behind her as though protecting her from Mike.

"Fever's down some. I can't see her until late this afternoon. Dr. Mortenson's sent me home to shower and shave and get some sleep."

"Have you had anything to eat?" Mrs. H. asked as she headed toward the kitchen.

"Thank you, Mrs. H., I'm not hungry."

"Eat something, please." She sounded plaintive.

"Maybe later. You and Walter going to church?"

"We're going down to the hospital," Walter said.

"Nothing you can do."

"Can't tell Melba that. She says she'll sit in that waiting room and wait all day if she has to."

"Thanks, Mrs. H., but—"

"Save your breath, Michael Whitten. I won't be comfortable anywhere else. So you just take your shower and get some rest. I'll call you if anything breaks before you get there." Mrs. H. picked up her handbag. Walter put a hand on her shoulder in a possessive gesture. "Oh, did you call Liz Matthews? Tell her how Pat is?"

Mike shook his head.

"Why ever not? She was frantic last night at the hospital."

"I know. I'm sorry." He turned away.

"Call her. If you don't, I will."

"She's at the horse show. I can't get her. I'll call her later."

"You promise?"

"Of course."

"She's blaming herself for all of this, you know," Mrs. H. said.

Mike looked at her in genuine puzzlement. "I wouldn't want her to think anyone blames her for any of this."

"She blames herself because she didn't listen to you."

"That's stupid. I promise I'll talk to her. Just go on, Mrs. H."

She took one look at his face, shook her head and left, hanging on to Walter's arm and hugging herself close to his spare frame.

Mike walked into Pat's room and saw it for the first time as Liz had described it to him. As sterile as a prison. Too neat. How would he balance Pat's need for a little healthy chaos with his need to keep her healthy?

His head was pounding. He walked back into the

living room and his eyes caught the flash of color from Sandi's portrait.

He stared up into her face. He still loved her, but looking at her portrait, he felt as though he were looking at the picture of some strange woman from another era, a portrait of someone he had never known and could appreciate only for its artistic value. He could see Pat's eyes in her eyes, however, and the way Pat tilted her head when she wanted to wheedle something out of him.

Suddenly everything crashed in on him. He walked into his bedroom and fell facedown on the bed without even taking off his loafers. He longed to have Liz's warm body to cradle in his arms. He'd never have her close to him again.

He recognized his need for sleep as escape. Even in the darkest days of Pat's illness he had always been able to sleep. That ability to recharge his batteries had preserved his sanity. He rolled over and stared at the ceiling for a long time. This was a man who had forgotten how to cope with disaster when he had opened his life to love. Finally he drifted into sleep.

The ringing of the bedside telephone woke him. He shook himself groggily and stared out through the blinds. Surely he couldn't have slept until dark, yet the sky outside was a solid blanket of near blackness. He cleared his throat and answered the phone.

"Mr. Whitten?"

He came fully awake in an instant. The voice was Mrs. H.'s and she sounded frightened.

"Melba?" He had never used her given name before.

"Oh, Michael, it's Pat."

His heart stopped beating.

"She's run away."

"I beg your pardon?"

"They took her IV off this morning, and sometime later she got her riding clothes out of the cupboard and snuck out."

"How could she do that? Wasn't anyone checking on her?"

"The nurses were letting her sleep. And there was a shift change. Sometime between eleven and a few minutes ago she just walked out."

Mike glanced at his watch. "That's four hours. My God, she could be anywhere."

"I know." Melba began to cry. "She still had fever, Mr. Whitten. She must have been groggy from the medication. She's not thinking straight."

"She didn't have her purse with her. She couldn't take a cab anywhere. She must still be in the hospital."

"She had two twenty-dollar bills in the fob pocket of her riding britches," Melba wailed. "I gave them to her. She wanted to buy a present for you and Liz at the horse-show shops. Oh, Mike, what have I done?"

He sat on the edge of the bed. "Calm down, Melba. Are they checking the hospital?"

"Yes. Roof to basement. Nobody's seen a child in riding gear. Should we call the police?"

"Not yet. Look, if she's delirious she may have taken a cab back to the showgrounds to check on Traveller. Call the horse-show office. Alert them. Tell them to page Vic and Liz. Get people hunting for her. If you can't get Liz or Vic, get Albert. He'll find her if anybody can."

"All right. Are you coming down here?"

"No. She may be on her way home. I have to stay here and wait for her. I'll call her friends. Hell, I don't know her friends. Except for the horse-camp kids and they're all at the show with Liz and Vic.''

"Call the headmaster. He'll have a list of her classmates and their phone numbers.''

"Good thinking, Melba. He can fax them to me here and I'll start calling. My God, why would she do a thing like that?''

He heard noise in the background. He recognized Walter's voice and several others, male and female. "Melba, what's going on?''

"Wait!" Melba said. He heard the chatter in the background again, and then Melba came on the line. "One of the nurses found something, Mike. It's a letter. It's addressed to you. It's in Pat's handwriting.''

Mike took a deep breath. "Of course. She's telling me where she's gone so I can come get her. Open it.''

"Mike, are you sure you want me to?''

"Open it, Melba. Read it to me.''

He heard the sound of paper tearing, then silence. Then a muffled sob.

"Melba! Melba! For God's sake, woman!" He began to beat on his thigh. Pat was delirious, frightened, disoriented, afraid, as he was, that her disease had returned. Surely she wouldn't have done anything crazy?

"Mike, I don't think…''

"Melba, read the damned letter.''

"Yes. All right. It says, 'Dear Daddy, please don't try to find me and don't worry. I'll be fine. I have a plan. I've been so happy I can't stand going back to before. I can't face all that stuff again. Please don't blame Liz. You always hunt for somebody to blame when it's nobody's fault. Stuff just happens to some people. You and Liz need each other. I know you love her and I know she loves you. So please hold on to each other, Daddy. I love you.'"

"Dear God."

"You don't think she'd hurt herself, do you?"

"I don't know." He dropped his head in his hands for a moment, then raised his head. "No, dammit, I don't. She's not a coward and she's not a quitter. She means what she says. She's planning to face whatever's coming to her alone. She's doing this to get out of my way, mine and Liz's. Dear God, how could she be so wrong?"

"She's twelve years old, Mike. She's feverish and she thinks she's dying and she thinks she's being gallant. Oh, Mike, she could be anywhere!"

"No, she couldn't. She's going to be where she can be happy. And that means she's going to ValleyCrest."

Suddenly a crash of thunder exploded close enough to rattle the windows of the apartment. Mike turned in time to catch a second flash breaking the sky to the west sideways like an egg.

"Melba?" he said into the telephone just as the lights went out. A moment later he heard only a dial tone.

CHAPTER TWENTY

LIZ DREAMED she was awake. She knew something was out of kilter, but she couldn't seem to get a handle on it. She was trapped in the middle of a battle somewhere. All the people she knew were being bombarded and she couldn't get through the machine-gun fire to rescue them. Finally, she managed to struggle up from the depths of sleep and open her eyes.

At least the bombardment was real. Thunder rumbled in an almost-continuous volley. All four dogs were pressed tight against her body. She scratched the nearest head, which happened to be basset. They were well-trained. They knew where they belonged in a thunderstorm.

Another rumble. Her shoulders hunched. Her mouth tasted like the bottom of Jacko's cage. She lay back and felt all of it flood back into her consciousness.

"Pat!" she said and shoved the Labrador out of the way so that she could stand up. Why on earth hadn't somebody called her? Melba would have called even if Mike had forbidden it.

She caught herself on the nightstand. Whew. She must have been more tired than she realized to have slept all day. A crisp rattle like snare drums made her jump. The clock on the bedside table read 1:00 p.m. She frowned. So dark? She wandered out to the living room and saw that the light on the answering machine was blinking furiously. One message. She hit the play-back and heard Vic's voice, "Liz, forgive me. I put a sleeping pill in your hot chocolate and turned off the ringer on the phone. Thought you needed the sleep. I'm at the show. No word on Pat. Go to the hospital. Don't worry about us."

Liz slumped onto the couch. Sleeping pill? No wonder she felt so groggy. Vic had never done anything that sneaky before. She must really have been worried. She looked up the number for the hospital and called the pediatrics floor. Pat was "progressing nicely." Whatever that meant. No, Mr. Whitten was not in the hospital.

Liz dialed Mike's number but hung up before the phone began to ring. If he was home and asleep, the last thing she wanted was to wake him. If he was home and awake, she didn't think he'd want to talk to her.

She let the dogs out and left the front door open so they could get back in, then she climbed into the shower, scrubbed fiercely, dressed in jeans and pad-dock boots, picked up her purse and drove down by the barn. The sky was a filthy smegma green-gray. The trees bent almost double in the hot wind.

She turned on her truck radio to catch an announcer giving details of thunderstorm watches and tornado warnings. Lovely. Guaranteed to make the horses act even crazier on the course than usual. Vic and Albert would have their hands full at the show. She'd have to stop by to give them a hand on her way to the hospital.

Her stomach rumbled nearly as loud as the thunder. She'd had nothing but that drugged hot chocolate since the cold cheeseburger she'd wolfed down ringside at midafternoon yesterday. She'd pick up fast food in a drive-through on her way downtown.

She climbed out of the truck. Her legs were no longer wobbly, but she still felt alienated, as though there were a sheet of glass between her and the rest of the world. It was like having a hangover without having enjoyed the party the night before.

Kenny met her at the door. "Got all the stable horses in, Liz," he said, falling into step beside her. "Barn's clean."

"That's fast. How long have you been here?"

"Only half an hour or so. Uncle Albert said he'd feed and water this morning. He just needed me to pick the stalls and refill the water buckets."

"Right."

"Can I go on home? This storm's going to be bad. My mama hates storms."

"Don't we all? Sure, Kenny. Thanks for checking on stuff."

The young man turned away, then hesitated. "Oh. Almost forgot. When I got here this morning I found this on the floor outside the office. Guess it blew down." He handed Liz a folded sheet of paper with a piece of cellophane tape along its edge.

"Thanks."

"Sure. Bye. Hope they cancel the show and get home before this hits."

"Me, too." Liz opened the sheet of paper. Probably a bill. She read the first lines and caught her breath. "Oh, no. No. You wouldn't." She sank onto the nearest tack trunk.

Liz dived for the office and snatched the telephone off the hook. She knew the number of the horse-show office by heart. "Come on, come on!" She tapped the note impatiently on the desk while the phone rang and rang unanswered. Finally a voice said, "Horse-show office." It sounded frazzled.

"Hey. This is Liz Matthews. Could you page Victoria Jamerson for me? It's an emergency."

"We've got our own emergency, Liz. Show's been canceled. I think I saw Vic and Albert loading up to go home earlier, but I really don't know."

Liz heard a noise in the background.

"Oh, Lord! Liz, one of the tents just blew down. We've got horses loose. Bye." The line went dead.

Liz knew she couldn't wait any longer. With every moment Pat and Traveller were riding farther away.

But where were they going? They'd have to be traveling east. There was nothing to the west but a big city and a very wide river. And Pat had written that she was going to look for jobs cleaning barns.

The new interstate was Liz's best guess. Had to be. Ran not three hundred yards beyond the back pasture fence of ValleyCrest. And on Sunday there wouldn't be a soul working on it.

Liz raced to her truck, unplugged her cellular phone and stuck it in the pocket of her shirt. She prayed the thing was fully charged, because it would be her only lifeline out on that road.

Her truck would never make it through the mud once the rain started. She had to do what Pat did, take a horse. Only she could ride faster than Pat ever could. Piece of cake! She'd have them all home and safe before the first raindrop hit the ground.

On who? Trusty? Hardly. Most of the other horses were at the show.

She closed her eyes. There was only one that was appropriate. Her absolutely least favorite mare, Squirrel.

Squirrel was furious at being rousted out of her cozy stall in the middle of a squally afternoon. Liz tacked her up, packed her up and started to unhook her from the wash rack to mount.

She stopped. She could at least leave Vic a note. She raced to the office, stuck Pat's note under a brass horse-head paperweight, added a note of her own saying that she'd gone after Pat, had taken the cellular phone and would be back with Pat safe and sound before dark. As an afterthought she added, "Tell Mike not to worry."

She was halfway down the pasture before she remembered she hadn't said precisely where she was heading. She considered going back. Nah. She'd be home before anyone would be overly concerned. How far could a delirious twelve-year-old girl and a green pony get, anyway?

CHAPTER TWENTY-ONE

VIC AND ALBERT were opening the doors of the six-horse van in the ValleyCrest parking area as Mike pulled in behind them.

"Where's Liz?" Mike shouted over the din of the downpour on the metal roof of the barn.

"Don't know," Vic shouted back. "Got to be around here somewhere. Her truck's over there. How's Pat?"

Mike ignored her, ran into the barn in a crash of thunder and a slashing rain. His shouts for Liz reverberated.

"Leave the horses, Albert," Vic said, ducking her head against the storm. "They're dry in the trailer for the moment. I've got to see about Mike."

Albert nodded and followed her inside. He flicked the switch to turn on the lights in the aisle, then flicked it again. "Electricity's out," he grumbled. "Figures."

"She's not here," Mike said. He dashed the rain out of his eyes and swept his hand over his short hair. "She wouldn't have walked up to the house. Not in this."

"What is it, Mike? What's the matter? Is it Pat?" Vic tugged at his arm and turned him to face her. He looked distracted, frantic.

"She's gone. I was sure she'd come here. Maybe Liz took her up to the house to get warm."

"I'll call. What do you mean she's gone?" Vic

walked into the office, reached for the phone and saw the note prominently displayed under the paperweight. She slipped both it and the sheet behind it, read first one then the other. "My Lord," she said, and sat down hard in the chair. She handed Mike the notes without a word.

His gaze flicked quickly down both pages, then convulsively he crumbled both sheets in his fists. "They're both crazy."

A flash of lightning illuminated the dingy office, followed almost instantly by a huge crack of thunder.

Vic jumped. "That was close. Too close."

"We've got to go after them."

"Where? How? We don't know where they went."

At least two sets of tires screeched in the parking lot. Mike raced to the door as Angie slid out of her Cherokee while Mrs. H. and Walter opened their doors and ran toward the shelter of the barn. "We heard at the show," Angie said. "Kevin's on his way over. The Simpsons and the Jessups and the Morehouses aren't far behind. Have you called the sheriff's office yet?"

"I'm about to," Mike said.

"Okay, Albert and I will unload and get the horses taken care of. You talk to the sheriff." Angie glanced over her shoulder. "Here's Kevin. He's hopeless on top of a horse, but he can handle them on the ground in a pinch."

Mike turned back to Vic, who was busily dialing the telephone repeatedly. "That stupid computer keeps saying the cellular customer I want is not answering or some fool thing," Vic said. The eyes she turned to Mike were brimming with tears. "She can't be out of range. Why oh why didn't she leave us at least the direction she went and the time she left?"

"God knows."

"I know," Vic wailed. "It's all my fault. I gave her a sleeping pill last night so she'd sleep. She's probably as groggy as Pat is." She jumped at another peal of thunder. At that moment the heavens opened. The rain no longer blew, it poured straight down. Water ran off the eaves and pelted the parking lot as though the whole place were sitting under a waterfall.

"Hope they've found some shelter," Kevin said as he walked by holding Wishbone's halter. Another crack of thunder. "But not under a tree. Those things are lightning rods."

Mike took the phone from Vic and called information for the closest sheriff's substation. By the time a voice answered, he could barely hear over the roar of the rain on the roof. And the man at the other end could barely hear him. He kept having to repeat himself. Finally he managed to get through to someone with more or less good sense, but when he explained the situation, the man answered apologetically.

"Sorry, sir. We've got our hands full. Trees down all over. We're pulling people out of flash floods. We've had four cars float away on the bypass. And we've got a report of a tornado touching down west of Macon. I don't have the manpower to mount a search and rescue. You don't even know for sure they need rescuing."

"Hell, man, of course they need rescuing!" Mike snapped. "They're out there somewhere—a woman and a twelve-year-old girl on a pair of horses."

"Listen, sir. After this blows through in a couple of hours if we're lucky, maybe we can break a couple of guys loose to help you. In the meantime, sit tight and don't add to the problem, okay?"

"I can't sit here and do nothing!" Mike nearly screamed.

"Best thing you could do, sir. We don't want to have to rescue you, too."

Mike was about to mount a scathing reply when he heard noise from the other end and the man came back on the line.

"Sorry, sir, we've got live power lines down across Cayce Road. Fire department's on its way, but we've got some people trapped in their vehicles." He hung up.

Mike turned to see the doorway filled with people all looking at him solemnly. He took a grip on his emotions and told them as carefully as he could what he'd learned.

"We'll look," Angie said. "Vic, you man the phones. We've all got cellulars. We'll head in different directions. We'll find them."

Mike opened his mouth to answer her and heard the stillness snap shut around him like a vacuum. Suddenly the horses went crazy in their stalls, stamping, screaming, lashing out at the wooden walls.

"What the hell?" Kevin said. "What's got into them?"

Machine guns answered him. "Hail," Vic said. "Oh, damn. It's hail. We've got to get to some shelter, people. That could mean a tornado's coming."

Mike simply gawked at her. A tornado. It figured.

"Git in the feed room," Albert said, and grabbed Angie's arm. "Git, y'all. Git now." Everyone but Mike broke and ran. Vic started toward the feed room, stopped, turned and grabbed his arm. "Come on, Mike."

Albert shoved everyone into the feed room, shut the

door and pulled a couple of hundred-pound bags of feed against it. "This room's built out of concrete blocks," he said. "The roof's solid and braced to hold the weight of all that hay and keep the rats out. Ought to hold up unless we get a direct hit."

"What about the horses?" Vic demanded.

"Can't worry about the horses now. Hunker down, Vic. Right now. I mean it."

Kevin grabbed Angie and pulled her into his arms. She huddled against him. Albert shoved Vic into a corner behind the feed sacks. He started to do the same to Mike, but Mike reacted more quickly and shoved him first. In silence they listened to the rattle of the hail, the sough of the wind, and then everything went silent once more.

Albert stood up. "Whatever it was, it passed us by. Listen to the horses."

"I don't hear anything," Mike said.

"Right."

They came out of their improvised bunker to find the horses once more munching hay unconcernedly in their stalls. The rain had become just that—rain. Water ran down the aisles where the force of the wind had driven it over the tops of the stable doors. Otherwise there seemed to be no damage.

They all felt the change in pressure. The temperature had dropped from ninety-five to sixty-five in less then ten minutes. The front had passed.

"Now we've got to find them," Mike said. "Even if they haven't been hurt, they're bound to be wet. In this temperature they could get hypothermia if they stay out too long in the wind."

"Okay. Everybody. Let's go play hide-and-seek," Angie said. "Which way, Mike?"

"Let Vic give you directions. I don't know the area that well." He headed for the office. "Now the sheriff's got to give me some help." He picked up the telephone. "Dead. Lines must be down." He reached in his sodden pocket for his cell phone and turned on the power button. The flickering sign read no srvs. "Hell, one of the cells must be out too."

The sound of a siren coming up the driveway made them all rush to the front door. A sheriff's car ground to a halt and a man in a brown uniform slid out. "Thank God," Mike said and went forward with his hand extended. "You did come."

"Sir?" the deputy said. "I've come for Dr. Kevin Womack. We were told he was here."

"Right here," Kevin stepped forward.

"Great. Doctor, you've got a couple of women in labor and the hospital's lost power and phone service. They're operating off the emergency power in their auxiliary truck. Plus we've got some injuries from the storm. We're bringing in every doctor we can find. Your service said we could find you here."

Kevin turned to look at Angie. She huddled close to Albert with her arms hugged across her chest. Mike watched her square her shoulders, put a smile on her face and run to her husband. "Go on, honey," she said. "I'll stay here until we find them."

"Ange, if you want me to stay…"

She shook her head. "Nah. You got babies to deliver and cuts to suture. You do remember how to sew up a cut, don't you?"

Kevin grinned. "Yeah, vaguely."

"Uh, Doctor, you'd better get what you need and come with me. We're restricting traffic where we can. Trees down all over. I've got a radio."

"The hospital will have what I need. Okay, let's go." Kevin reached an arm around his wife's waist, hugged her and kissed her passionately.

Then he ducked into the passenger side of the sheriff's car. The car backed up and drove down the lane with its siren blaring.

THEY PACKED in the search teams at dark, which came early. The air was chill now with the feel of September and autumn. The storm still rumbled and sent shock waves of lightning that lit the sky far to the east, but it had left the earth scoured clean and shining. By eight in the evening the night sky shone with a million stars and a new moon clearly cradled in the old moon's arms. Mike wished he could hold Pat and Liz in his.

The power came back on just before seven, and by nine Mike's cellular phone was working, although he was unable to get in touch with Liz. Janey's parents had gone home after searching for three hours. He'd sent the Simpsons and the Jessups home shortly thereafter.

Kevin had called from the hospital a dozen times to say that he had everyone in all the trauma centers checking to see whether anyone matching Liz's or Pat's descriptions had been brought in.

Mrs. H. and Walter worked the phones in Mike's apartment until Mike told them to switch the barn phones to ring in Liz's house. They picked up burgers and fries for everyone on their way out.

Mike couldn't eat, but stalked around inside and out, speaking to no one. The bad times were always like this. Powerless. Waiting. Unable to influence the outcome or even to know what was going on with the people he loved. For a man who dedicated his life to action, to control, to bullying his way into a powerful position in every situation, this was worse than hell.

The others gathered around Vic's big dining-room table in her ramshackle old house. He sat alone on the front steps of Liz's cottage. Alone, that is, except for the dogs. One "What a jerk" had earned the parrot a covered cage. Mike didn't need any reinforcement. He knew he was a jerk.

Liz had warned him that sooner or later Pat would run away from him. She hadn't warned him that she'd run after her.

He prayed a good deal, and most of his prayers were in the nature of bargains. Finally, he gave up offering alternatives to God. He began to make promises to himself. *I've got to stand aside and let them choose, even if the choices tear me up inside. If we get through this, I'll try to make them happy the way they want to be made happy, and not the way I choose to give them happiness.*

When the phone rang at ten, he fell over three dogs before he reached it. "Liz?"

"Sorry, Mike. This is Jake Mortenson. Any news about Pat?"

Mike sat. "Not so far."

"Look, I feel so bad about this."

"Yeah. Not your fault."

"We never dreamed she was faking. She must have been awake for hours planning this thing. She was probably not feeling too swift, but she's not out of her head or anything."

"That's good news? That your damned hospital didn't even monitor her properly?"

"Look, can we talk about that later? I called with some good news."

"Good news?"

"Right. I pulled strings. Pushed the lab work through, Sunday, thunderstorms, tornadoes and all. It's not a recurrence, Mike."

Mike sat down hard on the telephone chair. "Then what?"

"Your kid has a particularly nasty case of chicken pox. And if we'd waited until tomorrow morning, I promise you it would have been very evident. By now she's probably broken out in spots."

"Chicken pox?" He began to laugh.

"Uh-huh. At her age and with her background it could be serious. I don't think so, but the minute you find her she's got to come back to the hospital. Chicken pox in the eyes can be very dangerous."

"But treatable?"

"Absolutely."

"Chicken pox. God, I've never heard more beautiful words in my life!"

"Then hear this, my friend. You did the right thing to bring her in. Her fever with her history was damned scary. But Mike, you can't go through life like this. She can't. It's not healthy for either of you."

"Yeah. I'm discovering that."

"Okay. Bring her in tomorrow morning. We'll treat her symptoms and send her home with a bucket of calamine lotion."

"I hope by tomorrow morning chicken pox is the only thing I have to worry about."

"Keep the faith. It's about time you did." The doctor rang off.

Mike sat in the darkened living room for a long time. He didn't cry. He was too wiped out to cry. They were only halfway home. Somewhere out there were two females that meant more to him than life, and a pair of horses who deserved better. He reached for the phone and buzzed Vic's extension to tell her and the others the news. He heard the whoops of joy down the line.

"Tell everyone to go home," he said wearily. "Tomorrow morning, if we haven't heard from them, I'll hire an army if I have to."

Angie came on the line. "Listen, Mike, Liz is one sensible cookie. She'll be all right and she'll make certain Pat is fine as well."

"Sure she will," Mike said, trying to infuse his words with a confidence he didn't feel. "Now go home to Kevin where you belong. Oh, and Angie. Thanks."

LIZ URGED Squirrel into a full gallop as soon as the horse's muscles had warmed. She'd found pony tracks at the start of the trail into the back pasture, and knew for certain that she'd figured out Pat's course. Behind that pasture lay the new road.

The crazy kid was headed for parts unknown with a high fever and a green pony. The first raindrops splashed on the dust at Liz's feet. Within five minutes she cursed herself roundly for not wearing her racing goggles. She had to dash the water off her eyelashes continually. She had no idea where Pat would have jumped the pasture fence to get onto the right-of-way that bordered the new road. The child had never jumped any fence higher than eighteen inches. The pasture fence was four feet. She prayed she wouldn't find Pat lying in a heap.

Of course she wouldn't. If Pat had fallen, Traveller would have come back to the barn like any sensible horse. Unless she'd fallen on the far side.

Liz wasted precious minutes cantering along the

fence line to be certain that Pat had not fallen into a patch of weeds or worse. At last she saw hoofprints already filling with water. Somehow Pat and her green pony had jumped that fence. She shook her head. Crazy kid! But it proved both pony and rider had guts.

She turned along the right-of-way toward the slope of what would be the access road to the interstate. She had to slow Squirrel on her way up the incline. The clay-based mud had already begun to turn slippery.

Around every curve, over every rise she expected to glimpse Pat and Traveller. With every step farther away from ValleyCrest, with every clap of thunder, she grew more worried and more frightened. Out in the open she was an invitation to the lightning. She had no desire to wind up frying either herself or her horse. She shivered in her windbreaker and knew that it wasn't from cold, but fear. "Bother!" she snapped, and turned her face up to the sky. "Couldn't You make it just a little easier?"

She and Squirrel both jumped at the answering thunderclap. "Fine," she said, and pushed Squirrel to a canter.

If this blasted storm was her penance, it was a doozy. She'd never felt more alone or abandoned in her life. Even in the worst moments of her life she'd had Vic or Albert to offer her a modicum of protection. Now she didn't have either of them, and obviously she didn't have Mike. He hadn't even bothered to call to update her on Pat's condition.

She was relegated to the position of ex–Whitten's Wench, like Rachelle and all the others. Strange that she'd feared just that—the public humiliation of being known as an ex-girlfriend. Now she didn't give a damn what people thought of her relationship with Mike.

What mattered was that she'd loved Mike with her whole soul, and had lost him by her own stupidity. And might lose Pat. She'd endure any amount of humiliation, let the gossipmongers have a field day if only she could find Pat safe and bring her home to Mike in one piece. She would have to be content to know that he had loved her.

For he had felt love. For a few short moments ringside, she'd been sure of his love. Had all those other women been equally certain? She didn't think so. This had been different, if only for a little while.

Not all the water in her eyes came from the heavens. The salt in her tears stung. Once the mare stumbled, but recovered her balance. Liz settled herself more solidly. Wouldn't do Pat a bit of good if they were both lying out here unconscious or hurt.

She felt as though she'd been condemned forever to ride this lonely stretch of mud and concrete, past piles of metal girders and the silent monster earthmovers. Everyone in the world had vanished and left her galloping through a nightmare.

Not quite everyone. She glimpsed a flash of movement by an equipment shed, and slowed Squirrel to a trot. It was Traveller! But where was Pat?

She trotted up to the shed in time to see Pat disappear behind a big earth grader.

"Pat!" she shouted above the din of the rain. She pushed free of her stirrups, leaped out of the saddle, realized she'd forgotten to bring lead lines and halters and looped the soggy leather reins around a metal support pole. Squirrel nickered and danced sideways. Traveller raised his head and answered.

"Pat, I saw you. Neither one of us can run in this slop and I've got both horses."

No answer.

"Come on out here. I'm so tired I can barely stand up." She took a breath. "I've got some of your birthday cake with me. You're bound to be hungry."

Movement. Small but distinct.

"Look, I won't jump you. I've got to get out of this mess. I'm drenched, for Pete's sake. Come on out."

Pat's head surfaced behind the earthmover. "I won't go back."

Liz took a deep breath to keep from screaming, "You will if I have to drag you." That would be counterproductive. Persuasion first. Chains and handcuffs later if need be. "I'll swap some cake for some talk."

Pat walked out. She was spattered with mud from head to toe. Her hard hat hung from her forearm by its chin strap.

"We've got to get these horses farther up under shelter but far enough from those earth thingies so that if they kick out they won't break a leg."

"Yeah."

"I forgot halters and lead ropes. You obviously remembered to bring along stuff for Traveller."

"Yeah. I had a good teacher." Pat cracked a tiny smile. "Aunt Vic."

"Oh, thank you. Just what I need, a comedian."

"I forgot to bring anything to eat, though."

"Hah." Liz inched forward then stopped. "If I come past you, are you going to try to jump on Traveller and run off again?"

Pat shrugged.

"Because I promise you, you do not want to be out in what's coming just behind me." Liz shuddered. "You sure can pick 'em. We've got tornadoes and thunderstorms hitting all around us."

"We do? The sky was kind of yellow when I left. I thought it looked weird."

"Understatement. Okay. Look, There's some light cable on that earthmover behind the shed. If we can stretch it across to that stanchion and hook it around, we can make kind of a corral for the horses. You feel like giving it a try?" Then Liz realized she was talking to a child with fever. "Never mind. I can do it."

"It's okay, Liz," Pat said kindly. "I'm not dying. Yet."

Liz caught her breath. "Right. Okay. Heave-ho."

It wasn't as easy as it looked, but after half an hour or so of labor, they had managed to wire off an area about twenty feet by ten. Liz led each horse inside it, stripped off saddles and bridles, tied Traveller to a stanchion by his halter and Squirrel across from his—safely out of kicking distance—by her bridle.

"Okay. Cake." Liz said and sat down on her saddle. She split the now-damp cake with Pat and handed her a flask of water. "Now talk. You have any idea how terrified you have everybody?"

"My daddy?"

"For starters."

Pat leaned back against the earthmover. "I know. I guess I was kind of crazy. I mean, nobody's going to hire me to work in their barn. And my daddy'll have the FBI on my tail by now."

"Again, for starters. So why'd you do it?"

Pat's jaw set in a solid line again. "I won't go through that stuff again. I just won't. I'd rather die."

"One, you don't know you're going to have to go through anything."

Pat sniffed in annoyance.

"Two, you've got too much living to do to think about dying at this point."

Pat sat silent for a moment, then she turned to Liz. "You ever been bald?"

"I beg your pardon?"

"Bald. Skinhead."

"Uh, no."

"You've got that great hair, you know. And if I have to go through all that stuff again, even if it works, which it probably won't this time, I'll go bald again. No eyebrows or eyelashes, either. I won't do it."

Liz sat silent for a long moment. "Point taken. Okay, I'll make you a deal."

"What kind?"

"I know your father is going to want you to stay away from ValleyCrest..."

Pat wailed.

Liz held up her hands. "Wait. Hear me out. And away from me probably. I mean, this is all my fault, after all."

"No it isn't."

"That's not the way Mike will see it, and it's not the way I see it, either. Anyway, that doesn't affect the deal I'm offering."

"So, go on already. What deal?"

"You come back with me as soon as we can get out of here." As if to punctuate her statement, the heavens opened and rain began to drive all the way to where they sat.

"Yuck!" Pat said, picked up her saddle and slipped back into the corner. Liz followed.

"As I was saying, you come back, you do what they want you to do."

"What a great deal. I can hardly wait."

"You haven't heard my side yet, miss," Liz said. "The first clump of hair you lose, I shave my head, and I keep it shaved until yours grows back." Liz said back, horrified at what she'd offered. Pat was right, for a woman, bald was no joke. Liz's hair was her only good feature. But it was only hair, for pity's sake. Life mattered, not hair.

Pat gaped at her. "You'd do that?"

"Absolutely."

Pat stood and walked around to check on Traveller and Squirrel. She hunched her shoulders and wrapped her arms around herself.

Liz watched her. "You've still got fever."

"I'm okay. I got here, didn't I? I mean, I wasn't too sick to ride or anything."

"Just too sick to think clearly. All right, I've made my offer. What about it? I shave my head when you lose your hair."

Pat nodded. "Deal."

Liz closed her eyes. "Done." She sat up. "I've got to call Vic and your father." She dug her cellular out of her shirt pocket, turned it on and after a moment snapped it shut. "No service. Bother."

"Can we just go? We can call on the way."

"We have to wait until this storm passes. Then, if I can't reach anybody on the cell phone, I'll ride home and drive the pickup back to get you."

Pat began to sniffle. "I'm not staying here by myself." She curled on her saddle in the corner. "I'm cold."

Liz laid her hand against Pat's forehead. It felt hot, but not burning. Pat's teeth began to chatter and she closed her eyes. Liz pulled her jacket off and draped it over Pat, then pulled the blanket off the back of her saddle and settled it over Pat as well. Pat sighed and began to relax. After a moment she opened her eyes.

"I don't want to stay here all night," Pat said. "I can ride back, I know I can. I'm not that sick."

So this was what being a parent was all about. Making the decisions without having the answers. The rain was slackening. There was only another hour until dark. Liz had no idea how to get the horses down off the roadbed in daylight, much less in darkness. "You sure you want to try it?" she asked.

Pat threw the blanket off. "I want to go home."

They saddled Traveller and Squirrel, cleaned up their mess, put on their hard hats, mounted and rode out from under the shelter just as the last drop hit the mud at their feet.

"Yuck! This stuff is like glue," Pat said. "We'll have to go really slow."

"It'll take us forever to get home, Miss Expert," Liz said, but she knew Pat was right.

"Did you bring a flashlight? I never thought I'd be out after dark."

"As a matter of fact, I did," Liz said, and reached around to the fanny pack on Squirrel's rump.

At that moment a small branch still covered with green leaves materialized out of the dusk and flew right into Squirrel's face.

The horse freaked.

Liz found herself flung up in the air and she knew she had broken the cardinal rule. She was not going to come down in the center of the horse. She felt like a cartoon character. For a moment she hung suspended in midair, then she landed with a *whump* in the mud, and her right temple smacked into the edge of her hard hat. She didn't just see stars, she saw galaxies.

"Liz!" Pat screamed.

Liz sat up and saw Squirrel standing six feet away looking at her as though she had no idea what Liz was doing in the mud. Not Squirrel's responsibility.

"Get the horse," Liz croaked.

Pat swung off Traveller, squelched through the mud and grabbed Squirrel's reins.

"Got her. Can you walk?" Pat called over her shoulder.

Liz struggled to her feet and stood swaying in the gathering darkness. "If I have to. But I'd rather not." She sat down again in the mud. Her head was spinning, her stomach felt nauseated.

"Ohmigosh, ohmigosh," Pat repeated. "Sit there, just sit, don't move. I'll put the horses in the shed and come back for you."

Liz nodded and knew instantly that she should not have.

Pat slogged back and helped Liz to her feet. "We've got to go back. I can call my daddy from the shed. He'll come get us. He'll know what to do."

"Fine," Liz said and allowed herself to be walked back under cover. The wind had already dried the mud on her back to a solid cake of what felt like ice. She let Pat sit her down on the step of the earthmover.

"Let me have your phone," Pat said.

Liz reached into her shirt pocket. No phone. She looked toward the entrance wildly. "I must have dropped it when I fell."

"Ohmigosh! We'll never find it in the mud," Pat wailed.

"I'm sorry," Liz said. She leaned her head against the cool steel of the mover.

"Okay, okay," Pat said. She made shushing motions

with her hands. "We'll find it in the morning. We had a first-aid course at school, and my teacher said people who get hurt need to stay warm." She went to get the poncho and the blanket off Squirrel's saddle.

"The horses..."

"They'll be okay one night without feed." Pat got down on her hands and knees in front of Liz and stared up into her face. "Liz, talk to me. Please, say you're all right."

"I'm fine." Liz thought her voice sounded very far off.

"Sure you are. Oh, *bother*," she said, echoing Liz's favorite expletive.

CHAPTER TWENTY-TWO

WHEN THE TELEPHONE rang, Mike jerked awake and realized he was surrounded by dogs, all pressed as close to him as they could get. He coughed, sat up and reached for the phone. The clock on Liz's bedside table read 5:20 a.m.

"Yes?" he answered, and coughed again. His voice seemed to have disappeared somewhere during the night.

"Daddy?" The voice was faint, but clear.

His heart lifted. "Pitti-Pat? Baby, is that you?"

"It's Pat, Daddy. Pat, remember? Just Pat?"

He laughed so loud the dogs woke up. "Just Pat! Where are you? Are you all right? Have you seen Liz? She went out after you. We all went out after you..."

"Daddy, listen, okay? I don't know how much battery this phone has. It's kind of a mess. It fell in the mud."

"Fine. Yes, I'm listening."

"I couldn't find it until dawn. Okay. Here's the deal. Liz and I and the horses are fine."

Mike shouted. The dogs dived for the floor.

"Daddy! We're in an equipment shed on the new interstate they're building."

"The interstate!" Mike struck his forehead with the heel of his hand. "Of course. We should have known."

"Liz knew. She came after me."

"You're all right? Let me talk to her."

"Well, the thing is…"

Mike picked up the hesitation in Pat's voice and his heart did a loop in his chest.

"She's asleep. She kind of fell off a little last night."

"She's hurt?"

"Not really. She's maybe got the tiniest little concussion, and she's starting to get a really black eye where she fell on her hard hat, but she's fine, Daddy, really. She's fine. She's sleeping and I hate to wake her up."

"Wake her up. Now. You should have been waking her up every hour or so all night."

"Oh, Daddy, that's old-fashioned. Now if people get a concussion you just let them sleep and make sure they're breathing. I learned that in my first-aid course."

"Then check her the minute we get off the phone. Where are you? Tell me right now."

"I'm not real sure. About maybe ten miles east of where you are. I don't know whether you can see the shed from the side roads or not."

"Pat?" Mike said frantically. "Pat, you're fading."

"Get Aunt Vic to bring the horse trailer, Daddy. Come find us." Her voice was fading fast. "Oh, and Daddy, bring some food. We're st—"

"Pat?" he shouted. He broke the connection, dialed the number of Liz's cell phone one final time, but this time got that same computerized woman whom, had she been a live person, he would have cheerfully put out a contract on. He dialed Vic's extension. Albert answered sleepily.

"I thought you went home," Mike said.

"I came back."

"Listen, tell Vic I just heard from Pat. They're fine."

"Hmmph. I get my hands on those two, I'm gonna kill 'em both."

"Stand in line. Tell Vic we've got to get the two-horse trailer hitched up. Pat didn't know where they were exactly, but they're in an equipment shed maybe ten miles away. We'll have to hunt. I'll go ahead. You follow."

In the background, Mike heard Vic's voice. "Albert? What is it? Are they all right?"

"Fine," he said. "Until I get my hands on 'em."

"Oh, and Albert, could Vic bring some sandwiches or something? They're starved."

"I'll starve *them*. See if I don't," Albert said. As he hung up the phone, Mike heard him whisper, "Thank you, Lord."

Mike waited impatiently until he heard Vic's truck ten minutes later. He opened her door and gave her a hand out. "You need help hooking up the trailer?"

"Never have yet. Tell me where you're going. We'll follow."

Mike told them precisely what Pat had said, including the part about Liz's fall and her "little black eye." Albert rumbled ominously in the background, but Mike saw he had a large brown paper sack filled with what must be sandwiches.

"Did you call Angie?" Mike asked.

"Yes. Kevin's fine, as are the three babies, not two, that he delivered last night. She'll be out later."

"Good. I owe her. I owe everybody." He climbed into the Volvo, waved out his window, drove out and turned left.

He had no way of knowing whether or not Pat had

assessed the distance they'd traveled accurately, so he began exploring side roads only a couple of miles down the road. It wasn't easy going. For one thing, there were trees down everywhere, and despite the devastation, traffic was heavy with people trying to get into the city for work. At least he was going against the heaviest flow. Before he'd been driving twenty minutes he saw Vic's truck flash her lights behind him. She'd caught up. He pulled into the next side road and waited. She pulled up beside him. "I called the highway department," she said. "They gave me a list of equipment sheds between here and Nashville."

"I never even thought of that."

"Not surprising. Anyway, the next one is about six miles up this road and there's a good paved access road to your left. It's called Whitman. Lead on."

Mike felt his heart soar in his body. He was nearly there. He didn't care whether Liz had a dozen black eyes. He had to make all this up to her. He'd been the biggest fool in this history of the universe. To think he was being singled out. Talk about vanity. She'd been right. It had all been about him, what he wanted, the way he wanted to protect his cushy life.

He jammed on his brakes. Whitman Road. He could just glimpse the long embankment of the interstate ahead. He drove carefully. Wouldn't do to hit a tree this close to the end of his quest. Vic followed. Finally he could go no farther. He stopped the car, saw that there was a banked road that would eventually become an entry onto the highway and began to slip and slide his way up it toward the roadbed. The mud was like glue, slippery glue. But he made it.

There was the shed. And there was Pat, slogging her

way to him on boots so caked with mud they looked like snowshoes.

"Daddy! Daddy! Daddy!" she shouted. He picked her up, mud and all, and swung her around his head. He looked over her shoulder. "Where's Liz?"

He saw her then in the shadows, her face framed by that wild hair. He slipped his way to her, but stopped half a dozen paces away.

"I know, I know," she said, touching the left side of her face in embarrassment. "I look horrible."

"You look beautiful."

"Yeah. Right. I'm—we're sorry we put you through this." She sounded very formal.

"Daddy, Liz said last night that if I lose my hair she'll shave hers and go bald too."

Mike glanced from Pat to Liz. "You said that?"

"What the hell, it's only hair."

"No, it's a good deal more than hair," he whispered. He wanted desperately to haul her out of there and into his arms. But there was still this barrier between them he didn't know how to break. He shook his head. "But you won't have to do that," he said, and turned to Pat. "You're going to be fine."

"I don't have to go back to the hospital?"

"Yeah, you do."

Her face fell.

"But as an outpatient. You've got chicken pox."

Pat took a step toward him, swept her muddy hair back from her face and tilted it toward the sun. "Well, duh," she said.

"Good Lord," he whispered. She was covered in small red spots.

"I am gonna smack your bottom for you scarin' us all like that," Albert snarled in the background. He was wheezing badly and had fallen in the mud at least once, to judge from the slime on his coveralls.

"Sorry, Albert," Pat said.

"And you too, missy," Albert said, pointing at Liz. "*She's* a child. *You* oughta know better."

"Sorry, Albert," Liz echoed.

"Come on, let's get these horses in the trailer," Vic said. She walked past Pat without looking at her, then turned and grabbed her. "Never, ever do that again, young lady, do you hear me?" She crushed Pat to her and held her hard.

"Aunt Vic, I can't breathe," Pat said.

"And don't deserve to," Albert finished. He walked into the shed. "Come on, you old fools. Y'all need some breakfast."

"Oh, Daddy, so do we!" Pat said. "Did you bring us something to eat?"

"We did," Vic said. "In the truck. Go get it."

"Yeah." Pat began to slide her way across to the far side of the road.

Vic watched her go, then turned to Liz. "Couldn't you at least have told us which direction?"

"I'm sorry. It's your fault."

"My fault?"

"I finally figured it out. You drugged me! I cannot believe you did that."

Vic threw up her hands. "We'll talk later." She glanced at Mike. "Take Liz with you. We'll bring Pat and the horses." And to Liz, "You can walk, can't you? Didn't break anything?"

"No, but I warned you that horse was a menace."

"Got you here, didn't she?" Vic said. "Now scoot."

"I'll ride in the truck."

"The hell you will," Mike said, grabbing her hand. "You ride with me. We have to talk."

He half dragged, half slid her down to his Volvo, opened the door and shoved her inside.

"Oh, Mike, the upholstery!"

"The hell with the upholstery." He walked around to the other side and slid in behind the steering wheel. Instead of turning the key in the ignition, however, he swiveled to face her. "Are you really okay?"

"Except that I look as though I've gone ten rounds with Evander Holyfield, you mean?" She put a hand to her swollen eye. "I'm fine, thank you. Hadn't we better get started?"

"In a minute." He heard the coolness in her voice and sighed. She wouldn't make this easy. "I'm sorry I was an ass. I shouldn't have locked you out like that. I took out my fears on you. I'm sorry. You were right, it wasn't a relapse."

She turned a furious face to him. "And what if it had been? Would we be having this conversation? Or would you be out of touch in some world of your own where nobody could reach you, where I couldn't reach you?"

"I know. I wasn't thinking straight. And yes, we would be having this conversation even if Pat really were facing the same horrors all over again. I can't keep her under a glass dome because I'm afraid of losing her. You told me. She told me. You said she'd run away from me."

"Oh, Mike, I didn't mean it that way."

"You were right. I didn't get much sleep last night. I spent most of it worried about the two of you, but worrying even more about how to go on from here."

Liz caught her breath. "Is there any way we can do that?"

He reached over and took her hands. "It's not how long any of us lives that matters, but how fulfilled we are while we're here. You knew that instinctively the first day you met the pair of us. I should have listened to you."

"You really mean that?"

"Yeah. Took me a while, but yeah."

Liz laughed mirthlessly. "And here I am swinging around to your point of view. I was ready to sell Traveller and lock her up in that stupid apartment of yours for the rest of her life if it would save Pat."

"Pat doesn't need saving. She has to look after herself whatever happens. And make her own choices—within reason. She's still only twelve years old."

"Oh, she's a lot older than that."

"She once told me that." He grimaced. "We're the ones with the problem."

"Who we?" Liz asked.

"You and me."

"And what problem might that be?"

"I am in love with you and I think you're in love with me."

"Who says you love me?"

"I said. At the show, remember?"

"You were just being a proud parent."

"No, I was being a proud lover."

She turned away to stare out the window. He waited without releasing her hands, but not pressing her for an answer. He had to learn to wait. It wasn't easy.

Finally, she turned to him. "I'm not sure loving you is enough. We have absolutely nothing in common except our love for Pat. I don't want to fit into your world and you've made it abundantly clear that you loathe and detest mine.''

"Not anymore." He shook his head.

"What changed?"

"It's been gradual. But last night... The way everyone tried to help when you and Pat were out there lost. I've never been part of a community before. You've built a pretty fine little world. I'd like to try to become a part of it.''

Liz gaped at him. "You're serious."

"Absolutely. I love you. Whither thou goest. If you'll have me.''

"For how long? Until I fall off another horse? Until Pat breaks an ankle? My God, until you have your first coronary?'' Her eyes widened. "Oh, Mike, for the first time in my life I'm scared to death. I never knew what risk was. It was only me before. I can stand to lose me, but not you, not Pat.''

He pulled her into his arms. "Listen to me, my dearest love. Life is risk. I've finally come to terms with that. Every day we have together is gravy. But we can't store up happiness to offset the bad times. They're just as bad when they happen. So we live with it. Everybody does, every hour of every day. In four years Pat gets her driver's license. We stand in the doorway and wave as she drives away. About that time she'll start bringing home slavering juvenile delinquents with rings in their noses and sex on their minds. Two years after that we pack her off into some college dormitory. Then marriage and with luck, babies. Meanwhile, I'll stand by the ring and watch you jump fences. You'll kiss me goodbye at the airport and watch me take off for Singapore and Toronto. It's all risk, dearest heart.

We just have to love each other so hard that there's no room for the fear.''

"Oh, God, Mike.'' She raised a tear-stained face. "I can't bear it. I've got to have something to hold on to.''

He kissed the tears on her cheek and tasted the salt against his tongue. "We do. This love we share. You and I and the Polka-Dot Kid out there love each other. Nonnegotiable, unchanging, even when you and I are sitting side by side on the front porch of the retirement home watching our great-grandchildren play.''

"Whatever happens?''

"Whatever.'' He bent his head and touched her lips gently. "My love, will you marry me?''

She caught her breath. "When?''

"How does today sound? Mississippi will marry us in one day.''

"Yes,'' she said and opened her lips to him.

He held her fiercely, ignoring the end of the gear-shift, which dug into his ribs, and the steering wheel, which pressed painfully into his left kidney.

The knock on the driver's-side window startled them both. "Hey, you two. Knock it off and move it. The horses are hungry.''

Mike let Liz go, turned the ignition on and lowered the car window.

"Liz just promised to marry me today.''

"Oh, no!'' Pat wailed. "Daddy, you can't.''

Mike gaped at her. "I thought you'd be happy.''

"Happy? Are you crazy?'' Pat pointed at Liz. "Is she walking down the aisle wearing an eyepatch like Blackbeard? Do you expect me to play junior brides-maid looking like I'm in the final throes of the bubonic plague? Daddy, you never think.''

"Uh, what do you suggest?" he asked with suspicious meekness. His right arm squeezed Liz's waist. She giggled.

"Two weeks minimum. Two!" Pat held up two fingers. "Aunt Vic and I have already got half of it planned and we'll have the rest done before we get home." She leaned into the car. "Okay? Liz? Two weeks?"

Liz nodded. "If you say so."

"Good." Pat grinned. "Welcome to the family." She frowned at her father. "Now, move this thing so we can take these horses home before they start kicking down the trailer."

"Certainly," Mike said and turned on the switch. Pat stepped back and stood in the mud with her hands on her hips. He pulled gently out of the mud.

Neither he nor Liz spoke until they were out on the highway. Then Liz began to giggle.

"She certainly is a lot like me," Liz whispered.

Mike roared with laughter. "Good God, what kind of life have you let me in for?" He took one hand off the steering wheel and wrapped it around Liz's. "I wouldn't miss one minute of it."

Behind them, the truck and trailer pulled slowly into the road and caught up quickly.

The birds woke, the breeze sang softly in the trees. And the little convoy drove off into the red-gold joy of morning.

HARLEQUIN SUPERROMANCE®

FAMILY MAN

He's sexy, he's single...and he's a father!
Can any woman resist?

January 1998—IF WISHES WERE HORSES
by Carolyn McSparren

Ten years ago Mike Whitten made a promise to his little daughter—a horse for her twelfth birthday. Liz Matthews knows why it's so hard for Mike to keep that promise. But somehow—for the sake of both father and child—she has to convince him.

February 1998—A FATHER'S PLACE
by Joan Kilby

When Daniel returned to Canada from Australia, he was determined to mend his fences—for his daughter's sake. Karina offered them a place to start, a place that soon began to feel like home....

Be sure to watch for these and other upcoming FAMILY MAN titles. Fall in love with our sexy fathers, each determined to do the best he can for his kids.

Available wherever Harlequin books are sold.

**Look for these titles—
available at your favorite retail outlet!**

January 1998
Renegade Son by Lisa Jackson
Danielle Summers had problems: a rebellious child
and unscrupulous enemies. In addition, her Montana
ranch was slowly being sabotaged. And then there was
Chase McEnroe—who admired her land and desired her
body. But Danielle feared he would invade more than just
her property—he'd trespass on her heart.

February 1998
The Heart's Yearning by Ginna Gray
Fourteen years ago Laura gave her baby up for adoption,
and not one day had passed that she didn't think about
him and agonize over her choice—so she finally followed
her heart to Texas to see her child. But the plan to watch
her son from afar doesn't quite happen that way, once the
boy's sexy—*single*—father takes a decided interest in *her*.

March 1998
First Things Last by Dixie Browning
One look into Chandler Harrington's dark eyes and
Belinda Massey could refuse the Virginia millionaire nothing.
So how could the no-nonsense nanny believe the rumors that
he had kidnapped his nephew—an adorable, healthy little boy
who crawled as easily into her heart as he did into her lap?

**BORN IN THE USA: Love, marriage—
and the pursuit of family!**

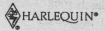 

Look us up on-line at: http://www.romance.net

BUSA4

WELCOME TO *Love Inspired* ™

A brand-new series of contemporary inspirational love stories.

Join men and women as they learn valuable lessons about facing the challenges of today's world and about life, love and faith.

Look for the following January 1998
Love Inspired™ titles:

Night Music
by Sara Mitchell

A Wife Worth Waiting For
by Arlene James

Faithfully Yours
by Lois Richer

Available in retail outlets
in December 1997.

LIFT YOUR SPIRITS AND GLADDEN YOUR HEART with *Love Inspired* ™!

Steeple
Hill™

LI1198

Don't miss these Harlequin favorites by some of our top-selling authors!

HT#25733	THE GETAWAY BRIDE	$3.50 U.S.	☐
	by Gina Wilkins	$3.99 CAN.	☐
HP#11849	A KISS TO REMEMBER	$3.50 U.S.	☐
	by Miranda Lee	$3.99 CAN.	☐
HR#03431	BRINGING UP BABIES	$3.25 U.S.	☐
	by Emma Goldrick	$3.75 CAN.	☐
HS#70723	SIDE EFFECTS	$3.99 U.S.	☐
	by Bobby Hutchinson	$4.50 CAN.	☐
HI#22377	CISCO'S WOMAN	$3.75 U.S.	☐
	by Aimée Thurlo	$4.25 CAN.	☐
HAR#16666	ELISE & THE HOTSHOT LAWYER	$3.75 U.S.	☐
	by Emily Dalton	$4.25 CAN.	☐
HH#28949	RAVEN'S VOW	$4.99 U.S.	☐
	by Gayle Wilson	$5.99 CAN.	☐

(limited quantities available on certain titles)

AMOUNT	$	_____
POSTAGE & HANDLING	$	_____
($1.00 for one book, 50¢ for each additional)		
APPLICABLE TAXES*	$	_____
TOTAL PAYABLE	$	_____

(check or money order—please do not send cash)

To order, complete this form and send it, along with a check or money order for the total above, payable to Harlequin Books, to: **In the U.S.:** 3010 Walden Avenue, P.O. Box 9047, Buffalo, NY 14269-9047; **In Canada:** P.O. Box 613, Fort Erie, Ontario, L2A 5X3.

Name: _____

Address: _____ City: _____

State/Prov.: _____ Zip/Postal Code: _____

Account Number (if applicable): _____

*New York residents remit applicable sales taxes.
Canadian residents remit applicable GST and provincial taxes.

Look us up on-line at: http://www.romance.net

075-CSAS

HBLJM98